"Well?"

"Well, what?" She leaned back and [illegible] make an ass of either of them.

"Well, don't you like the flowers?" Marley didn't know what he was thinking when he put the flowers on the car windshield. He assumed that she would like the idea of having someone feel that she was important enough to receive the gift. But he honestly didn't think it through. It wasn't as if Kayla was going to come running into his—a virtual stranger—arms just because had left a bouquet of flowers for her. This was an older, more sophisticated woman. He was going to have to step up to his game if he wanted her to pay him some attention.

"What? Look, I got to go to work." She pushed the button to automatically roll her window up. So the flowers were from him. Why?

"Wait . . . wait," he yelled, almost putting his hand into the window's path. "Will you have dinner with me tonight?"

"No." She shook her head for emphasis. Then without further delay, she pulled off. The nerve of him asking her a question like that right in front of her daughters. And where the hell had it come from anyway? He had never shown her any interest before.

THREE DOORS DOWN

MICHELE SUDLER

Genesis Press, Inc.

INDIGO

An imprint of Genesis Press, Inc.
Publishing Company

Genesis Press, Inc.
P.O. Box 101
Columbus, MS 39703

All characters in this book have no existence outside the imagination of the author and have no relation whatsoever to anyone bearing the same name or names. They are not even distantly inspired by any individual known or unknown to the author and all incidents are pure invention.

ISBN: 13 DIGIT : 978-1-58571-332-5
ISBN: 10 DIGIT : 1-58571-332-5
Manufactured in the United States of America

First Edition

Visit us at www.genesis-press.com
or call at 1-888-Indigo-1-4-0

DEDICATION

This book is dedicated to
Mitchell
The Man Three Doors Down

ACKNOWLEDGMENTS

Besides my family and friends (you all know who you are and that I love you), I have to acknowledge a few people who I didn't get to thank before due to timing issues. They are Rona Long, Vincent Raymond Turner, Hiroka Yasude, Carlaina Rose, and Shami Simmons, who work with me and make my day very eary.

To Doris Funnye Innis for all your hard work. Thank you.

To everyone who has ever read any of my books. Thank you.

To my friends, Theirdre Carey, Vera Smith, Loretta Martin, Denise Anderson, Carol Johnson and anyone I may have missed who emailed me after reading STOLEN MEMORIES to give me their honest opinions. I appreciate your feedback and will try to reply to all emails. Thank you.

And to anyone I might have missed, I'm thinking of you.

CHAPTER 1

Kayla Logan's cell phone rang the tune of R. Kelly's "Slow Grind", rousing her from a dreamless sleep. She hit the side of the phone quickly to silence the music, then stayed in bed for another two minutes. She lay completely still and listened to make sure that no one else in the house was awakened by the alarm. Her heartbeat quickened as, like in a covert operation, she slithered out of bed without making a sound.

Having showered and applied lotion before going to bed, all she had to do was spray herself in the sweet smells of her vanilla musk perfume and put a dab of gloss on her full lips. Her hair was kept in place by a scarf, which she now unwrapped. Running her fingers counterclockwise several times like a mad woman, Kayla lifted her short locks into an almost standing position. Wasn't nothing like a get-up-and-go hairdo. After putting on her black lace bra with its matching thong and garter belt, she covered herself with a long black satin robe to complete the ensemble.

Kayla looked at the clock on her nightstand: 1:35 A.M. Both her excitement and nervousness mounted. Soon, she thought, soon. Then, she waited until she heard the signal. In no time at all, the familiar chime of a car being locked automatically sounded outside. The double beeping of the car's alarm activation was the sign she had been longing to hear. Her inner walls clenched in response. Careful not to make any noise, she crept down the long hallway, going past two bedroom doors and down the stairs to the first floor. Pushing aside guilt, Kayla kept her mission firmly in the forefront of her mind. Stay focused, she told herself. Don't stray from the plan, she warned. Remember the payoff.

Once she was through the living room, she relaxed a little, but just a little. She wasn't home free yet. She still had to get across the kitchen floor, which would be a challenge, especially in her three-inch heels. It hadn't occurred to her that she could have simply taken the shoes off. Instead, she tiptoed across the floor until she reached the sliding doors leading to her wooden deck. Still careful to make not a sound, she slowly slid the doors open.

The moon's brightness seemed to reflect her mood perfectly: romance, intrigue, and fillfulment. Goosebumps peppered her skin, testifying to the intensity of her emotions. Though nervous and apprehensive, she was too fascinated by the promise of this adventure to renege, or regret, the agreed-upon plans. Her breath in her throat caught and her nipples hardened against the lace of her bra when she saw the silhouette of a man coming toward her deck.

Dressed only in a white wife-beater t-shirt and pajama bottoms, his sexual appeal dwarfed that of any man she had known in the two years since her divorce. Her mouth went dry, but her sexual fluids went south and settled in a warm pool between her thighs.

His gaze was bold and intense. His eyes coolly explored her body, beginning with her bright pink nail polish with the teddy bear design on her big toe and proceeding up her long legs to a teddy bear tattoo with balloons displaying the names of her daughters. He had seen it all before, but he still took appreciative note of her hourglass figure, her flat belly, and her large breasts. She was beautiful.

"Hello, love." His voice was deep and husky, his words soft and caressing. The vein in her neck pulsed uncontrollably.

Nervously, expectantly, she replied, "It's nice to see you."

"Why so formal, love?" he asked, keeping his voice low as he closed the space between them. His unhurried style was what had made her take notice of him, and right now it was keeping her enthralled.

"I-I guess I'm just a little nervous," Kayla answered truthfully. She had never done anything like this in all her life. Had never thrown caution to the wind. Suddenly self-conscious, she looked away and then down at herself.

"There's no need for that," he said firmly, his six-foot, two-inch frame less than a foot away. Chest muscles bulged invitingly beneath his t-shirt. She was just now noticing how magnificently sculpted he truly was. His arms were big and rock hard, tight and thick. This was the closest they had ever been. "It's just you, me, and the moonlight," he said, looking from side to side, as if to reassure her.

"This is just a little new for me," she confessed.

Hoping to put her at ease, he switched tactics. "You look beautiful, love. I'm almost speechless," he breathed, once again slowly perusing her body from head to toe. He was rewarded with a becoming blush.

"Thank you. I thought you might like it."

"Yes, I do," he assured her, his voice raspy and vibrating with pleasure. "Come here." Taking her by the arms, he brought her closer to him until their bodies were flush. "I've been thinking about this all day," he whispered near her ear.

"So have I," she confessed.

The softness of his lips surprised her when they touched her neck. The electrical current that followed the path he took en route to her shoulder stirred her, causing her to moan softly.

Encouraged by her reaction, he pulled his head back and looked at her. Putting one hand at the back of her head, he moved her forward until their lips met. Kayla shyly followed his lead, allowing her lips to move in concert with his, although nervousness prevented her from fully enjoying the kiss. But then he tightened his hold around her waist, pulling her even closer to him. She felt his imprint against her leg and, as his expert tongue glided between her lips, she matched the swirl of his tongue.

As her fears subsided, Kayla began to relax. His practiced tongue continued its steamy exploration. Wild, barely controlled, she responded in kind and, before long, she had become the aggressor. A longing began in the pit of her stomach and continued upward until her entire body was suffused by long-repressed desire. Needs that she had tried to bury could no longer be denied.

"Let's have a seat, baby," he suggested, guiding her to the patio lounger.

In all her thirty-seven years, Kayla had never imagined herself in this place, at this time, or with this man. But just because she had never done it didn't mean that she never should. For the past year, she had been furtively watching him, trying to read his habits, his lifestyle, what he did, who he did. Despite her determined efforts, she had come up with a complete blank. Her need to demystify this man had become a near obsession—probably because she didn't have a life of her own.

As soon as they sat, he leaned forward and recaptured her lips. Kayla shifted her body into a comfortable position, all the while responding to his kisses. He slipped the robe off her shoulders; she did not object and was left practically nude in the darkness. She liked that, and it excited her when he pushed away from her to get a better view of her body in the moonlight. His jet black eyes on her moon-touched skin created a sensation that made her stomach quiver.

Then he began fumbling with the lounger's side latch until it was fully reclined. Kayla was overjoyed; he wanted her, desired her, just as badly as she wanted him.

He pulled his t-shirt over his head. She gasped when she finally saw what she had suspected all along. He was a study in chiseled perfection from his neck to his . . . damn. She couldn't see beyond his navel, but it wasn't because of the moonlight or for not looking.

Reading her mind, he stood up, slyly smiling. He turned slowly, showing off his wide back. The span of wide shoulders was nestled with hard muscle covered by tight skin. Tight chocolate skin. She didn't know the difference between a glute and a quad, but he had plenty of both. It was a definite turn-on.

His body was his own work of art. He must have been lifting weights and exercising regularly since his teenage years. His stretching and turning in front of her intensified the atmosphere on the patio.

Kayla's mouth popped open each time her eye caught something new. And just when she thought she could handle all that she had seen, he tucked his thumbs into the band of his pajama bottoms.

"Oh . . ." she heard herself say as his pants drifted to the floor, revealing the hardness of his thighs, the hardness of his legs, the hardness of his hardness. Her stomach quivered, her insides tingled, and words failed her. Speechless, yes, but the message her body was sending was clear. *Join me on the lounger.*

And he obliged. He bent over and slowly covered her body with his. Kayla reveled in the way her body was responding to him. He touched her leg, and a muscle twitched. He lightly caressed a breast, and the nipple became a tight knot.

He unsnapped the bra's front hook and skillfully paid due attention to each breast.

Pliant and willing, she lay in his arms, waiting for him to do whatever he had a mind to do. Forgotten was the fact that it was the middle of the night and they were on her back porch in a development comprising over 200 townhouses. His kiss drove her to the edge of absolute mindlessness. The hand tugging at the string on the right side of her thong had her frustrated. *God, how she needed this.*

He delicately touched the folds of her core through the skimpy thong material, causing her senses to reel.

"Enjoy, love," he said confidently. Moving the thin fabric aside, he felt her surging excitement. Her scent floated into his nostrils, compelling him to keep exploring. He pleasured her with his hands until her sobs became uncontrollable moans.

Overwhelmed by feelings she had almost forgotten and wanting to be filled, Kayla reached for the hardness against her leg. Her fingers closed around him. She stroked his length, feeling the silky smooth skin surrounding his pleasure wand.

"Now, please," she pleaded.

Between kisses, he picked up his pajama bottoms and reached into one of the pockets. He found a foil-wrapped condom and immediately ripped the package. He covered himself with the prophylactic, and then refocused his attention on her. Using his arms as leverage, he positioned himself over her. Just as he was to plunge into her softness, he froze.

"What's wrong?" Kayla asked, bewildered. Why had he stopped?

"Shh . . . I think somebody's up," he whispered. "The bathroom light just came on."

"What?" She turned so fast he was almost pushed off the lounger.

"Shhh," he urged again, scrunching down low.

Kayla looked up, too. He was right; the bathroom window was now a bright yellow instead of black.

Horrified, she rushed to get off the lounger, accidentally kicking him when she swung her foot over. "Uh, sorry. I gotta go." She stood up, frantically straightening her clothing and nervously readjusting her disposition at the same time. "Go. You gotta go," she said without so much as a second glance at him.

Utterly confused, he quickly leaped off the lounger and grabbed his pajama bottoms. He stepped into the legs almost simultaneously and started moving closer toward the steps. "Kayla," he whispered.

"Go. Just go," she said, still trying to rearrange herself. "I should have never let this happen. God, this is so stupid."

"Wait a minute, love. I thought you wanted to be with me."

As if just noticing he was still there, she turned and looked at him. "Not now; please leave," she said, dismissing him.

He was flabbergasted. And offended. "Look, Kayla, I'm not somebody for you to toss aside as you please." Unmoved by her 'please', he was apparently prepared to stand there and argue with her.

"*Please.*" Minutes ago, Kayla thought she would be begging him to make love to her, to be inside her. But here she was begging him to leave. "Go before she comes looking for me."

Increasingly insulted, he stubbornly stood his ground. "This isn't over, Kayla."

"Yes, it is. It never started," she hissed before walking away. She didn't want to say it, couldn't believe the words were coming out of her mouth. As badly as she had wanted this man, had longed to be in this very position, she was now sending him away.

"Like hell," he grabbed her arm and pulled her close to him, his eyes deadly serious. "You want me, and I want you. Don't deny what you feel. This is hardly over, my dear."

Violently shaking her head and pulling her robe closed, she pleaded for the last time, looking him straight into the eyes. "Leave." No, she didn't want him to go, but what choice did she have? *God, how she desired him, even now.* His eyes glowed bright with anger and, she imagined, frustration. But she had made a vow, and she'd had her moment of weakness. It was time to get back on track.

This was the kind of confused and unsettling life she had whenever she let a man into it. Kayla couldn't let herself do it again. Maybe this was a sign, a sure sign that she was about to make a big mistake.

"I'm sorry, but this is over," she said, lowering her voice when she thought she heard a sound behind her.

"Mom?" they heard someone call from inside the house.

Like the proverbial deer in the headlights, she froze and stared at him with pleading eyes. "Just leave, please."

He finally took pity on her vulnerability and went down the steps of the deck as quickly and quietly as possible. As soon as he was out of sight, the sliding doors open.

"Mom, you out . . ."

Kayla sat straight up in bed. In quick, short movements, she swiveled her head to drive the dream from her consciousness. Letting out a long sigh, she ran her hand over her face and collapsed back on the fat, fluffy pillows crowding her queen-size bed. When was it going to stop? When would she be able to have a peaceful night's sleep instead of having the same dream over and over again? She had to get it out of her system. Get him out of her system.

She grabbed one of the pillows and placed it between her legs, desperately holding on to it as if it were a life preserver of some kind. Rocking back and forth, she tried to stop the urgent pulsations that were becoming more and more insistent between her thighs. It didn't help. The edge of the pillow only served as a conductor for the fire within as it found its way past her freshly shaven folds and rubbed against her.

She was supposed to be strong, keeping men out of her life so that she and her daughters could stay focused on their lives. She needed to stay focused. No more men bringing her down, destroying her willpower and lowering her self-esteem. But, for reasons she could not fathom, she was having the hardest time keeping this man off her mind.

It was driving her crazy. Kayla had to get over him, but she didn't know how. At least for the time being she could relieve some of the tension he was causing her.

She pounded her fist into the pillow in frustration before moving off the bed. She opened her walk-in closet, or so they called it when she bought the house. Bending over and reaching to the back of the closet, she moved the garbage bag holding her wedding dress and pulled out a black Nike gym bag.

This black bag had been her lifesaver as of late. Ever since the first day she had seen him, he had been invading her mind slowly but surely with unspoken promises of what his body could offer. Her only relief was within the bag.

She slowly slid back the zipper, and inch by inch by marvelous inch her savior appeared in the form of eleven inches of hard white plastic. Kayla pulled Adam out of his hiding place. *Adam*, she smiled. In her wicked little mind, there was something both wrong and so right about giving her toy a name. That name. But it was perfect. Adam was thick and heavy. Veins carved down and around its length from the fat head, which sported a crease and indent on the tip, to the swell of its base, which was surrounded by two huge, severely ribbed round mounds.

She smiled with excitement as her inner muscles tightened. They knew what to expect. Satisfaction.

Kayla pulled Adam out of the bag. Beneath him were his partners. From a paper bag she pulled out one of the multicolored condoms. She covered her friend and moved back to the bed. Relief was on its way.

Lying back on the bed, she rubbed Adam's head against her inner thighs, moving slowly toward her middle. With her left hand, she squeezed the tight nipple of her left breast.

Having been there so often, Adam knew exactly where to go. She flipped the switch on his side and brought him to life. The veins around him surged alive as fluid pulsed through them. That turned her on more than the constant hum of his juddering.

This was one of the best investments she had ever made in her life. He was a true friend, always there with a pick-me-up when she needed it. Adam never complained, never let her down, never broke her heart, and he never cheated on her.

Her fingers played between the soft hairs of her mound until they found the nub at the tip of her folds. The stickiness of her enthusiasm was evident.

While Adam performed, a face flashed before her tightly closed eyes. And she envisioned the man who was already her lover in her mind. It was him wildly exploring her insides, pushing her higher and higher into a state of ecstasy. The orgasm caught her off guard. It was hard and fast and disappointing. Kayla knew her body too well. It took her no time at all to please herself. She was going to have to do something about that.

Kayla clutched her body together, drawing her legs up until she was lying on her side in a tight ball, breathing heavily, exhausted.

"Mom was up late last night, Kaitlyn," sixteen-year-old Kamry said to her sister as she poured her favorite cereal, Pops, into an empty bowl. "I heard her moving around in her room when I got up to use the bathroom. She's always up in the middle of the night. I wonder what she's doing."

Kaitlyn put down her spoon, not really hungry. She didn't like to eat breakfast, but her mom insisted that it was the most important meal of the day. Her figure was the most important thing to her. At seventeen, she was very conscious of everything dealing with her weight, figure, looks, and clothing. This was her junior year of high school, after all. She had to look her best at all times, and gaining weight would make her just as inconsequential as the flabby girls that her girlfriends made a point to make fun of. "Oh, yeah? What did it sound like she was doing?"

"I don't know. It seemed kind of weird. Mom used to sleep like a log. Lately, she's been a little uptight. Haven't you noticed?" Kaitlyn's silence assured her that her sister hadn't noticed that their mother was acting a little strange. She would have been surprised if it were different. Kamry hunched her shoulders and carefully carried the bowl of cereal, nearly overflowing with milk, to the table. Kamry wasn't as worried as her sister about her physical appearance. She never gained weight that she noticed. At five feet, ten inches, she was a forward on the girl's basketball team, so she exercised daily, and her metabolism was high. She never worried too much about acne or having her nails done. She was a true tomboy. Not that there hadn't been one or two boys that had caught her eye. She just wasn't concerned with having a boyfriend right now; she was trying to have fun. And sports were fun.

"Maybe she misses not having a man in her life. I know I do." Kaitlyn walked over to the sink, having ignored Kamry's question, and emptied her half-eaten bowl of cereal. Then she picked a banana out of the fruit basket on the kitchen counter.

Kamry rolled her eyes. *Here we go again,* she thought to herself. Kaitlyn was about to start acting like she was deprived of one of life's most precious treasures again. "You've never had a man in your life. How can you miss something you've never had?"

"And I'm about the only one in school who hasn't. I'm a junior, Kamry. Every single one of my friends has a boyfriend. The only people at school who don't have boyfriends are the nerds."

"All you ever worry about is what other people think about you, Kaitlyn," Kamry stated, shoveling Pops into her mouth.

"Mom's just lonely. That's what I think. She'll get over it. All she has to do is find a man," she said quietly, briefly glancing toward the stairs to make sure her mother wasn't on her way down.

"You better be quiet. That's what I think," Kamry fired back, laughing. "If she hears you, she's going to bust your behind, and you won't have to worry about any boy wanting you. I think it's more than her being lonely. I don't think she's happy with her life."

"She's not busting anything. I'm too old for beatings," Kaitlyn said confidently. "She's still mad because

Dad left her for that woman. If she got a man, she'd be much happier."

"So what? I'm still mad about that, too. And at last check, so were you. What? It's okay now because Mom won't let you have your way about something? If you remember correctly, Dad did a lot more to her than just cheat with another woman. It's funny how easily you forget things when it suits you, Kaitlyn. And a man's not the answer to everything."

"I didn't say that. But I bet that if I lived with Dad, I'd be dating right now." Her hands moved to her hips to help her prove her point.

"If you lived with Dad, you'd probably be doing a lot of things that you shouldn't. He doesn't have time for you. If he wanted us to live with him, he'd at least be calling here more than once a month." Kaitlyn had always been a daddy's girl. All he did was spoil her rotten, let her get away with everything, and buy her anything she asked for.

"He's busy," Kaitlyn responded, defending her father.

"Yeah," Kamry said under her breath, "busy chasing women."

"You don't know what he's doing."

"And neither do you. I swear, you are so stupid if you think that he's thinking about you. Like I said, he doesn't have time for us."

"You're just jealous because he loves me more." Kaitlyn turned her face into a triumphant smirk, knowing that she had hit her sister's highly sensitive spot.

"And you're dumber than your grades show. It doesn't matter who he loves more, because he's not trying to see you just like he's not trying to see me," Kamry retorted, passing her sister as she moved toward the sink. Her anger was visible in her eyes, as well as by the way she braced herself as she walked, fist clenched. Kaitlyn didn't want to mess with her this morning, and definitely not on this subject.

"Hey," Kayla said, entering the kitchen, "what's going on in here?" Her voice was much louder than either of theirs had been. They had been arguing. Although their words had been unclear, Kayla could hear the tone of their voices from upstairs. She waited a moment, giving each girl time to answer. "Oh, nobody has anything to say now? A minute ago, it seemed neither of you wanted to shut up." She looked from one daughter to the next. "Get your stuff together so we can get out of here."

Kayla loved her girls to death, but most times they got on her damn nerves. They were as different as night and day. One a prom queen, the other a tomboy. Kaitlyn was pretty, but she knew it. That was dangerous to Kayla. There had been girls just like Kaitlyn when she went to school, and she could remember how hated they were. With Kaitlyn's clear mocha skin, bright ebony eyes shaped like perfect ovals, her sparkling teeth, and full lips, no one could tell her different. She made sure her thick, jet black locks were straight and always in place. The wrap she sported was full-bodied, making her look older than seventeen.

Kaitlyn kept her body in shape by not eating, which concerned her mother. Young ladies needed their nourishment. However, despite all of her attempts, she couldn't rid herself of her worst nightmare. Wide hips. It was hereditary.

Kamry, on the other hand, was beautiful. But she hadn't realized it yet. How could she, standing in Kaitlyn's shadow? With Kaitlyn always in the limelight, Kayla was afraid she never would. Kamry was a true athlete. She played field hockey and basketball, ran track and played softball for the high school. Her hair was constantly in braids and ponytails, which were more comfortable for her active lifestyle. She maintained her grades, hoping to get into a good college, and she never watched what she ate.

As she continued to look at her girls, Kayla marveled at how they were both like her at different stages of her own life. But she didn't need this first thing in the morning. Her own frustrations were still too high after last night. Kayla didn't feel like arguing with the girls, so she let the incident pass. And if she did snap, she would most likely take out her problems on the girls, and that wouldn't be fair.

She remained quiet while they retrieved their jackets from the hallway closet. They grabbed their backpacks and made their way out the front door. She followed, grabbing her purse from an end table on her way out. This school-day routine was done in complete silence.

Kayla was checking her blouse when she heard Kaitlyn squeal. "What now?" she asked without looking all the way up.

"Mom, look. Oh, my God, this is so romantic," Kaitlyn exclaimed, practically running to the car. A big smile appeared on her face. David had actually been bold enough to bring flowers to her home. David was the boy at school that she was secretly dating. Only her closest friends knew. They could only "go together" during school hours, and only when Kamry was nowhere to be seen. But so far everything had been working out just fine.

Kamry stopped in her tracks and watched her sister. *She is so stupid, and obviously so was David.* Why in the world would he bring flowers to the house if their relationship was supposed to be a secret? Yeah, she knew about it. There wasn't too much that went on in school that was secret. But Kaitlyn was her big sister, and no matter how much it hurt that they weren't closer or how mad Kaitlyn made her, she would never tell on her. That wouldn't be right.

"Oh, there's a note," Kaitlyn continued, hoping that if her mother saw how romantic and thoughtful David was, she wouldn't object to them dating. She eagerly opened the small piece of paper. "*Thinking about you.* What does that mean?"

"Let me see that," Kayla said, rushing to her oldest daughter's side. She couldn't believe the audacity of some people. Who would leave a note like that on her car? Boy, she had a good mind to . . . suddenly, she remembered where she was and who was watching her. With one hand on her hip and one foot tapping rhythmically on the tar road, she sent a clear message to the girls. *Don't ask. Let's go.*

"Mom, who are the flowers from?" Kamry asked, ignoring the warning. Their mother was acting strange. Something was going on, and she wanted to know what it was.

"No one important," she replied quickly. "Get into the car," she said, taking the lead.

"But, Mom, they're from a man," Kaitlyn interjected, ready to leap in with assumption after assumption until she won her own battle. "You've been seeing someone," she accused. "I thought you said men were off limits to all of us, yourself included."

"I did," she said, glancing at both girls. "And I meant it."

"Well, then who—"

"I said 'nobody', didn't I?" she snapped as she started the ignition. The beat of her heart had slightly increased. *Damn him.*

Him, she assumed, was Rydel Simmons, who worked with her in the billing department at Kent General Hospital. For the last two weeks, he had been asking her every day for a date. She had politely refused him, but it seemed that hadn't been enough. As soon as she got to work, she was going to have a talk with Mr. Simmons and their human resources representative. He had gone too far.

After checking her review mirror, Kayla put the car in reverse and was backing out of her driveway when the door to the townhouse three doors down opened.

Marley hadn't planned to make a big scene, just a simple gesture. He had less than forty minutes to get to JP Morgan Bank where he worked as a service manager. He knew that her daughters would be with her in the morning, but he was determined to make sure that she noticed him every chance he could. Dressed for work in black pants, pink dress shirt, and black tie, he rushed out of the house. His arm in the air, he attempted to make contact with a simple wave.

Kayla ignored him. Oh, she had seen him as soon as he walked out the house. With both girls behind her exclaiming excitedly, how could she miss him? He was too sexy for his own good. The short, wavy hair and bright smile. The pile of muscles around his neck and shoulders that made his shirt seem too tight. Small waist, nice ass, thick thighs. *Damn him.*

Again, he had her silk panties wet without having any idea of what he was doing to her.

"Mom, look, the man three doors down," Kamry said, pointing. That was the girls' name for him. The man three doors down. If only they knew how close he really was. Then he would be the man in mommy's head.

"Girl, if you don't get your hand down . . ." Kayla yelled, slowly pulling out of the driveway.

"I think he wants you, Mom," Kaitlyn said next, already suspicious of her mother's behavior. "You should stop to see what he wants."

"He does not," Kayla replied, refusing to look in the man's direction.

"But he's waving at you. Look," Kaitlyn said.

"No, he's not." Kayla's denial was at a high. She didn't know if it was because she didn't want to be bothered or because she was afraid that he would be able to take one look at her and tell that thoughts of him woke her every night.

"Mom, he's coming this way."

"Kaitlyn, stop exaggerating and mind your business," Kayla answered, putting more pressure on the gas pedal. Once in the street, she shifted the car into drive.

Marley was nowhere to be seen, or so she thought.

From the side of a parked red pickup truck, he jumped out into the road, almost in front of her car. Instinctively, she slammed on the brakes. Kaitlyn and Kamry slammed against their seatbelts with more force than necessary. She knew that they were trying to be smart with their exaggerated movements. Before she could pull off, he was coming toward her car. Kayla's face was filled with dread—and her mind with desire—as she watched him walk across the front of the car and stop at her window. She didn't want to roll the window down.

"Mom? What's he—"

"Shhh, Kamry . . . I don't know," she answered, hesitantly lowering her car window.

"Well?"

"Well, what?" She leaned back and hoped he didn't make an ass of either of them.

"Well, did you like the flowers?" Marley didn't know what he was thinking when he put the flowers on the car windshield. He assumed that she would like the idea of having someone feel that she was important enough to receive the gift. But he honestly didn't think it through. It wasn't as if Kayla was going to come running into a virtual stranger's arms just because he had left a bouquet of flowers for her. This was an older, more sophisticated woman. He was going to have to step up to his game if he wanted her to pay him some attention.

"What? Look, I got to go to work." She pushed the button to automatically roll her window up. So, the flowers were from him. Why?

"Wait . . . wait," he yelled, almost putting his hand in the window's path. "Will you have dinner with me tonight?"

"No." She shook her head for emphasis. Then without further delay, she pulled off. The nerve of him asking her a question like that right in front of her daughters. And where the hell had it come from, anyway? He had never shown her any interest before. Usually, she only saw him when he was wiping down one of his vehicles. His two Cadillacs, one white, one cream. And he was constantly cleaning them. Wiping them down, spraying off the tires, waxing the tires. Triceps flexing with every movement, glistening formations of solid muscle. She squirmed in her seat and shook her head. At any rate, she was mad at him. Now he had put her in an awkward position with her girls.

"Mom, what was that all about?" Kamry asked innocently.

"I don't know, dear. I think the man's crazy." She tried rationalizing the situation. Tried clearing the foggy memories of the night before from her mind.

Where he had gotten the notion to ask her for a date she didn't know. She didn't even want to think about it. She didn't care to ask why he had chosen that moment to ask. He was better off being a figment of her imagination. They had barely even had anything longer than a two- or three-minute conversation.

Kayla didn't want him to be human and make her heart melt with sweet sentiments. After all, he was pure evil; equivalent to that cookies-and-cream cheesecake she had ordered from the little girl down the street and was eagerly awaiting. It wasn't any good for her, but she knew that once she got a little nibble of him, it, she wouldn't be happy until she had consumed the whole thing.

"Well," Kaitlyn said, interrupting her thoughts, "I think he likes you. I think that you should go to dinner with him." This might be her only opportunity to get her mother out there in the dating world. And she needed that before David decided to dump her because he couldn't date her openly. As far as Kaitlyn was concerned, Marley was her light at the end of the tunnel, and she was going to do whatever she could to help both of them.

"I'm not going anywhere with him. Didn't I say no men in our lives? I mean it. You need to concentrate on school, and I need to concentrate on this job. No men."

No men, she thought, not even when they look and smell that good at eight in the morning. Not even when every muscle in his upper body looked like the honey bun she'd been craving for the past two weeks.

"But, Mom . . ."

"Don't 'But, Mom' me. I said no. See? Already you're letting one get up into your head. But I tell you right now, get him out of it. I don't want to see, hear, or think that you're at school flirting with one of them good-for-nothing boys. Do you hear me, Kaitlyn?"

"Yes," she mumbled, recognizing defeat.

CHAPTER 2

The fear that showed on her face had him confused. It was more than a fear of being talked to or asked out. It was a look of complete horror. Like she had something to hide from him. He knew that she lived in the house with her two children, teenage daughters. There wasn't any man there; if fact, he hadn't even seen any men visit the house at all. He had been watching the house for the past two months just to make sure.

Marley Jarnette wasn't a stupid man. He had made a lot of stupid mistakes in his lifetime, but he wasn't stupid. He purposely watched her and her house for the last two months to make sure it would be okay to approach her. When he saw her either coming into or leaving the house, he made sure to be cordial and speak. He wanted her to notice him, but it seemed that his plan hadn't worked.

He hadn't met to ask her on a date in front of her girls, but the look on her face told him that he wouldn't have gotten another opportunity. Marley figured he had no choice but to take his chance now.

From the first time he saw her six months ago when she was trying to drag a mattress into her house, Marley was interested. Unfortunately, at the time he was in the process of ending a relationship. It ended up taking three months before the breakup was official. He'd spent a month working on his own problems, then two months watching her.

But Marley had always liked what he saw. The full breasts, wide hips, the fat ass; they caught his eyes first. He loved a voluptuous woman. A big girl. He had her pegged for a size 16 or 18. Right up his alley. She was even pretty without all the makeup that her oldest daughter seemed to love. He hated makeup. It was too messy.

Over the last couple of months, he had made it his mission to get to know as much as he could about her and her daughters without being intrusive.

Since they both had moved into the new development a little over a year ago, it made sense that he should meet his neighbors. He had met everyone on his street at least once. And although he paid extra attention to her and her family, none of his overtures to her could be considered out of the ordinary. They had talked in public on most occasions, and he was mindful to make sure their conversations seemed innocent to everyone else.

Inside his house, Marley walked up the carpeted steps to his bedroom and retrieved his car keys. His mind wandered over the morning's events. It was jammed with both misery from not being able to express his desires and a renewed determination to get closer to Kayla Logan. He just had to figure out the best way to maneuver himself into her life. But how do you make a strong and independent woman not just want you, but want to keep you, when she outwardly did not want a man in her life at all?

As Marley left for work, he wondered if maybe he had dug himself into a hole. He was infatuated with a woman who didn't seem to want anything to do with him—or any man, for that matter.

"Come on, Kamry, help me," Kaitlyn urged, unlocking the front door to their home. She had a plan and was ready to put it into action, but she needed her sister's help.

Kamry knew her sister was up to something. From the moment Kaitlyn got on the bus, she knew something wasn't right. Usually, Kaitlyn was the life of the school bus. She liked to entertain people and enjoyed being the center of attention. She would start the jokes and the fun and play the music. And it seemed that all the other kids came to depend on her for that. When Kaitlyn was out sick, the bus ride home was dead and boring. Today, too, the bus was quiet, and Kaitlyn was sitting next to the window in deep thought—at the front of the bus.

At first, Kamry thought someone had upset her or that David had broken up with her. Kamry had automatically made a special note to find out what the problem was. She didn't have a problem taking up for her sister. Even though she always fought with Kaitlyn, nobody else had that right. But when Kaitlyn was the first off the bus at their stop and began walking home at high speed, Kamry realized that it had to be something else.

"Would you hurry up? We don't have a lot of time." Kaitlyn was saying as Kamry walked into the living room. She threw her book bag in the middle of the living room floor.

Mom's going to bust her behind, Kamry thought. Their mother didn't play that. Nobody and nothing out of the ordinary was allowed in the living room. Kaitlyn was in the dining room, pulling at the patio blinds like a madman.

"What are you doing? You better get that bag out of the living room. You know you're going to get your ass beat, right?"

"Just help me. We got to do this before Mom comes home."

"Whoa, I ain't gotta do nothing. Don't put me in the middle of whatever you're cooking up." Kamry threw her hands up. She turned around and was on her way up to her room when her sister stopped her.

Kaitlyn looked her right in the eye. "Kamry, I'm doing this for both of us."

Kamry didn't believe a word she was saying. In fact, she knew Kaitlyn was lying; Kaitlyn never thought about anyone but herself. But the desperate look on her face hit a spot. Kamry gave in with a long sigh.

"What do you want me to do?"

"Help me take one side of these blinds down." Kaitlyn knew her sister would have her back. No matter how much they pissed each other off, she had to admit that her sister always looked out for her. Always.

"I don't understand what you're trying to do. When Mom comes home, we're both going to be in trouble."

"Fifteen minutes before it's time for Mom to come home, you're going to run three doors down and get Mr. Marley."

"Do what? I'm not—"

"He'll be here trying to fix it when Mom comes in."

"Have you lost your mind? I'm not going down there."

"Yeah. You have to. Mom won't suspect anything if you get him. You know she trusts you more than me. Didn't you see the way he was looking at her this morning?"

"Of course I saw, but that doesn't mean anything. You're just trying to get Mom hooked up because you think it'll make things easier on you. That is not going to work."

"Mom needs a man in her life. That's why she's so anal all the time."

"Kaitlyn, you're only thinking about yourself. Just admit it."

"Well, it's true that she might ease up a little, but I'm doing it for both of us. You might not believe it, but sooner or later you're going to want to date, too. Then you'll look back on this and wish that you had listened to me. You're not going to be a tomboy forever, Kamry."

"Whatever. I'm not a tomboy now," she lied. "All I know is that we better hurry up because if we get busted, I'm going to bust you up."

Together they pulled on the edge of the blinds until it had successfully come loose from the wall.

"She's going to kill us," Kamry whispered.

"Just be ready to go get him." Kaitlyn had already checked to make sure that his cars were there when she walked home from the bus. "We got exactly two hours before Mom pulls up."

"We're going to get killed. I don't know why I listen to you."

"Look, all you got to do is go get the man. I'll start dinner for you." Kaitlyn knew it was Kamry's turn to cook, but she didn't want her to have any more excuses to waste time. The quicker she got Kamry on her side, the better.

The clock on the wall above her tiny four foot by five foot cubicle read 3:45 P.M. Kayla hated the last hour of her workday. It was always the slowest time of the day, and it seemed to stretch on forever. Glancing down at the stack of bill statements she had just pulled off the printer, she figured she would be finished by the end of the workday. She began separating the statements she would mail from the copy she filed and saved for the hospital's records, imagining each tear was Marley's neck separating from his shoulders.

"Hey, girl," Wanda yelled, maneuvering her wide hips past the two desks at the front of the office. She didn't speak to the ladies that occupied the desks, and they knew not to speak to her. Unfortunately, because the hospital was located in Dover, the state's capital, when temporary employees were brought on board, they were usually through Delaware's "Moving to Work" program, an initiative to help low-income single mothers and families work toward moving out of the state's housing tenements. These temperamental hood rats, as Wanda called them, came into the office fully stocked with attitude and resentment. Kayla didn't know where either came from, but there was so much estrogen in the office that arguments and conflict were common occurrences.

Kayla just shook her head knowingly when one of the girls smirked as Wanda walked by. Wanda just waved a hand at her dismissively. Though the job was filled with drama, everyone in the office seemed to know his or her place. They all knew not to fool with Wanda, not even on a good day.

Wanda was more than a handful. She was a weak sistah's worst nightmare. She was a secure, sophisticated, hip, and successful white woman married to a black man. The lady was beautiful, with thick, dark hair that hung in long, graceful curves over her shoulders and green eyes that held a gleam no makeup could improve. Her body was fierce, with up-tilted breasts and curved hips that tapered into long, bowed legs. And she confused the hell out of most people. With her cool and confident laid-back swagger, Wanda was more comfortable around the tension that often arose at work than Kayla was. Neither temps nor perms—not even upper management—easily intimidated Wanda. She made Kayla's day every time she wandered into the office.

"What are you doing tomorrow night?" Wanda asked, leaning over the desk to snatch a Reese's cup from Kayla's candy jar.

"Nothing." Kayla continued to rip the statements. She knew what was coming next. For the last few weeks, Wanda had been bugging her every Friday to go out with her on Saturday night. And every week, she declined the offer. She didn't have any reason to hang out in some club.

People only went to the club to meet other people, and she wasn't interested in meeting anyone. She didn't need the complications or the headaches. No men, that was the rule.

"Girl, you already know what I'm going to ask you." Wanda put her hands back on her hips. She couldn't stand when Kayla tried to play tough. The girl was stiff as a board, and she needed to get out. A little socializing never hurt anybody. What harm could it do to get out and breathe a little fresh air?

"I'm not going out with you, Wanda." Kayla didn't even lose her rhythm; the ripping of the paper stayed at a steady pace.

"Why not? You need to come out and shake your booty. You would have a really good time."

"No, I wouldn't."

"Yeah, you would. I think you're afraid."

"There's nothing to be afraid of. I just don't want to go."

"I know, I know. No men, right? I think that's part of your problem. A lot of good men will be there."

Good men. Men weren't anything but trouble. In fact, she had been having a hard time getting her work done for thinking of a good man all day long. "I'm sure there will be," she replied, "but that's not what I'm looking for right now."

"I'm not talking about what you're looking for. I'm talking about what you need." Wanda stopped talking for a moment and looked at her. "Kayla, did you ever think about going to that support group I told you about?"

"Wanda, look, I really appreciate your concern, but I'm not going—to either." She gave her friend a stern look that she hoped would convey her message better than her words. Support group? She did not need a support group. Kayla did not need a stranger telling her what her problem was; she knew what it was. Men.

Wanda seemed to get the hint. It was, after all, the same hint that she was given every other week. She just wished that her girl would get over the hurt from the past so that she could move on with her life. They had already had the whole conversation about how Wanda felt she was going about getting over the mental and physical abuse she suffered from her ex-husband the wrong way. There wasn't any need to go there again. If Kayla wanted to live like a nun, who was she to judge? Some people needed a little more time than others to get over a bad relationship. Even though it now had been a few years.

Wanda had been in bad relationships before, but fortunately, she had realized the relationships were a total bust before they had gone too far. If she had been with the same man for close to twenty years, she hoped that it would take her a little while to be ready to move forward. That made sense. She would actually worry about Kayla if she weren't going through some things.

"Okay, girl," she said backing off. "I won't pressure you, but you know my number if you change your mind."

"Thanks," Kayla replied, glad that she didn't have to go into any further detail with Wanda. Glancing up at the clock, she stood up and smiled. "Oh, and thank you for making the last half hour of my time speed by."

"Well, I'm glad to know that I'm good for something," Wanda laughed.

"You know what I mean." Kayla turned around and gave her a brief hug. "I gotta get on home."

"Kayla, your girls are old enough to be home by themselves for a minute. You have to stop treating them like they're still babies. Why don't you go out with a few of the girls and me? We're going to happy hour over at the pub."

As she searched her purse for her car keys, she looked at her friend. "You know I can't. I'll see you Monday."

"Can't blame a girl for trying. Have a good weekend."

"I would say the same to you, but I already know that you will."

Kamry looked at Kaitlyn for a split second before turning and rushing out the door, mumbling about her hatred for her sister. As she walked up the steps three doors down, Kamry silently prayed that Mr. Marley would answer the door quickly and not give her a hard time about coming down to the house. Remembering the way he had looked at her mother, she doubted the latter would happen. She wasn't an expert on love or romance or even lust, but in Mr. Marley's eyes she saw the possibility of all three.

And Kaitlyn was right about one thing. Their mother did need to get a life. Kamry understood the whole taking-time-to-get-over-your-ex-husband ordeal her mother had been going through, but it was three years already. She had long since gotten over the fact that her father wasn't that great of a dad. It shouldn't have been hard for their mother to realize he wasn't a good husband. Kaitlyn was the only one still in denial. So, for vastly different reasons from Kaitlyn's, she agreed that the plan was a good one, and she would try to help her sister make it work.

On the doorbell's second ring, Kamry looked over her shoulder. She was sure that at any moment her mother's black Nissan Altima would turn the corner and she would be caught standing on this stranger's doorstep. Then Mr. Marley opened the door.

"Kamry?" His shock and surprise could not be hidden. "What are you doing here? Is everything okay?" He figured that something had to be wrong for her to be knocking on his door.

"Ah, yes. Hi, Mr. Marley." Kamry looked him up and down. Perfect, she thought. He was dressed in a wife-beater t-shirt and blue sweatpants. "Um, can you come down to the house for a second? When we got home, we found the patio-door blinds on the floor. Kaitlyn and I couldn't fix it, and Mom will be home soon. Can you come look?"

"Sure, no problem," he eagerly agreed, and followed her toward her house, stopping at his cream Cadillac to retrieve his toolbox from the trunk. "Um, are you sure it's okay for me to be in your house? I don't want to do anything to disrespect your mom." The last thing he needed was trouble from their mother, especially when he was trying to get to know her.

"It's okay. Mom should be home in a second. We can leave the front door open just to be on the safe side. Believe me, I don't want to get hollered at, either." They were laughing together as they walked into the door. Standing by the fallen blinds, Kaitlyn wondered what the laughter was all about.

"What's so funny?"

"Oh, nothing," Kamry answered. "We just made a joke. Let's hurry. Mom will be here soon."

Kayla pulled around the corner and became immediately alarmed when she noticed the front door of her townhouse open. *What the hell?* If those girls were up to something, she was going to whip somebody's ass. She didn't know why in the world she had to put up with this kind of shit. As much as she spoiled them, you would think that they would be responsible enough to take care of the house when she was away. They were teenagers, for God's sake, and they knew right from wrong. She stomped up the front steps.

"What in the hell is goin—" *Damn, why did he have to look so good?*

Marley was lifting the patio blinds back into place. The muscles of his back stretched and folded and stretched and folded as he moved from one side to the other. She stood there with her mouth open and a churning in her stomach.

He hadn't seen her come in, but the girls had. They stood stock-still in the kitchen and held their respective breaths as the tension in the room grew.

Kayla quickly snapped out of her lapse into stunned silence. "What's happening?"

"Oh, Mom, when we came home, the blinds were down." Kaitlyn said, nonchalantly bending over to put the prepped meat into the oven. "We didn't know what had happened. I was scared to stay in here at first."

Kayla looked at her back suspiciously. She knew her girls. Nothing Kaitlyn did was unplanned. Kaitlyn was cool and calculating.

Knowing her mother's mind well, Kamry came to the rescue. "I ran down to get Mr. Marley to see if he could fix it for us. I knew you would be home soon. And I left the door open because I knew you wouldn't want us in here with a man alone. I hope that's okay."

Kayla let out a long sigh after thinking the situation over. "Yeah, it's all right, I guess." Kayla put her bags down on the dining room table. "Dinner straight?"

"We got it, Mom. Don't worry," Kaitlyn replied.

Kayla turned to go upstairs, thinking she could make a quick getaway. She was wrong.

"There you go. All done. Hello, Kayla. How was your day?" Marley's voice seemed to vibrate right through her.

The closer he moved toward her, the more intoxicating the scent of his cologne became.

She knew he was close. Kayla had no choice but to turn around and face him. "Hello, Marley. I'm good. And you?"

"I can't complain. I meant to tell you this morning how nice you looked."

"Uh, thanks," Kayla replied, turning away from him to go up to her room. She was not in the mood to talk to him. He unnerved her and, until she knew how to deal with these unsettling emotions she had towards him, Kayla wanted to put distance between them.

"Wait." He grabbed her arm to stop her retreat. "I wanted to ask you something." She pulled away gently, making him feel that she really didn't like being touched.

"What?" She saw him reacting with lifted brow to the irritation in her voice. "I'm sorry. I've just had a long day."

"Uh, no problem. I can help you fix that."

"Fix what?"

"Fix the tension and irritation." He stood his ground, making sure she was focused on his face. His voice was smooth and mellow; confident and sure.

"Oh, yeah, and how's that?"

"Why don't you go to a little get-together with me tomorrow night?" Marley knew she would reject him, but there was a small part of him that was still in denial. He could tell that she was attracted to him. She wanted him, too, but she was too damn stubborn to admit it. He could deal with that, but he wasn't going to give up just because she said she should. And most important, he wanted her.

"Sorry," Kayla fired back with the first thing that came to mind. "I'm afraid that I already have plans for tomorrow night."

"You do?" Kaitlyn and Kamry looked at each other, dumbfounded. They were both thinking the same thing. Usually, on Fridays—and Saturdays, for that matter—Kayla was dressed in her green and blue-checkered flannel nightgown, sipping coffee and watching television.

"Yes, I do." Kamry insisted, looking form one girl to the other, daring to see any hint of disbelief. Back to Marley, she explained, "I promised my girlfriend that I would go out with her tomorrow night."

"Okay, well then, maybe some other time. I better get going." Carrying his toolbox, Marley moved past her. He wasn't upset that she had said no; he knew that she would. At least now he knew that she wasn't just sitting in the house. Now that she was getting out, maybe she wouldn't be so resistant to going with him next time.

"Thanks again for fixing the blinds." She hadn't meant to lie to him, but what harm could it do? Going out anywhere with him was not a good idea. It would be like jumping out of the frying pan into the fire. It was hard enough dealing with the man when she barely ever saw him. The worst mistake she could make was offering an opening into her life.

"Thanks, Mr. Marley," the girls yelled. "Mom, who are you going out with?" Marley was barely out the door.

"Huh? Um, Wanda from work. She asked me to go somewhere with her tomorrow." She watched Marley's back until he was completely through the door and had closed it behind him. *God, the man looked good coming and going.* Kayla headed upstairs.

Kamry could see the wheels in Kaitlyn's mind turning. That girl was always up to something. Okay, she had backed her up with this idea, but that was it. Kaitlyn wasn't going to pull her into any more of her lame-brain ideas.

"You know, Mom will probably change her mind before tomorrow comes," Kamry commented.

"Well, we're just going to have to make sure that she doesn't, won't we?" Kaitlyn looked at her, determination resurfacing in her eyes.

"And how do you plan to do that?"

"Give me until tomorrow morning. Don't worry, I'll come up with something."

"I just know you will. Anything to get you out of the house."

"Not even. Believe me, I'll sacrifice getting out sooner to make sure that she's happy and enjoying herself first. Sister, you got to start looking at the bigger picture."

"Bigger picture?"

"Yeah." Kaitlyn sat down at the table and opened her math book. "Why try to sneak out for a night when, if I make sure she finds love, I'll be able to go out every weekend?"

"I gotta hand it to you, Kaitlyn. You're close to being a genius."

"You think?"

"Yeah, an evil genius trying to take over the whole planet," Kamry laughed, dodging the book her sister tossed at her. "Hah, you missed."

Saturday afternoon, Kayla knew she wasn't going out. In fact, she had known that Friday when she said it. She and the girls had just finished cleaning the whole house. It was their Saturday-morning routine. They got up at five-thirty in the morning and went room by room, making sure the whole house was spotless. The week's dirty clothes were all washed, folded, and put away; by noon, they were all back in their rooms for a nap.

Nothing changed their schedule. Anything else they needed to do was done after their naps. Sometimes they went shopping, to the movies, or maybe even out to lunch. The girls often used Saturday afternoon to get their hair done, so after her nap, Kayla expected to be home alone.

Knock, knock. "Mom, someone's here to see you."

Kayla rolled off her bed. Who could be coming to her house on a Saturday afternoon? She didn't have too many friends, and the ones she had knew not to come without calling.

"Who is it, Kamry?"

"It's Stacey's mom."

Kayla let out a long sigh. Stacey was a friend of Kaitlyn's from school. Kayla didn't know the girl that well, but she seemed nice enough the few times she had met her.

"Hello," Kayla said, walking to the door in her nightgown.

"Hi, Mrs. Logan. I'm Trina Wisher, Stacey's mom."

"Nice to finally meet you, Trina."

"Yes, same here. Um, I was throwing a small slumber party tonight for Stacey and a couple of her girlfriends. Stacey got accepted to the New York Ballet School's summer-studies session. She worked so hard to make the cut that I wanted to celebrate, even though she doesn't leave until summer. Anyway, if it's okay with you, I'd like the girls to come. I'll be there all night long. I'll probably take them skating tonight, then come back home for cake and ice cream, movies, and girl stuff."

"Sure. That sounds like a lot of fun. What time would you like them at your house?"

"I'm headed home right now, so anytime would be fine. I only live around the corner, so I could leave Stacey here to walk them over."

"Okay. I'm sure it won't take them long to get their things together. Thank you."

"It's no trouble at all. They're good girls. Besides, I know sometimes it's good for us single moms to have a night to ourselves."

"Well, thank you again. I'll send them around as soon as they finish packing." Kayla shut the door, thankful that she would have the house to herself. She visualized a cold glass of white wine and a long soak in a hot tub.

As soon as she went upstairs, her girls came into her room with their packed bags in their hands.

"Mom, we're leaving," Kamry smiled. Her mom was stretched across the bed with her legs crossed, a smile on her face. "You don't have to be so happy to see us leave."

"Oh, no, baby. I'll miss you." Kayla's smile widened.

"Well, we need money." Kaitlyn held her hand out. She wasn't asking, she was telling. As her mom reached for her purse, she continued, "Oh, and Miss Wanda called for you while you were napping. I told her that you were sleeping but that you were excited about going out with her tonight. She said she would call you back."

"What? Why didn't you tell me? Damn." She shut her eyes slowly as she saw her perfect, quiet evening go up in flames. "Damn."

Kaitlyn was smart enough to keep her pleased smile to herself. She wanted her mom to get out of the house. Even if her plans involving Mr. Marley didn't come together, she had to make sure her mother got out and had a good time. It couldn't hurt. Either way, she would relax a little and then become more relaxed with them and her silly rules.

"Mom, money?" She waved her hand in Kayla's face.

"Girl, get out of here. What you need money for?"

"We'll need money at the skating rink."

"Five apiece for something to eat." Kayla handed them a ten-dollar bill. "Y'all have a good time," she said, collapsing on the bed as soon as they left the room.

Now how was she going to get out of going? *See,* she scolded herself, *that's what you get for lying. You reap what you sow. God don't like ugly.* All of her mother's old sayings came back to haunt her as she sat up on her bed and prepared herself to face the music. Pulling her cellphone out of her purse, she looked up Wanda's number.

"Hey, girl, you call me?"

"Yeah, I was calling to ask you one last time to go with me tonight, but then one of the girls told me that you had already decided to come. Girl, I'm glad you did. I promise, you will have a good time."

"Well, actually—"

"Uh uh, I don't hear you." Wanda was good at cutting people off and talking faster when necessary. If given half a chance, she knew Kayla would back out. That was a chance that Wanda wasn't going to give her. "I'll be there at nine-thirty to pick you up. Wear jeans."

Wanda hung up.

Damn. Kayla looked at the clock. 4:30. She only had five hours until Wanda showed up. Luckily, she had her hair wrapped in a scarf. She would just pick out an outfit now and lay it out. That way, she could rest for a couple of hours, then shower and dress and be ready by the time Wanda arrived. It also gave her time for that glass of wine. She was sure she would definitely need it. She set her alarm.

At nine-fifteen, Kayla was finally feeling a little buzz from the two glasses of wine she had. She was about to pour herself another glass, but wisely decided against it. Nervousness had caused her judgment to falter. Kayla knew that she shouldn't have drunk both glasses in a combined six gulps.

She went into the bathroom and checked her appearance for the fourth time. She ran her fingers through her dyed midnight black locks. After scrubbing her face nearly bare, her makeup was applied to perfection with heavy eyeliner and smoky-black eye shadow, which caused her eyes to appear large and luminous. The crimson lipstick and cinnabar liner accentuated her full lips. She was very satisfied with the end product. It had been so long since she had been out she had forgotten how much fun getting ready was.

She wore blue jeans, as instructed, with a black tank and low-heeled boots. Then she waited patiently for Wanda to arrive. Kayla was checking the time again when she heard a motorcycle purr to life in the near distance. She didn't pay it any attention; someone on her street owned one. She had heard it before.

Wanda pulled in front of the house at nine forty-five and blew the car horn.

"I should have known you'd be late, Wanda," Kayla practically snapped at her.

Wanda just looked at her. "Hello, and you look nice, too."

Kayla was silent for a moment. "Thank you." She fell silent. "You look nice."

They smiled at each other.

"Okay, you got me."

"Girl, just relax. I know you haven't been out in a long time, but ain't nothing changed. Besides, you think I would get you into anything that ain't right?"

"No, but—"

"No buts. All you have to do tonight is sit back, chill, and enjoy yourself. It's about a forty-minute drive."

"Is Jonathan coming out, too?"

"He'll be there."

Kayla liked Wanda's husband, Jonathan. Although she was uncomfortable the first time they met, he had made her feel very welcome in their home. She hadn't expected the six-foot-plus, chocolate bear of a man to be so warm and cuddly. With his neatly trimmed, full beard sprinkled with gray hair, a potbelly, and a loud voice, she had expected he would be off-putting. But he was well educated, and Kayla found him to be outgoing and fun to be around.

Wanda's jeans fit her hips perfectly. If she weren't so pale, you'd never know this was a white girl. For the longest time, Kayla assumed she was mixed, but Wanda told her that she was half-white and half-Irish, which meant all white in Kayla's book. But it didn't matter; Wanda was cooler than most of the black women Kayla had associated with in the past. Wanda reminded her of a Teena Marie type woman. Her laid-back style made you either love her or hate her. Kayla loved her and was glad they were friends.

"Just don't leave me," Kayla said. That had happened to her too many times in the past for her to count. Her hot-ass girlfriends would hook up with somebody or their men would show up, and she would be left high and dry to fend for herself in a sea of wolves. That was when she made it a rule to always drive herself to any social gathering. But that was a long time ago; luckily, she didn't hang with those kinds of women anymore.

"Just enjoy yourself. Ain't nobody going to leave you."

CHAPTER 3

They moved slowly through the busy parking lot. More than once, Wanda had to stop on a dime, pushing on the brakes hard, to wait for people rushing past the car trying to get into the club. As they moved through the fairly large, but crowded, lot, Kayla saw cars lined up and down the road.

"Why don't we just park on the road like everybody else?"

"Because those fools are going to have tickets on their cars when they come out of the party."

"They're parked on the side of the road."

"Those aren't legal parking spots. Ain't no curb over there; that's just the side of the road. The police know exactly what they're doing. When it's really crowded like this, they come out and put tickets on those cars to make their monthly quota."

"Well, I didn't see a 'no parking' sign."

"There's one over there. One sign for that whole long-behind road. Denton isn't exactly the city, Kayla. This is the country, and the police need to make their money just like everybody else does. Girl, please, they know what they doing."

Kayla assumed from looking around that the people walking around the parking lot ranged in age from the early twenties, maybe younger, to at least sixty. There were a number of men walking around wearing worn black leather jackets with identical logos on the back. Some were directing traffic as best they could; others were standing around watching the people walking around. The patches were big black circles outlined in silver stitching. Inside each circle was what Kayla assumed was the likeness of an African warrior holding a spear and shield and standing in front of a motorcycle.

Almost instinctively, Kayla went into a fearful mode. She looked out the slightly dingy car window. This was why she didn't like being in large crowds; you never knew what to expect. And these men didn't look affable and easy-going. They all looked as if they were on guard, waiting for something to happen. It had been a long time since she had been out in this kind of environment, and she couldn't hide the fact that she was nervous.

Kayla didn't like to stereotype folks, but this was one of those times that she couldn't help herself. After they parked and began walking through the parking lot, she was able to get a better look at the emblems on the jackets, and she realized that some were different. A few smaller groups of men sported the same designs, but were completely different from the ones with the African warrior. The Rebel Riders wore leather jackets; the Soldier Boys wore what looked like bulletproof vests. There were even at least three different girl groups that Kayla could identify. In all, she counted over twelve different bike groups at the party, but the men wearing the African warrior on their backs were the largest by far.

With such a mix of people in attendance, she only hoped the scene did not become volatile. That was her biggest fear when around so many people. The potential for some kind of conflict was always there. The worry she felt was plain to see. She was frowning and had a nervous look in her eye.

Wanda looked at her friend with a slight smile. Kayla was so obvious. What she needed was another drink, Wanda mused. The girl hadn't been out in so long that she had forgotten how to relax around people. The parties were always like this, a huge gathering of people. And even though Kayla didn't know it, the parties usually went off without a hitch. Not too many people fooled around with the Zulu Nation; they knew the consequences.

Kayla's eyes darted from one group of people to another and from one spot to another as if she was trying to figure out the best escape route in case of an emergency.

"You can breathe, Kayla. Don't be scared. You're not in hell. You're at a party."

"Girl, where the hell you got me at?"

"It's a party, Kayla. That's all. You don't have anything to worry about. You see all of the security that's around?" Wanda used her hand to motion to the busy parking lot. "You're safer with these men than you would be with the police. Just try to relax."

"That's easy for you to say. But you got me out here, so if anything happens to me, it's on your head."

Wanda laughed at her before leading her closer to the clubhouse. "Come on here. You need a damn drink."

Kayla followed close behind, keeping her eyes straight ahead. "I was expecting a regular party."

"This is a regular party."

"No, this is some kind of biker's club. I thought it would be small group of mature and sophisticated men and women in a nice bar somewhere with maybe a little old-school music playing in the background."

"You need to get out more. This is the party. Pooh's bike club has dances all the time. What fifty-plus-year-old do you know who wants to be sitting around feeling fifty-plus? Fifty is the new forty. Kayla, you have to learn to enjoy your life every day and stop holding out for tomorrow."

"I guess you're right. Pooh's in a bike club?"

"Of course. You've never heard of the Zulu Nation? They're only the largest bike club on the East Coast. They've got chapters all over. That's why there are so many people here. It's this chapter's anniversary. Members from other chapters came here to celebrate and party. Then it's vice versa for every other chapter. We are always traveling with the club. God, you act like you've never been around black people before."

Kayla looked at her. "And you act like you're blacker than me."

"I am." Wanda laughed and kept walking, ignoring the push to her shoulder Kayla gave her. "Come on." On their way in, Wanda stopped numerous times to greet acquaintances. She introduced Kayla as she went along.

Kayla could tell that the members of the bike club and a lot of the ladies there held Wanda in very high regard. The men practically went out of their way to speak to her.

"Hello, Jaybird," Wanda said to a short, light-skinned biker who had stopped to give her a kiss on the cheek. "This is my girl, Kayla. Kayla, this is Jaybird."

"Hey, baby, how you doing?" Jaybird said, looking her up and down. He stuck his hand out to her then pulled her in for a quick hug.

Though unnerved by the close proximity to the stranger, Kayla returned his hug. "How you doing?" she said.

He was attractive. His curly hair and coffee complexion, along with those bright hazel eyes, had to make him stand out in any crowd. He was fine as hell, but she didn't feel a need to look him up and down as he had done her. She didn't want any men. He had a playful persona that made her think of him as a little brother.

"I got to run to the car real quick, Mrs. Bear. I'll be right back in." He looked at Kayla again, clearly sending a message that he was interested and was talking to her, too.

"We'll be inside. Did you see Pooh inside?"

"He's in there with Dang at the table." Jaybird moved by them, but he looked back to get an eyeful of Kayla's full lower shape. He liked that. "Kayla, you save a dance for me," he yelled to her before walking on.

"He's a sweetheart," Wanda explained. "Hardworking, single, no kids, a little younger than us, but still—"

"Wanda, stop it," Kayla interrupted. She knew her girl was about to get into her matchmaking mode, and

Kayla couldn't handle that. Not tonight, even though she knew that was why Wanda dragged her there.

"Stop what?" Wanda stopped in her tracks and moved out of the way of the opening door. "What did I do?" she asked, her face a study in innocence.

"You know what you were doing. I'm not trying to be hooked up, so just cut it out, *Mrs. Bear.*"

Kayla repeated the nickname given to her by the guys in the club so sarcastically that Wanda had to laugh. She threw up her hands in despair. Hey, you couldn't blame a friend for trying. But if Kayla didn't want what she needed the most, who was she to force it on her? She was a grown woman.

Wanda explained as they walked through that the building contained two rooms, which were separated by a large kitchen and restrooms. The larger of the two—the party room—could hold up to 750 people. The other room was much smaller and was usually reserved for club members.

"Hey, baby," Pooh yelled as soon as Wanda and Kayla approached his table. The long table was at the back of the room. Other long tables were scattered all around the back of the small room while round tables were scattered around from the back of the room to the dance floor. Two of the guys at his table immediately got up and stood against the wall behind the table.

Kayla didn't really know what was going on, but assumed they were being gentlemen by giving up their seats. Wanda took one seat, and she took the other.

"Oh, boy, don't tell me that my baby has finally done the impossible; she finally got you to come out with her, Kayla. Baby, I guess I owe you a couple dollars," he laughed.

"Yeah, she did. But I know y'all didn't bet on me. That's messed up," Kayla said, smiling.

"We've been making bets for the past two months," Wanda said, also laughing. "I want you to know that you've cost me over seventy dollars and a few favors."

Pooh laughed. "Well, although I am so glad you came out, I have to say that I'm disappointed that I didn't win again. The stakes were getting pretty high, but at least now I don't have to hear her complaining every Saturday night."

"She kept bugging me until I couldn't take it anymore. She wore me down." Kayla smiled at the big man sitting across from her, whose eyes were saying, *No surprise there.* When she looked at them together, she could see that they were a perfect match. Wanda was sassy and uncouth, and Jonathan (Pooh) was brawny and brainy.

Kayla was shocked to find that he was part of a motorcycle club. In his other life, Pooh was a high school assistant principal. She had always thought bikers were hardcore and dangerous, but she could tell that he was completely at ease among his biker friends. She had never been around bikers before, so she had a stereotypical impression of them, but he had given her a totally different perspective on the whole biker scene. She instantly began to relax.

Kayla had first met Pooh at her job when he had come to take Wanda to lunch. He was dressed in a suit and tie. He was an established professional. So she knew that if he was involved in this club, it had to be something worthwhile.

Now, someone else was helping to change her outlook: a tall, lean man came over to the table and sat next to Pooh. *Lordy.* Now, he was handsome, dark, and muscular. Truth is she was taking note of quite a few good-looking men in the room. She hadn't been with a man since the divorce, and maybe that long dry spell was causing her hormones to jump around like corn kernels in a heater.

Getting involved with a biker had always been the remotest thing from Kayla's mind; she had never really known any bikers. But this evening was giving her new possibilities to think about. She would never tell Wanda, though, because her girl would have her hooked up so fast that she wouldn't know what had hit her. Many of the men there had female companions that she assumed rode on the back of their men's bikes. *That would probably be fun, if I wanted a man.*

"You want a drink, baby? Kayla?"

"You know I do," Wanda replied. "And Kayla definitely needs one. She's not totally comfortable yet. Still getting her feet wet."

"Wanda!"

"It's all good, Kayla." Bear raised his hand in the air and motioned for one of the guys standing at the wall to come to him. "I need two Cap and Coke."

Kayla watched as they walked off. She was impressed, but didn't know why. Pooh obviously held a large amount of respect in the club if men just stood around to do his bidding. She didn't drink Cap and Coke, whatever that was, but she didn't seem to have the right of refusal. When she turned back, her eyes stopped on the eyes of the dark stranger who sat next to Pooh. He was watching her intently. A shiver went up her spine. It was as if he could see right through her clothes.

Pooh must have noticed, too.

"Kayla, this is my man Danger. Dang, Kayla."

"How you doing, miss?" His voice matched his eyes, dark and raspy, but in a sexy Ice Cube sort of way. He was sneaky. Fine, but sneaky. She could tell. She had known sneaky men. Dang was tall. His body was fit, but not too lean. His head was wrapped by a green bandana. Sexy.

"I'm fine, thank you," Kayla replied. She began to think that maybe, just maybe, she needed to re-evaluate some of her decisions. She needed a distraction, and thankfully Wanda was able to provide her with one. Wanda began pointing out girls that Kayla knew from work. The whole time she could feel his eyes on her. She was unnerved by it. And she was thankful when her drink was sat in front of her.

Sensing Kayla's unease and watching her down the tall glass of Captain Morgan rum and Coca-Cola in five minutes, Wanda was certain she would relax once she got the first two drinks out of the way.

Her friends always felt uncomfortable when they first met Dang. He didn't trust most women after having been married to a crazy woman for six years. Poor man. She had made his life miserable, until he finally realized that he couldn't change someone who didn't want to be changed. In the end, he was happy that he had listened to his lawyer and had secured a prenuptial agreement.

His wrinkled brow, clenched jaw, and thin mouth attracted a lot of attention, but he would ward off most advances. Danger was a self-made millionaire. At the age of thirty-five, he already owned two businesses and several pieces of real estate. He didn't have any kids, and he was her next project.

Wanda could only take on one hardship case at a time. She had hoped that he and Kayla would hit it off, and she would kill two birds with one stone. No such luck. She could tell by Kayla's expression that the interest hadn't been strong enough, but hell, the night was still young. You never knew what the night had in store once the evening progressed and everyone became comfortable.

Marley was mad as hell. After paying out over $2,100 to his mechanic, he was sure that his motorcycle would be ready by this weekend. Brian had been working on the bike for the past three weeks, and he had assured Marley it would be ready for the ride. But when Marley started it earlier that day, it sounded a little funny, so he had decided to have Brian listen to it again. The carburetor needed to be slightly adjusted. He had been unable to ride down with his brothers, and he'd had to take the long ride by himself. Everyone else was on bikes and had left hours earlier.

He arrived at 11:30 P.M. and, as he expected, the place was already packed. At least, he mused, the ride was worth it. Their club parties never ended before five in the morning. He couldn't count the number of times he had pulled his car into the empty lot to catch a couple of Zs before taking the long ride home. This night promised to be no different.

The only parking spot he could find was on the road. This, he knew, meant that when he came out from the party there was going to be a ticket on his windshield. Instead of parking, he rode through the parking lot one last time, hoping that someone was leaving. Luckily, on the second turn he saw someone waving him down. It was Jaybird.

"Yo, man, what took you so long?" he asked, leaning into the car window.

"Man, I had to drop the bike off at Brian's shop."

"Oh, well, come on, park the car over there on the end. Jaz held a spot open for you when I told him that you were driving down."

"That is what's up, man." Marley pulled into the spot and jumped out of his car, grateful that someone had been thinking about him. He went to the trunk of his car and pulled out the black leather jacket with the African warrior on its back. The worn jacket fit him perfectly, comfortable from years of wear and tear.

"Smooch. Man, what's up?"

"Jaz, how you doing, man? Thanks for the parking spot, brotha," Marley said to the short man standing at the end of the parking lot with two other men. He could tell they were prospective members by the plain leather jackets they wore with the word prospect on the back. Jaz introduced them all, and then walked a short distance with Marley.

"Smooch, why you not riding?"

"It's back in the damn shop."

"Man, you missed a hell of a ride."

"I bet I did. Have you seen Danger? Where did Jaybird go that fast?"

"That knucklehead Jaybird just went inside. He and Danger are probably sitting with Pooh. Mrs. Bear came with a friend. Fat ass, wide hips. Didn't get a chance to look at her face."

"You never do. I'll holler at you later, man," Marley smiled, shaking the older man's hand.

Inside, Marley walked around the outskirts of the dance floor. There wasn't any possible way a path could be made through it. He looked through the crowd of dancers, nodding at people he knew until he neared the tables at the back of the room. Pooh always sat at the table to the right side of the room. It gave the big man the most room for his girth.

"Hey, Smooch is here." Pooh's loud voice gave the others at the table a startle.

"Yo, man," Danger said, turning and throwing his hand high into the air. "Didn't think you were going to make it." The smile on his face showed genuine pleasure that his friend had finally arrived.

"Me neither for a—" Marley did a double take. A huge smile spread across his face. All but dismissing Danger, he walked around the other side of the table and stood next to Kayla. He bent over with both hands on the back of the chair and spoke close to her ear. "What are you doing here?"

His voice was low and steady and the music was loud, but she heard every word he said. She felt the vibration of his voice more keenly than the vibrations coming from the large speakers. His hand caressed her shoulder with just enough pressure to secure her undivided attention. The soft breeze of his voice forced her legs to close tightly. She gripped the plastic cup. *Damn him.*

"I'm here because I want to be. And because I didn't expect you to be." Kayla tried her hardest to be strong. She looked him right in the eye and silently dared him to say anything else.

"Oww, the lady has a quick tongue," Danger laughed.

Marley ignored him. He took the seat next to Kayla and turned his whole body toward her. He concentrated all his attention on her—from the sheen of her hair to the way her tongue darted out to wet her lips to her breasts heaving heavily under his perusal.

"You can fight it all you want to, but my determination is only second in strength to my patience. I know what your deal is. This thing between us is inevitable, and you know it." Then he leaned closer and whispered directly into her ear. "You know I want you."

"What the hell are you talking about, Marley?" Kayla stared at him, anger flashing in her eyes. He didn't have to do this to her. She was out for the first time in a long time and was having a pleasant time. He had no right to come into her space and sit so close to her that it made her body tingle with betrayal. "You don't know me that well. You don't know what I want or what I need. And I don't want to talk about this any more tonight. Is that okay with you?" she demanded, making no effort to lower her voice.

Now, everybody at the table was listening to the supercharged exchange, especially Wanda. Wanda saw something that she had never seen in her friend. In Kayla's eyes, she saw lust. In her voice, Wanda heard a lie. Kayla's voice was shaky and unsure. *This was a good thing,* Wanda thought. Wanda was an expert at reading body language. She didn't have a degree, but she should have one. Oh, yeah, this was good, better than she could have expected.

After listening for a couple of minutes, Danger decided to rescue his boy before he totally drowned. "Smooch, man, bar." Danger nodded toward the long bar on the other side of the room. His boy was dying, so he decided to throw him a rope.

Marley looked at Dang and then stood and moved away from Kayla. His eyes never left her. She was on his ground now, and he felt his desire for her grow.

"What the hell was that?" Wanda asked as soon as the men left the table. She wasn't quiet, and didn't care that her husband was listening to every word with interest.

Kayla looked from Wanda to Jonathan. It was very uncomfortable when you were blind-sided and all of your business was being put out there for everyone to see. She didn't know how to answer. She couldn't say that he was the man who lived three doors down from her and who she wanted to drag into her house, throw on her bed, and make love to until she was unconscious.

Pooh laughed loudly, "Wanda, I think we already know the answer to that question."

"Nah, I want an answer," Wanda persisted. She stared Kayla in the face. "I've been trying to hook her up with someone for almost as long as I've known her, and here she is with the finest man in here sniffing up her ass."

"The finest man?" Jonathan questioned.

"Besides you, baby." Wanda patted him affectionately on the belly.

"Wanda—"

"Kayla, don't try to dodge the question."

"I'm not. I'd just rather explain things to you later."

"I can walk away if you'd rather talk privately," Pooh laughed, pushing his chair away from the table.

"You don't have to do that, Jonathan, really."

He put his hands up and glanced at his wife. "Yeah, I do."

Wanda sat back with her hands crossed. She couldn't believe Kayla had been holding out on her. They had been friends for too long, almost since Kayla moved to Dover. She was happy that Kayla was finally showing interest in someone, even if she was hurt that she hadn't shared the news. And Kayla was interested, no matter how much she tried to deny it. It was written all over her face.

"Okay, okay."

"Why didn't you tell me about you and Smooch?"

"Because there's nothing to tell. Marley lives down the street from me. That's all."

"No, that's not all. Come on now. I'm not blind."

"He's asked me to go out with him. That's basically it."

"And you turned him down? Are you crazy?" Wanda looked at her as if she really thought she was crazy.

"Of course I turned him down. I didn't and still don't want to go anywhere with that man, and he doesn't need to be anywhere near me."

"But why? You want him."

She knew that a truer statement had never been spoken, but Kayla still felt a need to deny it. "No, I don't."

"Kayla, stop being an fool. There is nothing wrong with that man. And you have no logical reason not to get to know him better."

"How about I don't want to?" She held up her hand; a personal stop sign. "Just let it go, Wanda. Please."

"No problem. You want another drink?" Wanda wasn't a fool, and she knew how to play the game. There wasn't any need to press Kayla about something that was already in the works. Kayla could throw her hands up to stop her or shut her up, but there was not stopping God.

Kayla was about to say no, but then she looked up and saw Marley or Smooch or whatever his name was standing with Danger near the DJ's booth staring at her through the few people dancing between them. His eyes unnerved her even more than he had when he was talking directly to her earlier. In them, she saw determination and his willingness to be patient. But it was his desire that practically screamed out at her. She nodded her head yes and downed the rest of her drink.

"Man, what's up with you and ol' girl?" Danger asked curiously. "I had to get you out of there. I've never seen you turned down so many times in one conversation."

"You've never seen me turned down at all. That's the lady I was telling you about that lives down the street from me."

"And you've already fallen for her. This must be some kind of record."

"Nah, man, I'm just interested, that's all."

"You sure it hasn't gone any further than that? 'Cause it looks like it might be more than that to me."

"What?" Marley looked at his friend. "Come on, man, you know me better than that."

"Smooch, you look at her differently. I've never seen you look at any other woman that way." Danger didn't want to bring up the painful memories of Marley's past. He knew better than anyone how hard it was to move on. He had been going through such a struggle himself.

Marley looked across the room at Kayla, and then back at his friend, knowing that he couldn't hide his feelings from him. Hell, Danger knew almost everything that there was to know about him. "I don't know what it is, man. I'm just really feeling her for some reason. I've been thinking about her for a long time, speaking every time I see her or her kids, then when I asked her out, she shot me down fast and hard. She makes it very hard to get to know her. Maybe I should ask Wanda to help me out."

Danger laughed. "You know Cupid will. I'm sorry that she won't have anyone else to turn her attention on. If you accept her help, then she'll be all excited and looking to hook up everyone she can, including me."

They laughed, but the laughter stopped abruptly when Danger tapped him on the shoulder and pointed to Jaybird asking Kayla to dance.

Kayla was so tipsy by this time that she gladly followed him onto the floor. She was finally enjoying herself, with the alcohol's help, and didn't want the feeling to fade. It had been a long time since she'd had this much fun. Wanda kept her laughing, talking about the people they knew. And the liquor was definitely putting her in a better frame of mind.

Marley visibly tensed and was about to follow the two onto the dance floor, but Danger put a hand on his shoulder. Marley shrugged it off and moved to the end of the floor to watch.

Jaybird danced way too close for her taste. Kayla knew that on a fast song people still got close to each other, but it seemed that Jaybird wouldn't move away from her. His hands were constantly touching her on her hip or her waist to keep her close. After a few seconds of dancing, it was almost as if they were playing a game of tag, and she was trying to outmaneuver his hands. He made her uncomfortable, especially after she saw Marley watching them so intently.

Several women tried to pull Marley onto the dance floor, but he didn't move. He stood in his spot and kept his eyes on them.

Jaybird was a good guy; he was fun and playful, just a little too touchy for her taste. When the dance ended, Jaybird, against her wishes, kept his hand at her waist as they walked off the dance floor. Then Marley called him over. After that, Jaybird didn't bother her the rest of the night. He stayed very far away. In fact, nobody asked her to dance the rest of the night. Only Marley.

Toward the end of the evening, Marley finally pulled her onto the dance floor. Deep inside, she had been dying for him to ask her. And, with nobody showing her any interest, she had been forced to sit at the table with Wanda and Pooh. And now that she was a little intoxicated, she wanted to dance. But she took pains not to show her excitement when he finally came for her. Already two sheets to the wind, she simply followed him to the dance floor.

It was a slow song. She thought it was slow, anyway. The music was kind of fuzzy in her ears. But by the way he held her close, the way he wedged his hip between her thighs and led her in a smooth sway, it had to be something slow. Her heart began to beat unevenly, and her breathing became erratic. He had to know what he was doing to her.

Kayla felt a spasm in her belly, and then a shiver flowed downward until it landed right between her legs.

His hand tightened on the small of her back.

"You feel good in my arms, Kayla."

"I'm sure you tell all the girls that," she managed to say.

"I don't understand why you keep fighting this. We could have a good time together, but you keep pushing me away."

She was silent.

He pulled her even closer.

"You got everything I like."

"You don't even know me, Marley."

"But I know what I like."

His arm slowly moved down her back.

Kayla's knees shook, but she covered by moving into him.

"You better stop before you have me knocking on your back door," he laughed.

Kayla froze. In all her dreams, that was exactly what he had been doing, coming to her back door and seducing her.

"You all right?" He looked, his concern plain.

"Yeah, I'm fine, just fine."

"I know that's right."

"Marley, why do you want me? Anybody else would have taken my rejection at face value and gone on his way, but not you. Is it because I said no, and you're not used to that?"

"You're right. I'm not used to rejection, and I don't like it. But that's not the reason. The reason I'm not going away is because I want you. Pure and simple. I want you to be mine, to be with me, to spend time with, and to love. Are you saying that I should let what I want go? Would you tell your daughters not to go after their dreams?"

Kayla failed to answer. What could she say? With his sweet voice and commanding words, he had her right where he wanted her. And that body . . . she was having trouble concentrating.

Kayla was enjoying the feel of his body next to hers. She couldn't help but wonder how it would feel to lie next to him in a bed, with no clothes, doing God only knows what. Well, she knew what, and the thoughts were turning into vividly erotic images by the minute.

Kayla looked up briefly and saw Wanda walking out the door with her husband, Danger, and Jaybird. The song went on and on. They were dancing for so long it seemed their skin was fused when they finally pulled apart.

Kayla sat in the passenger seat of the white Cadillac pissed off—pissed off and drunk. She knew she should have stopped before that last Cap and Coke, but the tension of the night called for it. The drinks definitely did their job and calmed her nerves. She couldn't even remember how many drinks it had taken, but even as mad as she was about her predicament, she still felt the effects of the alcohol.

Marley's dark, penetrating eyes bore into her. They made her nervous and horny at the same time. He made her think about naughty . . . Kayla laughed loudly. Because of her intoxicated state, she found it hard to control herself. She blew out a long breath.

"Whoa, get it together, girl," Marley laughed as he looked over at her, shaking his head. He tried not to laugh at her, but this was too funny. She pretended not to pay him any attention. Instead, she looked out the window at the empty field next to the road. She wasn't about to let him know that he was on her mind.

"Are you all right?" Marley waited for her to answer. When she didn't, he used her silence as an excuse to put his hand on her thigh. Any reason to touch her was a good reason as far as he was concerned. He shook her leg. "Kayla?"

"Please don't. Don't touch me." She hated hearing those words come out of her mouth. It sounded more like a plea than a command.

"I'm just trying to make sure that you're all right. You had a lot to drink. Are you going to get sick or something?"

"No. I'm all right. Just drive. And don't touch me again." Yeah, she thought, that was more forceful.

Marley laughed. "So, you don't want me touching you?"

"No, I don't." She was lying, and he knew it. "I can't believe Wanda left me like that," she huffed.

"Well, she said Pooh wasn't feeling well. Besides, she knew you were in good hands. You can trust me, Kayla."

She rolled her eyes. It wasn't that she didn't trust him. It was herself. Although her mouth spouted lies, her heart was screaming the truth. She wanted Marley so badly, so intensely. It was agonizing to sit next to him while he slowly maneuvered the car onto the dark back roads.

The alcohol combined with the darkness of the night sky didn't help matters any. It made her sleepy, and it made her think of her dream from the other night. So, horny, tired, and frustrated, she sat next to the (literal) man of her dreams.

Marley wasn't tired. Having Kayla sitting next to him kept him wide awake. He was grateful to Wanda for giving him the opportunity to have some quiet time with her. Leave it to her to think up the perfect scenario—anything in the name of romance. When Wanda first told him of her plans, he knew Kayla wouldn't go for it. Apparently, Wanda didn't think she would, either. Instead of telling Kayla the truth, she just left, telling Marley to explain to her that Pooh wasn't feeling well and that she wanted to get him home as soon as possible.

Kayla glanced at him. His skin was so smooth. He was wearing a green bandana, but she knew he wasn't bald beneath it. The bandana seemed to look sexier on him than it had on any of the 200 other heads wearing the same color. His sideburns, mustache and beard were nicely trimmed. She wanted to reach up and run her fingers over his face. Her hand twitched just before she balled it into a fist on her lap.

His eyes closed briefly.

"Hey, you all right? Asking me if I'm all right. Are you all right?" she asked. One thing Kayla didn't do easily was trust other people's driving. She would stay awake until she got home, no matter how tired she was.

"I'm all right. It's just been a long day."

"Marley," she slurred, "I'm serious. It's dark as hell out here. Let me know if you're too tired to drive. I'm for real."

"What you going to do? Drive for me? Maybe you haven't noticed, but you're the one who is drunk. I only had a couple of beers, Kayla. I'm more tired than anything."

"Look, I'd rather drive than run up into something because you've fallen asleep." She sobered up a little—very little.

"Like you wouldn't have us in a building by tomorrow morning. I got this. Just let me drive."

"Honestly, tell me what I gotta do to keep you awake." Kayla sat forward in the passenger seat and looked him in the face. She was so drunk. "I can talk to you."

"What are you going to talk to me about? Tell me why you won't go out on a date with me."

"No, I don't want to talk about that."

"What should we talk about then?"

"I don't know."

"Then don't talk. Go ahead to sleep. You're drunk anyway."

Kayla giggled. "I'm not drunk. I'm in total control of myself." To prove it, more to herself than to him, she concentrated hard on pushing the radio's "ON" button. Barry White's baritone voice echoed through the speaker. Kayla only let him sing one verse before deciding that it wasn't helping. Barry always made her sleepier.

"Okay, that wasn't a good idea. We'll both be sleep if I leave that on."

Marley laughed and yawned.

"Okay, what to do, what to do?" she wondered aloud.

"Take your clothes off," Marley replied on another yawn. He didn't really think she would do it; he was just throwing out his own preference. He thought it would spark an interesting conversation.

"Really? You want to see me naked?" Kayla knew it sounded fickle, but suddenly that was how she was feeling—fickle and shy, almost high school-ish.

Marley looked over at her. Was she crazy? What kind of question was that?

"I mean—"

"Kayla, I'm not saying that's all I want, but hell yeah, I'd love to see you naked. You're a beautiful woman. What kind of fool wouldn't want to see you nude? I've been trying to get to know you for the last few months, but you've been pushing me away, and none too gently, I might add. Besides, if you let me see you naked right now, it's for a greater cause. You're actually trying to save my life, which I greatly appreciate."

He was telling the truth, but even drunk, she could see through the bull. She liked their light banter.

She blushed. The blood in her veins suddenly boiled. Kayla knew he was interested in her, but until he had just stated it in front of her, to her face, she hadn't realized how serious he had been. She didn't know if it was her desire, the celibacy, and loneliness getting to her or simply the alcohol, but she was turned on by his confession.

Marley tried to divide his attention between her and the road. He reduced his speed and practically stopped when her arms crossed in front of her and grabbed the bottom of her shirt. He thought at any minute she would turn to him, laugh, and announce she had been joking.

But she didn't.

Kayla pulled the blouse over her head with determination. She was wearing a strapless black bra underneath.

Marley licked his lips. Her shoulders were bare. The mounds of her breasts pushed against the bra, eager to be released from their hold. Quickly, he took a brief glance at the road.

The feel of his gaze on her made her feel confident, reassured. It had been a long time since she had felt so desired. He wanted her. He could barely keep his eyes off her.

As her excitement grew, Kayla's skin began to moisten. She rolled down the passenger-side window to let the breeze of the night air cool her. Acting before she lost her nerve, she reached behind her and released the bra's clasp, pulling it off and throwing it to the floor.

Taking a chance, Marley took his eyes off the road to watch her. Damn, she looked good. Squirming, he tried to find a more comfortable position. That wasn't working, so he reached into his jeans and straightened himself out. While he was fixing his pants, Kayla was unfastening hers. When he looked at her again, her pants were on the car floor next to her boots.

Marley wondered at the sudden change in her. It was like seeing a whole other person. Never in his wildest imagination would he have imagined that the quiet, unapproachable woman who lived three doors down from him could be so free, wild, and sensual. This had to be one of her multiple personalities emerging. *Okay, maybe this is going too far.*

The Kayla he knew was standoffish. Maybe she was not *really* that way, but he could only go on what she had shown him. Everybody had two sides, but she had never shown this welcoming, inviting side to him. Marley felt he had to take advantage of this opportunity. He had to make her realize that he was someone that she needed to get to know better.

If he had taken the unsolicited advice Wanda had given him seriously, he would already be lying between Kayla's legs. That was how he usually operated. For some reason, this time he wanted something different. He was unwilling to have this be a one-night stand. With the other women, it hadn't been necessary to get to know them. They hadn't made it a requirement, so neither did he. He wanted to know Kayla, wanted to know her inside and out.

Marley glanced at the road one more time. He somehow was unable to concentrate on both Kayla and his driving. The more she took off the more he forgot about the road.

CHAPTER 4

She had his full attention now. All she had left to take off was the lacy black panties, which were shielding his eyes from the prize he was waiting to see. Marley shut his eyes and swallowed hard. In the moonlight, Kayla appeared sexy and wanton. He knew it was the effects of the alcohol. He wished it were because she wanted him just as badly as he wanted her, but he knew better. She had been fighting him off from day one.

The tingling of her skin wasn't from the night air. Kayla was hyper-excited, hyper-energetic, and hyper-aroused. It felt good to let her hair down and lose control, if for only tonight. She had been closed up for so long, even if it had been at her own choosing. But every now and then, it was okay to just let go. And that is exactly what she was doing. She didn't have to be aware of her daughters' watchful eyes, not tonight. Tonight, she was a single woman, free and with no inhibiting responsibilities. And she could do whatever she wanted. Right now, she wanted to enjoy Marley's company and his attention.

"Keep your eyes on the road, Marley," she cooed teasingly. "We don't want any accidents."

"It's hard for me to keep my eyes on the road with you sitting next to me like that." He quickly glanced back at the road and then turned right back to her.

"Do you want me to put my clothes back on?" She liked playing with him. The glint in his eyes enticed her on. "I don't have a problem with doing that." Kayla forgot how much fun simple banter could be when it was used as foreplay. The light comments helped to fan the flames stirring between them.

"No, don't . . . I mean, it's okay. I got this. Just finish what you're doing." He wanted to see it all. What could he say? He was a greedy, selfish man. "Go ahead and finish."

"You sure? 'Cause I don't want to do anything that is going to distract you from your driving." She watched him watch her as she put her thumbs under the straps of her thong. Slowly, she pulled them down.

"I got the road. Go 'head." Marley glanced forward one more time, and further slowed the car down. As her panties slid lower, his eyes widened. Marley held his breath and didn't blink. He didn't want to miss a thing.

"Wait, wait. Don't move," Marley commanded once the panties were completely off. He reached up and turned on the car's interior light.

"Marley, if you don't get that light out of my face ..." She raised her hand and covered her eyes. "Turn it off," she yelled, shocked that he had done that. Granted, they were on a back road, and there weren't any other cars around and very few houses. But Kayla could just imagine some teenage boy unable to sleep looking out his bedroom window at four-o'clock in the morning and seeing the car drive by with her lying butt naked on the passenger seat. It was a little far-fetched, but that was how her mind worked.

"Hell, no. I can't see with the light off. I want to see you, Kayla."

Her nipples grew harder under his scrutiny. She didn't lower her hand.

"Damn."

"Marley, somebody might be watching."

"Ain't nobody watching. Ain't nobody out there."

"That's what they always say right before somebody comes out of the woods and jumps in front of the car carrying a hatchet."

Marley looked at her bewildered, and then he burst out laughing. "You know what? You got a very wild imagination. If somebody is watching, they got to be as happy as I am right now, looking at you. I'm sorry, but damn, I didn't expect this. I mean, I knew you would be beautiful, Kayla, but I didn't expect for you to look this good. You have a beautiful body. Don't ever let anyone tell you different."

She felt herself blushing and knew that he saw it when he looked at her with unexpected understanding.

"Hasn't anyone told you that before?" he asked softly.

"I've heard it a time or two. Now, could you please turn the light off?"

"I thought you were trying to keep me awake." He poked out his bottom lip playfully in an attempt to gain her pity. It didn't work.

"I'm sure you're up by now."

"Kayla, you have no idea," he replied, reaching up to turn the light off. As he brought his hand down, it grazed her left breast.

"Marley?" Kayla froze. Her eyes were wide with shock—not fear, but shock, because it was truly unexpected.

"What? I can't touch, either? For real, that's the only way to keep me awake. I'm about to doze off right now." Marley looked at her. "Just sit back and enjoy the ride. Because of your willingness to keep me awake, we'll get home safe and sound."

"I sure do hope so."

Kayla did as she was told and lay back in the reclined seat.

Marley kept one eye on the road and one hand on Kayla. He was sure to have a headache in the morning from moving his head back and forth so fast and so often. He rubbed her breast and licked his lips, wishing he could take his attention off the road and bend over her.

Her aroma filled the car. The scent of her perfume, the lingering smell of the clubhouse that embedded itself in their clothing, and her own whetted his senses like an aphrodisiac. It was more intoxicating than the beer he had drunk.

Kayla inhaled as his hand slid across her belly. She glanced at him briefly. Even though she was drunk, she was very conscious of his every move, and still self-conscious enough to notice his hand was crossing the evidence of her motherhood. The little bulge that filled the center of her midsection had been her cross to bear since she had given birth to her youngest daughter. She pushed his hand away.

"What you do that for?" he asked. "I'll stay awake if I can do what I want to."

"Whatever," she laughed. "You're full of it. That line is getting a little old."

Marley laughed with her. He liked the light-hearted side of Kayla, a side that he had never seen before and was surprised that she even possessed. She was absolutely beautiful. When she laughed, her eyes sparkled and small dimples appeared in her cheeks. He could tell that she was relaxed and enjoying their playfulness as much as he was.

Again his hand found its way to her midsection, but this time he didn't dwell too long in one spot. Instead, Marley moved his hand further down to the thin line of hair that he knew was a pathway to something good.

She inhaled again and slowly released her breath, but she didn't stop him. She forced herself to relax even more and enjoy the sensations he was provoking. Without his urging and after a brief hesitation, Kayla slowly began to let her legs fall open so Marley could continue his exploration.

At the offering, one of his eyebrows lifted. He hadn't been watching so much as feeling her, but this made him pause in his movements. Marley turned away from the road. His hand moved a little lower, testing her resolve. She didn't stop him. Marley glanced at the road. He let his fingers travel further down her legs.

Marley squirmed in the driver's seat. *Damn.* The band of his briefs was making him very uncomfortable.

"Kayla, you got to let me pull over."

"No," she forced out through clenched teeth. Kayla was trying to concentrate on his hand movement. She honestly wasn't even thinking about the road until he brought it up, but she knew that she wasn't about to be parked along some dark road in the middle of nowhere.

Moisture surrounded Marley's finger as he entered her. He didn't expect that much wetness and glanced down at his handiwork. The car swerved.

"Marley?" Kayla quickly sat up as much as she could.

"I'm sorry," he replied. His breathing was a little harsh as he tried to focus his attention on the road and off the naked body next to him. "I got it. Just lie back."

The movements of his finger made Kayla obey his order.

Before long, Marley found that he couldn't concentrate on the road, not with Kayla moaning and purring in his ear.

"Oh . . . that feels good," she murmured, going only slightly out of her mind. Kayla wasn't thinking about anything except the hand that was bringing her so much pleasure. She needed this, and she wanted it.

Kayla lay back and enjoyed the ecstasy that had gripped her. It was so easy for her to forget about the heartache and pain she had suffered in the past. Had she known that the pleasure he had to offer her was so thrilling, she would never have dismissed him so easily. She knew that Marley's interest in her had probably started around the same time as her interest in him had, but by that time the resentment and hurt was too deep for her to fight against it. She had been still angry with her ex-husband and had begun taking that anger out on men in general.

Marley opened Kayla wide and used his hands to satisfy her. He was like a kid in a candy store, exploring, playing, finding new and exciting . . . his lips spread into a smile as he watched her reaction to his hands.

"Please, let me pull over, Kayla," he begged, his confusion growing from the mixed signals she was sending him.

"No, we can't."

That is what she kept saying, but at the same time, she grabbed a hold of his hand and mindlessly rotated her hips in time with the bump-and-grind music that was playing on the radio.

"Oh, my God," Marley said, shaking his head to snap back into reality. The road. He quickly glanced at it, looking back at her immediately. Watching her, he thought, *mixed signals.* He wanted to just pull over and let the rest of the evening take its course, but he was afraid of her reaction, so he silently suffered.

She moaned and concentrated on how good she was feeling. It had been such a long time. Kayla soon forgot about her surroundings. She forgot about her uncomfortable position, the car's leather interior sticking to her backside. She almost forgot about Marley. It was feeling so good to be showered with this attention.

"Damn it," Marley whispered. He knew he had told himself that he would respect her wishes, but this was harder than he could have imagined. He was frustrated; he had truly reached his limit. It was time to move this up a notch. But as he looked down at her again, he could see that she was having a good old time. From the wetness, he could feel it. He could hear it, too.

If he had a free hand, Marley would have reached into his own pants, but he had to keep a hand on the steering wheel. *Would she notice if he pulled over for just a second before reaching town?*

Kayla opened her eyes. She could see streetlights. When the blurry flashes seemed to be more regular, she figured that they were approaching town. It was time for her to snap back into reality. She didn't want the night to be over. She was enjoying herself, but, like all fantasies, it had to end.

"No, no, no," Marley said, complaining when Kayla removed his hand from her body. Her moistness was running down his hand. There was no use trying to hide his disappointment. He was upset about three things. All too suddenly, they were closer to their houses. All too soon, he had to take his hand away from her body. And all too quickly, the night would be over.

He quieted down when she lifted his finger to her mouth. As she suckled him clean, Marley's mouth opened wide in amazement.

"Oh . . . shit," he muttered. "Come on. Don't get dressed." He didn't mean to sound like a whining baby, but he was used to being spoiled and getting his way.

"We're practically home." As Kayla pulled up her pants and put her shirt back on, she realized she had a decision to make. Although she was still a little woozy from the alcohol, much of its effect had worn off, thanks to Marley. She couldn't use her intoxicated state as an excuse for anything that might happen from this moment forward.

They turned off the highway and onto the road leading to their development in silence. Each was wondering what the next step should be. They knew what they wanted it to be, but every action had a reaction. The reaction was what was most scary for both of them.

In her mind, Kayla admitted that she had possibly gone too far with Marley for her to turn back now. In all honesty, she didn't want to turn back. There would be no better way to end a perfectly enjoyable evening than to go home with him or to invite him into her home for a little romper room. But now that she was sobering up, she had to think before she acted.

Tomorrow, would she be able to look herself in the mirror knowing that she had broken down and allowed her weakness to control her? She had promised herself that she would not let this happen to her again. The last time she got so enthralled in a man it turned into over twelve years of constant abuse, self-doubt, and self-esteem. She wouldn't wish what she had been through with her ex-husband, Quincy, on any woman. The physical abuse, the adultery, and the names he called her all contributed to Kayla thinking at that time that she didn't deserve better. She had allowed that man to break her down until she was nothing.

If it were not for the girls asking her why she was letting him treat her that way, Kayla would probably still be in the same situation. She never once thought that the girls knew or were being affected by her abuse. But of course they heard it; they had even seen it. The look in their eyes made her feel worse than any beating he had given her. The very next week, with the help of friends who obviously knew what was going on too, she packed up the girls and moved to another state.

She was only an hour and a half away from it, but it was far enough for her to make a fresh start. After a few minor incidences involving the police, Quincy got the picture and left them all alone. The promise, pact, she made was created for the sole purpose of ensuring that she accomplished the goals that she set for herself. It was simple: no men.

It had taken her nearly twelve years of a bad marriage and a divorce to realize that. She didn't want her girls to have to go through the same thing. So, for her girls, she had to stay focused and stand her ground. No matter how much she wanted this man for tonight, forever even, she couldn't let the feel of his hands on her overpower logic.

Marley wasn't sure which side of the fence he should put his faith in. He was still half blown away by what had just transpired in his car. The amount of sexuality that she possessed left him speechless. Never in his wildest imagination would he have thought that he would ever see Kayla's true self so soon. She kept her every emotion so carefully locked up. But he knew that what he had seen tonight was the real Kayla—relaxed, fun, and confident, and it made him want her even more.

As they neared their turn, he looked over at her. The struggle that was going on in her head was clearly fought out in plain view on her face. In that moment, he knew that their night was about to come to an end. The funny thing was, and he couldn't believe it, but he wanted it to. This wasn't the way he wanted to start off his relationship with her, not with all her doubt and confusion weighing her down.

She had shown a side of herself tonight that had been uninhibited, uncontrollable, and incredibly sexy. When she flicked her tongue around his finger and lapped up the residue . . . well . . .

Marley forced the image out of his head before he reversed his decision to be a complete gentleman for the remainder of the evening. He let out a long sigh. Despite the contrary wishes of his lower region, Marley had resigned himself to bidding her a goodnight and then going home to a restless sleep.

He didn't want to make love to Kayla tonight and have her wake in the morning with regrets. When he thought of what he could gain from her by being respectful, the decision was easy to make. He was determined to get to know this side of her a little better. As far as he was concerned, the cold, standoffish Kayla no longer existed. He would not even allow her to be that person around him ever again.

When the white Cadillac pulled into the parking spot, they both stayed in the car, not moving, not saying a word. Kayla's feelings ranged from one end of the emotional spectrum to the other. She steadfastly held to the spirit of the pact, but deep, deep down Kayla wanted to grab Marley's hand and drag him into the house to finish their evening.

"Um, Marley?" she began, unsure of what to say and how to say it.

"I'll walk you to your door, Kayla." Marley suggested the best solution, thus averting any potential mistakes. He knew one thing for sure: he was on Kayla's mind now. She wasn't likely to forget their evening together, and he was especially glad that he hadn't pressured her into doing anything that she didn't want to do. Kayla hadn't been forced or coerced any further than her own alcohol intake had taken her. She would have to question and answer for her actions on her own.

"Okay," she solemnly agreed. Her body was telling her something different, but it was for the best.

"But you got to do me two things," Marley said, taking her hand.

She looked at him. He was a good guy. Anybody else would have sat in the car and silently pressured her to ask him in.

"One, I want you to go somewhere with me tomorrow."

"I—"

Marley put his finger, the same finger he had used before, to her lip to silence her. He purposely used that finger to remind her that he knew her better now and to stop her from reverting to her old ways.

"Nothing fancy, just a barbecue. Second, don't turn back into the woman you were yesterday. I like you much better the way you were tonight. Friendly, approachable, not so mean and angry-looking all the time. You're beautiful when you're—"

"Drunk?" she questioned.

They laughed.

"I was going to say that you're beautiful when you're you. You don't have to get drunk to enjoy yourself. All you have to do is be your real self. I realize what happened tonight was partly due to the alcohol, but I saw you be free tonight. I saw you."

"Marley, you don't even know me." Kayla turned away, but he turned her back to face him.

"I'm trying to get to know you, if you'd let me." His eyes did not waver, and Kayla realized he was serious. He wanted to get to know her.

Kayla swallowed hard and opened the car door. He followed suit.

Luckily, it was nearly four o'clock in the morning on a Friday night. The chances of their neighbors seeing them were slim to none. Kayla still couldn't stop herself from looking around.

At her door, Marley made it simple for both their sakes. He said goodnight from the bottom step and watched her until she was safely inside. If he had gone all the way up her steps, he feared he might have continued into the house.

The vibe between them was strong. He could tell by her slow approach to the door that she wanted the night to end differently just as badly as he did. But now just wasn't the right time.

After she locked the front door, Kayla leaned against it briefly and then headed upstairs to her bedroom closet. It seemed the ending to her perfect night was going to be up to Adam. Fortunately, he was always ready and willing to please her.

Marley stroked his frustrations out in the shower. His first impulse was to take a cold shower. He thought the cold water would shrink his need, both physically and mentally. But it didn't work. He kept thinking about Kayla stretched out on the front seat of his car. He couldn't take his mind off the wetness of the cavern he was able to explore intimately.

Marley's breathing was irregular as he leaned against the shower wall, wondering how he had gotten himself into this situation. He wanted Kayla so badly that even taking care of the problem in the shower hadn't eased the pain of not having her.

Marley pounded his hand against the wall and looked down at himself. It was hard and stiff and looking right back at him.

In the morning, well, afternoon, Kayla stretched in her bed. She smiled to herself as she turned her head and saw that Adam had decided to stay over. It lay on the pillow, on its side of the bed like any other bootie call would. So, that's how she would treat it. Before sending him on his way—back into his little Nike bag—she would use him one more time.

Kayla realized that there was something a little twisted and weird about her relationship with Adam. It wasn't as if she was bipolar or psycho for becoming too attached to him, *it.* He, *it,* had just been around for a long time and was always there when she needed him, *it,* like any good friend.

Instead of lying on her back, she decided that Adam should join her in the shower. Occasionally, she would take him, *it,* into the shower and use the suction cup to stick it to the shower wall.

Kayla turned on the hot water and put on her shower cap. The steam from the shower filled the bathroom immediately. She stood directly under the shower and let the water flow over her.

Adam was already on the wall a few feet below the showerhead, stiff and hard, waiting for her. Turning away from the water, she backed up to the wall. Kayla bent forward, reaching between her legs and guiding him into her.

She loved the feel of the water beating on her back. Between the steady rhythm of the water, the vibrating against her G-spot, which she knew like the back of her hand, and her fingers working their magic, it took Kayla no time at all to complete her task.

If she had one complaint about the time she and Adam spent together, it had to be that it was too short. She knew her body too well after spending so much time with herself. Kayla knew exactly how and where Adam needed to go, how he needed to move, and where her hands needed to be.

Although she loved the time they spent together, it seemed that as soon as it started, it was over. She needed to spend less time with Adam and more time with someone else: Marley. *Who said that?*

Sunday morning was warm and sunny. Kayla had opened all the windows and doors to allow the house to air out. She had just finished sweeping the kitchen floor and was about to vacuum the living room floor when her girls walked in.

"Hey, Mom," they yelled in unison. "What you doing? We cleaned yesterday." Truth be told, she was bored out of her mind and nervous as hell. Bored because the girls were gone and she was home alone with nothing to do to keep her from thinking of her night with Marley and nervous because of her date with Marley. She didn't know what to expect after their escapade the night before. She was glad the girls were home to help take her mind off her dilemma.

"Hello," she replied, moving the vacuum cleaner out of the way. "How was the sleepover? Fun?"

"Yeah," Kaitlyn answered. "It was a blast. We stayed up all night. Ate everything in sight. You know, girl stuff."

"Their house is so cool, Mom," Kamry added. "They got this big room full of cool stuff. They got a pool table, darts, and a pinball machine. It was the best."

"Good. I'm glad you had a good time."

"So . . . how was your night, Mom?" Kaitlyn didn't follow Kamry upstairs to put her bag of clothes away. She needed to know the answers to her questions immediately. All night long, she had been praying that her mom was having a nice time at the party, and maybe even meeting a man. She couldn't enjoy the company of her friends for thinking of her mom. When she had been able to sneak a phone call to David, she told him of her plan to get her mom and Mr. Marley dating. He thought it was a good idea.

He had been telling her for the past week that he was thinking that maybe they shouldn't date anymore. But Kaitlyn was determined to get her mother to end the No-Man Pact that she had made without consulting her or her sister.

"It was just fine, dear. Nothing to talk about."

"Didn't you go out with Miss Wanda?"

"Yes, I did."

"And nothing happened?"

"No." As far as her children were concerned, nothing did happen. She didn't want to talk about last night at all. "We went out and had a few drinks, nothing major."

"You didn't even meet anybody new?"

"No. Was I supposed to?" At least that wasn't a lie. Kayla put her hand on her hip and looked at her daughter pointedly. Why was Kaitlyn asking her so many questions?

Kaitlyn caught herself just as Kamry came down the steps. "I was just, um, wondering."

Kamry frowned slightly, sensing that her sister was up to something suspect. Kaitlyn was so street-smart that she was usually dumb. Why would she come into the room and start firing off questions like that? *Kamry to the rescue again.* "Well, Mom, we were both a little worried about you last night. We know how you don't like going anywhere, and we hope that you didn't go through all the trouble of getting ready just to sit around and watch everyone else have fun."

Kayla looked at her girls. Maybe she had been a little closed off from the world. Was she closing her girls off, too? She never imagined they would worry about her having a good time.

"I had a good time," she assured them. "I didn't sit around all night. I even danced once or twice."

Both girls smiled brightly.

"You didn't meet anyone new who might have interested you?" Kamry asked.

"No, I didn't." That wasn't a lie either. Not really.

She glanced at her watch. Ten o'clock. It was time for her to start getting dressed. This was going to be the hard part. She didn't know what to wear to the barbecue or what to say to her girls. How could she explain to them that she was about to go out on a date with Marley when she had been preaching about not allowing men into their lives?

In another hour, she was going to have to walk out the door to meet the man three doors down for an official date. It wasn't really a date to her, but that is what he had called it. She had convinced herself that she was doing him the favor he asked for last night.

The girls, on the other hand, would see it for what it really was. A date. And on top of that, they would look at it as she was telling them one thing and doing another. She couldn't/wouldn't let her girls think that she was reneging on the promise that she had eventually dragged them all into. Even though she knew that Marley was just a friend, Kayla didn't think that the girls would believe it. They had already mentioned the way they had seen him looking at her. So, how would she keep her word to Marley *and* make the girls understand the situation?

Just Kayla's luck; Marley rang the doorbell at eleven o'clock sharp. She had been sitting in her room getting ready for the past hour, trying to decide what to wear. She still hadn't said anything to the girls. Kayla was a chicken; she knew it. In the end, she found herself walking down the steps in a soft orange flower print sundress with matching sandals.

Kaitlyn answered the door. Kamry was washing out a cup in the sink, but when she heard Kaitlyn greet him, she rushed into the room, curious about the purpose of his visit.

"Hi, Mr. Marley," Kaitlyn smiled sweetly. She stood at the door with her sister next to her. Marley was dressed in blue jeans, a green t-shirt, and black boots, and he wore a green bandana around his head. A teenager's dream guy.

"Hello, girls. How are you today?" he asked.

"We're fine," they replied, giggling.

"Would you like to come in?" Kaitlyn asked.

"Sure. Um, is your mom around?" he asked, stepping cautiously into the house. He hadn't called Kayla before stopping over to pick her up, and he didn't know what to say to them. He didn't how Kayla was going to handle the situation and didn't want to say too much.

"I'll go get her," Kaitlyn readily agreed, but as she turned around she saw her mom coming down the steps. Kaitlyn's mouth fell open. Her mom was all dressed up, and even without the smile on her face, she was beautiful, not that she wasn't already pretty. But Kaitlyn just noticed something different about her.

"I'm right here," she said nervously. When she reached the bottom, she turned to the girls and tried to be as nonchalant as she could under. "Okay, girls, I have to go somewhere with Mr. Marley."

The girls looked at each other then back at their mother, stunned. They could not believe they had heard right.

But their mother just kept talking—as if this were an everyday occurrence in the Logan household. She didn't have to explain everything to her daughters. She was still the mother, and this was not a date. "You know the rules. I don't want anyone in my house, over to my house, or in front of my house. Stay inside. I'll call you from my cellphone in a few."

She turned to him. "I'm ready."

Marley looked her up and down. She was beautiful. Unnerved, but beautiful. The soft colors of the dress matched her skin color well. Her hair, as always, was shiny and sharp. But she was dressed all wrong for the occasion. "You might want to change. This is a little less formal. Besides, we're riding the hog."

The girls squealed with delight.

"Hog?" Kayla asked. She hoped he wasn't saying what she thought he was saying. Hog meant big motorcycle. Everybody knew that. She wasn't going to be riding no motorcycle.

"Yeah, my bike. Got it out of the shop this morning. We're riding with the group." He glanced at his watch. "You'd better get a move on. We gotta meet the others in a few minutes." He saw the expression on her face, but he wasn't going to give her the opportunity to back out. Wanda bet him that he couldn't get her to come to the barbecue. And his mouth was watering from just thinking about the turkey necks that she was going to have to cook him. He was already in the house, and the girls already knew about it. There was no reason for her to back out now. He had her.

"So," Kaitlyn ventured, "is this like some kind of date or something?" Her heart was racing. Her plan was actually coming together faster than she could have dreamed. It didn't matter that she and Kamry had no idea how this all had come about. All that mattered was that it was happening just as she had hoped.

Even Kamry had to give her sister kudos on this one. It did seem to be coming together well. And they hadn't really done anything to prompt it—just a tug here and there.

"No," Kayla said.

"Yes," Marley replied. "It's a date."

Kayla gave him an *Are you crazy?* look. She couldn't believe he had used the word *date*. This was *not* a date. This was her doing a favor for a friend, or someone that she thought was a friend.

"No, it's not a date, girls. I'm just doing Mr. Marley a favor by going somewhere with him. I suppose he was afraid to show up alone, and no one else would go with him, so he asked me."

Both girls looked at her unbelievingly. Then they looked at Marley. He was a very good-looking man—tall, slim, muscular, and handsome. Their mother's reasoning just didn't make any sense.

"Mom," Kamry laughed, "Mr. Marley doesn't look to us like he couldn't get a date."

Then they both giggled.

It was the last thing she expected to come out of Kamry's mouth, of all people. Maybe it was a little naive, but she had never thought that Kamry even looked at men. The girl was so much of a tomboy that it never crossed her mind that she would have to worry about Kamry and boys. Now, Kaitlyn she watched day in and day out. But Kamry wasn't into girly things. She didn't care about looking good, just presentable. Kamry wasn't supposed to be worried about makeup, hairstyles, and especially not boys.

"Mom," Kaitlyn stepped up. She took her mother's hands. "If it is a date, it's okay. We're not going to be mad or anything. Kamry and I understand."

"Understand what?" Kayla's hand went to her hip, and she leaned back on one leg and waited for a reply. When none came, she continued, still insisting, "It's not a date. Look, I'm going to go up here and change into some jeans and a shirt. When I come back, I'm going with Mr. Marley as a favor, not a date. I repeat, not a date. You two go finish your work." Kayla stumped up the stairs. She looked over her shoulder and gave Marley a dirty look before snapping her eyes.

Marley smiled and followed the girls into the kitchen. Kamry finished washing her cup; Kaitlyn was making herself a sandwich.

"Your mom's one tough nut to crack," he laughed. "She doesn't take to people easily."

The girls looked at each other silently.

He watched them closely. Something was up. He didn't know a lot, but he knew kids. Young kids, teenaged kids, even young-adult kids. They were all the same.

"Okay," he approached them, standing on the other side of the kitchen island, both hands planted on the counter. "What's up?"

"Nothing," they said together, too innocently.

"Come on. I can tell you two are up to something. It's written all over your faces."

"I'm not," Kamry volunteered.

Kaitlyn looked at her, and then turned to him. She whispered, "Can you keep a secret?"

"I'm pretty good at it," he assured them, keeping his voice low, too.

"Okay," she exhaled. "It's not really a secret. We were just hoping that you and Mom would, you know, hook up. That's all. My mom is kinda strict. And she has made up this pact thing, like a promise, for all of us. She doesn't want us to have any boyfriends. But Kamry and I don't want to be a part of it anymore. We're getting older now, and—"

"I get it. You're talking about your mom not letting any men into her life." Wanda had told him a while ago that one of her friends had come up with the idea of not having men in her life. At the time, he hadn't known she was talking about Kayla, but it wasn't hard to figure out later.

"Yeah." They looked at each other excitedly. "It was okay when we were younger. We weren't interested in boys then, but now, well, we need her to kinda start dating so we can."

He looked from one girl to the other, smiling inwardly. They almost looked identical, except where Kamry's hair was pulled back in a ponytail of braids, Kaitlyn's was in wavy extensions, long enough to wear loose or flip into some kind of up-do. They were both pretty, Kaitlyn wearing a little makeup, Kamry none. As angelic as they looked, Marley knew the two were devilishly smart. Fortunately, their plan was his plan, too.

"You two are pretty crafty," he said, smiling.

They looked at each other.

Kaitlyn was about to say more, anything to convince him to help them. She wasn't sure who was telling the truth about the date or what exactly was going on, but it was a step in the right direction for their mother to be going outside of the house on a Sunday with a man on a motorcycle. Kaitlyn could see everything going according to plan. She was practically jumping for joy inside.

Basically, they needed this man's help.

"Mr. Marley—"

"Okay, I'm in." He might have seemed too eager, so Marley tried to correct himself. "I'm willing to start putting the pressure on your mother to date me. I don't mind helping you out."

Kamry smiled. "Mr. Marley?" She looked at him closely. "You're agreeing a little too fast. And you sure didn't take much time to think about it. I think you've wanted to date my mom all along."

They all turned when they heard Kayla's footsteps on the stairs.

"You're a smart girl, Kamry." Marley smiled at them. He walked toward the front door to meet their mother.

CHAPTER 5

To her surprise and delight, Kayla found the motorcycle ride exhilarating. She loved the feel of the wind whipping her face and the sense of freedom that being on a bike gave her. Before they headed off, Marley had given her a quick lesson in bike safety and had talked a little about bike riding in general. He wanted to make sure that she felt safe and was also comfortable.

Bear and Wanda were the first club members they saw when they pulled into the gas station, the rendezvous spot. Wanda was smiling ear to ear, and Kayla walked toward her friend to get the expected interrogation out of the way.

"Well, look what the cat drug in," Wanda laughed, tapping her husband's shoulder and pointing at Kayla.

"More like a wolf," Kayla retorted, running her fingers through her short locks.

"Girl, you might as well not try to lift you hair back up until we get where we're going. You'll drive yourself crazy trying to keep it up. Just keep the scarf on. That's much easier."

"Yeah, we argued for about five minutes about me wearing the helmet. Then I had to go back in and pull out this old backpack purse from the back of the closet."

Wanda laughed. "You'll get used to it."

"I'm not trying to get used to anything."

Wanda just looked at her, doubt evident in her eyes and in her *If you say so* posture.

"I'm not."

"You know you made me lose my bet."

"What bet?" Kayla asked, already suspecting what it was.

"I bet Marley that he wouldn't be able to get you to come with him today."

"You bet on me, Wanda?"

"Yeah, I just knew he wouldn't be able to do it. And I needed a new helmet."

"You bet a helmet? What did he bet?"

"I owe him a dinner. Turkey necks, greens, sweet potatoes, macaroni and cheese. You know, the works."

"Why did you bet him?"

"Because I thought that I knew you."

"I'm glad you lost," Kayla joked.

"How did he convince you to come today?" Wanda asked.

Kayla answered honestly. "He asked."

Wanda just stared at her, a small smile working at the corners of her mouth. She was glad she didn't know Kayla as well as she thought she did. Two down, she mentally noted. She decided to drop the subject for the time being and focus on introducing Kayla to a few of the other ladies riding with them.

"Hi, ladies, this is my friend Kayla. Kayla, this is Tonya and Donna."

"Hello," she said. The women were both short and skinny, each being under five feet, three inches. Kayla had to look down at them. Donna was light-skinned and her hair was pulled back into a ponytail. Tonya was a little darker. Her hair was braided to her scalp in zigzag designs and hung past her neck. Like Wanda, they were holding scarves in their hands. But Wanda was the only one wearing a leather vest with the bike club's insignia on the back.

"Hi," they cheerfully replied.

"So you're riding with Smooch?"

"Smooch?" Kayla replied, momentarily forgetting his club members' nickname for him. "Oh, yeah, I am."

"Hmmm, this should be interesting," Donna said, half under her breath.

"Don't start, Donna," Wanda warned, giving both of the younger women a stern look.

"What's up?" Kayla asked, looking at all three for answers. Somebody needed to tell her what Donna meant before they moved any further in the conversation.

She looked over at the group of six men, standing about ten feet away talking while filling their bikes' gas tanks. She figured it had something to do with one of them.

The three women suddenly became dumb, but Kayla had no intention of letting the matter drop.

"Wanda?"

"Okay. Look, it's nothing serious," Wanda said. Whether it became relevant or not depended on Kayla and Marley, but she needed to give her friend a heads-up. "As I told you last night, Smooch hasn't brought anyone around the group in a while. It's a long story, but the last woman he was seeing tried to play him. She cared more about being with the club than being with him—a true biker chick. So when Smooch didn't come to some of the events, she still showed up, sometimes on the arm of a member from another chapter."

"She ain't nothing but a trick. She went from one member to the next," Tonya said, inserting her two bits into the conversation.

"Now she realizes too late that she lost a good man. She's been trying to get Smooch back lately, but he won't give her the time of day," Donna added.

After the heads-up Kayla still didn't know what any of it had to do with her. She was just doing Marley a favor. And if she kept telling herself that, eventually she would believe it. "Okay, and?" she persisted.

"And," Wanda answered, "she's going to be there today. She comes to all the functions. She'll probably be there with someone else, but she'll be looking for Smooch."

"And she will not like seeing you with him," Donna laughed.

"Well, Marley and I are just friends. I have nothing to do with whatever their problem is."

"Friends?" Donna sauntered closer to her. "Kayla, nobody just wants to be Smooch's friend. If I wasn't so wrapped up in trying to get Jaybird into a commitment, I'd be after Smooch myself."

Wanda looked at her and laughed, "Yeah, right? Girl, you aren't Smooch's type. He likes his women tall and thick with a brain, ambition, and mostly respect for themselves."

"You saying that ain't me, Wanda?"

"No, baby, of course not. All I'm saying is that you're not his type. But you're perfect for Jaybird, because he hasn't fully gotten out of his boyish ways yet. The two of you are kinda maturing together." Wanda looked quickly at Kayla, who immediately saw what her friend was trying to do, and that she was succeeding. You just had to know how to talk to some people.

Donna accepted that answer because it was the truth. Neither she nor Jaybird was ready to completely settle down. She didn't want to get married or start a family. She just wanted him to commit to her exclusively, and she didn't think that was too much to ask of a man.

Then their attention shifted to the roar of approaching motorcycles.

"How in the hell did you do it, man?" Pooh Bear asked admiringly, patting Marley on his back. "How did you get Kayla to agree to come with you today? Wanda couldn't believe it. Don't tell her that I said so, but I'm glad you won. That's a meal for me, too."

"I just used a little of my charm," Marley replied.

"According to Wanda, it should have taken you a lot more than charm to get her here. It doesn't even matter. I'm just impressed, that's all."

"Come on now," Jaybird interjected. "You know Smooch is the man."

"Hell, I ain't going to lie to you. It wasn't easy. And I wasn't trying to be the man; I was just trying to be me. I guess she knows a good man when she sees one."

"I bet it wasn't easy. Well, tread lightly, my boy. A good woman is hard to find because they won't put up with any bullcrap." Marley listened to Jonathan's words as he always did. Because Jonathan had been good friends with Marley's oldest brother Robert, they had always know each other, but it wasn't until he joined the club that they became really close. Jonathan had been the club's president for the past ten years because of his easy-going personality and honesty. He won the five-year election easily both times.

The remaining ten bikers pulled into the gas station. They all had passengers—except Dang. As usual, he was riding solo.

"Fellas? What's up?" he asked, coming up to Marley and Pooh.

"You, Dang. Just waiting to pull out. Anybody else coming?" Pooh asked, shaking his hand and giving him a quick hug.

"Everybody is here. Muttley and I are riding solo, so we'll take the front. Cool?"

"Good idea," Pooh agreed. "Well, let's round them up."

Marley, Jaybird, and Dang headed for their bikes.

"I see you doing big things, Smooch," Dang said. "Was kinda surprised when I pulled up and saw her here. You go, dog."

"I do what I can, man," Marley replied.

"Yeah, I see that. Just be careful, man."

"Dang," Marley said, stopping, "man, you got to get over it. Sure, Tabby messed up. But you have to move on and find a good woman. We've all been fooled once or twice. Look at Vanessa and me. But I'll be damned if I'm going to let that trick . . . I'm sorry, that woman, and I use the term loosely, stop me from finding happiness. And you're a fool if you let Tabby stop you. You give that girl too much power, and she is not even around."

Dang seemed to be absorbing what he was hearing, at least outwardly. "You know what? You just might be right." He patted Marley on the back and walked over to his bike.

Dang loved this life. There was nothing like sitting on his hog, roaring down the highway, the wind stinging his face. It was like being totally free, and nothing else came close. But maybe Smooch was right. And he was beginning to wish he did have someone to share this life with. He actually didn't like being alone. Watching the others mount up with their wives and girlfriends, he wished it hadn't taken him so long to begin realizing that his staying single was a mistake.

They were all lined up, two by two, and Kayla's excitement began to rise. Years ago, she had ridden on the back of a bike, but never in an actual pack. As the bikers waited for an opening to pull onto the highway, the noise made by the sixteen bikes was thunderous. Kayla noticed how much attention the group attracted. Everyone was watching them. People in cars turned their heads toward the group, the people at the gas station watched as they filled their cars, and people walking into the nearby McDonalds and auto shop stopped in mid-stride to observe as the group moved into traffic.

"Hold on to me tight, Kayla," Marley said as they started off. "I mean you got to press your body close to me. Become one with me."

"Marley?" she laughed, punching him in the back.

"I'm serious. Hold on."

"I will. You think I want to fall off?"

They were riding in the middle of the pack. Kayla had actually started enjoying her day with him. After Dang and Muttley pulled into the middle of the road to stop any oncoming traffic, the bikes filed out onto the highway. When the last bike was out, Dang and Muttley caught up and took their place in front of the group.

Once Marley stopped shifting gears, Kayla eased her hold on him a little, but every time she relaxed her hold, Marley would grab her hands and pull them tight around him again.

She knew he was doing it on purpose; Kayla even played the little game a couple of times. She noticed that Wanda wasn't holding Bear as tightly. Wanda was smiling—more likely laughing—at her.

It was a forty-five minute ride to their destination. Kayla enjoyed the ride, and enjoyed sitting behind Marley with her arms wrapped around his hard body even more.

When she got off the bike, Kayla's legs were a little stiff, still vibrating from the ride. She stood aside while Marley turned the bike off and parked it.

He fastened both of their helmets onto the hooks hanging from the bike's seat. Their fingers touched accidentally, and he paused and looked at her. Kayla looked away.

"That's okay. You don't have to say anything about that yet." Marley understood that she was still somewhat in denial about their relationship. And they *were* in a relationship.

"About what?" she asked, trying to downplay whatever it was he was suggesting.

"Kayla, I thought we had an agreement. You were supposed to be yourself around me, remember?"

"Yeah, I remember," she said, looking at him. Kayla had been hoping, apparently in vain, that he hadn't remembered. Okay, if that was what was expected of her, she was just going to have to relax. She could do that. Her main girl was here. She was with an attractive man who made her laugh and whose company she enjoyed. What was there not to like? Why shouldn't she be having the time of her life?

She ran her fingers through her hair, lifting the short locks to a nearly straight position.

Watching her, Marley wondered how she could fix her hair without a mirror or comb and have it looking like she just walked out of the hair salon.

"Years of practice," she said, answering his unasked question.

Laughing hard, he pressed his hand against the small of her back and led her through the park to a large pavilion.

Kayla's eyes grew large when she saw the number of people at the barbecue. The park was huge, and people were everywhere—more people, in fact, than had been at the clubhouse party.

"Kayla, let me talk to you for a minute," Marley said, softly touching her elbow to slow her down.

His light touch caused a shiver to run up her arms and down her spine. Kayla was aware of her reaction, and she couldn't ignore it.

"Listen, Kayla," he said, once they were completely alone, "I love this bike club. It is I, and I am it, but not everybody in this club is like me, if you get my drift. This can be a pretty rough crowd. I just want you to be aware of your surroundings at all times. Don't go too far away from me and my crew, okay?"

"Okay," she promised. That was a given as far as she was concerned. He didn't have to tell her to stay close; she had no intentions of straying off. Everybody seemed to be having fun, but she wasn't a big fan of crowds. Ten chances to one, Marley would be pushing *her* away before the day was over.

Rows of long tables were set up under a large, white tent. One long table along the far edge was laden with aluminum pans of food. From the parking lot, Kayla could smell barbecued chicken, ribs, hot dogs, and hamburgers cooking. Her mouth was already watering, and her stomach growled in agreement.

Marley held her hand as they maneuvered through the crowd, stopping occasionally to greet someone he knew. He never failed to introduce her and included her in his conversations. There were men, women, and kids all around the picnic area. Everybody seemed to be doing something recreational: people played cards and board games at tables; a tag football game was underway; horseshoes were being tossed; and some girls were playing jacks at another table.

At last it was time to eat, and Pooh and Wanda led the way to the food line. Kayla piled a little of each dish onto her plate; she was that hungry. She sampled everything, even dishes that she wasn't so sure of. Marley did the same thing, but he filled two plates to her one.

"Marley, why do you need two plates?"

"One for my meats and one for my sides," he replied, looking at her as if what he did was common practice. He dug in after saying a brief prayer and didn't come up for air until both plates were completely clean. Not surprisingly, he finished before Kayla.

Two hours later the food was gone. Most of the men had left the eating area and were either standing around talking or gathered in small groups near the bikes. Kayla sat at a table with Wanda, Donna, and Tonya. The younger ladies would provide Kayla with a little intel when someone they knew walked by—as if she was going to remember or needed to know. After a few minutes, Kayla gave up even trying to keep track of the names and faces. Just too many people at one time.

She watched Marley almost continuously throughout the day, taking note of the way he stood when talking to others; how his long, confident stride took him across the grass. He was so handsome—so relaxed and comfortable around his friends.

Sometimes he would catch her looking at him and would smile. Then she would catch herself and quickly turn her head. But in minutes, she would be searching for him again in the crowd.

"He's pretty easy on the eyes," Wanda said the last time she saw Kayla turning from him.

"Huh?" Kayla looked around. Donna and Tonya had left; she hadn't even noticed.

"I said Smooch is pretty easy on the eye, isn't he?"

"I guess," Kayla said, shrugging.

"He must be. You haven't taken your eyes off him since he walked away."

Kayla turned a questioning gaze on her friend.

"You can stop the game with me, Kayla. It's written all over your face, and it's okay. Nobody ever said it would be wrong for you to like Smooch."

"Nobody but me," she replied, half under her breath.

"If you ask me, you're having a good time. There's nothing wrong with that, either, so don't ruin your day by thinking too much about things. Just go with the flow."

"Wanda, that's easier—"

The sudden hammering of Wanda's fist against her leg stopped her in mid-sentence.

"What?"

"Look." Wanda pointed toward Smooch. Kayla had turned from him just a second before. A tall, thin, bronzed beauty was walking towards him. Dressed in tight blue jeans that fit her like a second skin, she walked like a runway model. Her high-heeled black-leather boots came up to her kneecaps. A green scarf was belted around her waist, and she wore a green sleeveless, low-cut tank under a black leather vest like Wanda's.

"Vanessa. She's the one we were telling you about earlier."

Kayla watched her shake her long, curly black hair. "Confident, ain't she?"

"Confident and cocky; unfortunately, she's also fickle. Smooch isn't the first guy in the club she's screwed over."

There was no way Kayla was going to turn away from the scene that was about to unfold before her.

"Hey, Marley," Vanessa said, walking up to him.

"Hey, Vanessa," Marley responded. Dang and Jaybird had been standing with him, but walked away without speaking to her. Watching them leave, Marley smiled. Only the guy she was currently screwing liked her. The smart members kept her at arm's length. Marley was so glad that he had smartened.

"I've been watching you. How you doing? You looking good."

"I am good, thanks." He looked around warily. Whomever she was dealing with at the moment was bound to be jealous if he saw them together. It wouldn't be the first time she would have maneuvered two members into a confrontation.

Vanessa moved closer, putting her arm around his shoulders, her breast against his arm. "I've missed you."

Marley lifted her hands off and put them at her side. Then he stepped away. "Really?"

This was going to be harder than she thought. Marley was acting like he couldn't stand her, didn't want her touching him. "Well, of course. You know I do."

"I don't know anything. Besides, aren't you here with someone?"

"Yeah, Calendar, but—"

"No buts. Look, I'm here with somebody, too. You know what, Vanessa? You need to stop playing these games of yours before somebody really gets hurt. I'm not for it. I don't want to listen to your lies, and I don't have anything to say to you. So I'll see you around." He left her standing there and went to catch up with Dang and Jaybird. Seeing her was a lot easier than he had expected. He knew he was over her, but it was good to prove it to himself.

He caught up with his friends and looked over at Kayla. She had probably seen the entire exchange, and Wanda was no doubt now giving her a play-by-play accounting of his and Vanessa's history.

"You good, dog?" Jaybird asked.

"Real good, man. Don't even sweat it."

"That's what's up," Dang added. "So, Kayla? You really trying to build something with her?"

"I'm trying to, but she's a tough one."

"It's still good. I like her. She'll be good for you." Dang balled his hand into a fist and pounded Smooch's fist to show his support.

"All right, enough of all that. Dang, it's your turn," Jaybird joked. "You always trying to make sure other brothers are on the right track. What about you, man?"

"Whoa." Dang put his hands up. "Ease up, fellas. I'm taking it real slow. I'll let you know."

"Oh, damn," Wanda said, "here she comes."

Kayla turned her attention from Marley to Vanessa, who was heading straight for them. She wasn't too happy. The scowl on her face changed her whole demeanor, and she was looking, not beautiful, but evil, vengeful. Her shoulders were higher than before, and her head hung low. And she did not look so much the runway model as she did an angry bull stalking a bullfighter in the ring.

Wanda's smile brightened, leading Kayla to wonder what she was up to.

"Hey, Vanessa, girl. Long time no see. I didn't know you were going to be here today. Who you with?" she asked cheerfully.

"Hey, Wanda. How you doing?" Vanessa asked, putting on a passably friendly face but sounding out of sorts.

"What's wrong with you?" Wanda asked. "Why you sounding so down?"

"Nothing," she mumbled.

"Oh, okay." Wanda knew she wouldn't say too much with the others around, but she had to show some concern. "Who you here with, Vanessa?"

"Calendar," Vanessa replied, sounding not too happy about it.

"Oh, he's a nice guy. But you know he's married, don't you?" This was the kind a shit that galled Wanda. With all the single men in the club, why would she degrade herself by latching on to one who was married? But Vanessa was an equal-opportunity groupie; she didn't much care who the man was—as long as he had a patch on his back and a bike between his legs.

"Yeah, I know. But he did say they aren't getting along."

"Oh? And you believe that? I know that man's wife. And she's a good woman—probably too good, staying home all the time and letting him do whatever or whoever he wants. She's crazy. Well, how long have you been seeing him?"

"Only a couple of months. You know how it is." She showed no remorse, not a glimmer of regret.

"No, actually, I don't." Wanda stopped just short of telling the girl to get away from her, but Vanessa wasn't taking the hint. She hated to be mean, but some people really needed reminding that their actions hurt other people. Vanessa made it hard for good women like Donna to find and keep a good man, especially when someone like her comes along practically giving her stuff away. "Oh, I'm sorry. Vanessa, this is my girl, Kayla. Kayla, Vanessa."

"Hi, Kayla," Vanessa said, looking her up and down, but smiling.

"How are you doing?" Kayla replied, not smiling back. Something about Vanessa didn't sit well with her, and it wasn't the fact that the girl used to sleep with Marley or that she still wanted to. Vanessa wasn't just a beautiful girl, she *knew* it, and that knowledge oozed from her every pore, her every move, her whole attitude. Kayla was turned off by that.

"Kayla is—"

"Kayla!" It was Marley motioning for her to join him.

"That's my cue," she said to Wanda, slowly getting up from the table. "I'll see you in a minute, girl."

"All right," Wanda replied. The disappointment she felt when Marley interrupted her introductions disappeared when she saw Vanessa's expression. Her girl knew how to play the game. Kayla had remained cool and confident even when she had seen Vanessa with Marley. And she now walked over to Marley with the same attitude. That was the difference between a woman and a girl. Luckily, Kayla's back wasn't a bull's eye, and Vanessa's eyes couldn't shoot darts.

Kayla walked into Marley's open arms willingly, letting him put his arms around her and pull her close. As they walked away, arm in arm, talking and laughing, Kayla could feel the fire from Vanessa's eyes burning through her.

"Umm," Marley smiled. "If I had known I would get all this, I would have had Vanessa around way before now."

"Is that why you think I let you hug me?"

"Why else? Before you saw us talking, I would have never been able to hold you like that, not in public, anyway."

"Oh, whatever. I'm not prudish. I just need to know whom I'm dealing with. Obviously, you may be used to a different kind of woman."

"Some people are deceptive. And regardless of what I'm used to, I know what I want." His looked into her eyes, not blinking, never wavering.

Kayla's knees began to shake, and she was sure that by now they were being heavily watched, so she started walking, leading him away from the group.

"I want you, Kayla," Marley continued. "It's not a secret, but I don't just want your body. I want all of you. Most of the girls I've dated in the past were just like Vanessa. Kayla, you're very different, but you're everything I want. Strong, beautiful, loving, and smart. Those are the qualities I want in my lady." Then he laughed, lowering his voice. "Plus, you're a freak." He moved out of the path of her arm when she swung at him. "And a fighter," he joked. "I couldn't ask for more than that." She chased him for about thirty seconds before he let her catch him and wrapped his arms around her.

Kayla laughed with him. She wasn't going to tell him that she actually wanted to be close to him, held in his arms. The truth was, the good time she was having made it easy for her to forget that she was only doing him a favor by being there. Sure, she was adding a little show to their lollygagging for Vanessa's sake, but she was doing it more for herself than she would ever be willing to admit.

At five-thirty, the autumn sun was just starting to move towards the horizon. It was still warm, though the wind was blowing softly. Kayla was glad she had agreed on this outing.

"We'll be mounting up soon. How 'bout we go for a quick walk?"

"Walk where? There are people all over the place." She made a sweeping motion over the picnic area. "I didn't realize your club was so large."

"Yes, we're large. These are only the members in the area. We got chapters all up and down the coast."

"I know. Wanda told me."

"If you really want to see a lot of people, you'll have to travel with me some time."

She looked at him, and he looked deadly serious. "Um, maybe one day." She could just see herself lying up in some hotel room in a strange city with Marley.

They got as far as the cement walkway that led to the parking lot before they heard Dang and Jaybird yelling for everyone to mount up.

"I guess I moved too slow to get you on the nature trail." Marley smiled and pulled her toward the motorcycles. "I should have called you earlier."

She looked over her shoulder and saw a sign with an arrow under the words *Nature Walk.* He was a slick one. She hadn't even noticed that he had been leading her into the woods.

"You think you're slick, Marley Jarnette. I'm going to have to watch myself around you."

"Don't worry about that. I watch you enough for both of us. Come on, let's mount up. Are you ready for the ride home?"

"I'm always ready to ride," she replied.

Her words stopped Marley in his tracks. "Be careful, baby. The game might get too dangerous for you."

Kayla ignored him. "I'm glad I came. It's been a good day."

"The day's not over yet," he responded. "I'm glad you came, too."

They held hands on the way to the motorcycle, walking and swinging their arms as if they had been a couple for years.

As they neared the parking lot, Vanessa was standing not too far away with a man who looked to be about four inches shorter than she. She held her head high and smiled as if she had not a care in the world.

Vanessa's acting was so good that she had everyone believing that she really wasn't miserable deep down inside. But she was. Marley was walking around flaunting Kayla as if he was in love or something. At one time, it had been she he had showered with attention and affection. Once upon a time, he cherished her. Vanessa realized she had made a mistake, which she had been trying to rectify, but she still needed her bills to be paid.

Kayla had spotted her as soon as they started toward the bike and could see the subtle change in her. An air of confidence or determination had come over her. Kayla didn't know if Marley had seen her, but he acted as if he hadn't, walking by without the merest glance in her direction. She simply wasn't on his mind anymore. It was as if she didn't even exist.

Kayla thought that Vanessa might mistakenly see her as mean and childish, but she couldn't help waving goodbye to her with one of her friendliest smiles. She didn't think that Vanessa would wave back. She knew how improbable that was. And Vanessa didn't.

Kayla just followed Marley back to his bike. She didn't have anything to do with whatever had gone on between them, and she didn't want Vanessa to think there were any hard feelings between them. One woman's trash was another woman's treasure. She should have appreciated him when she had the chance.

The synchronized moment of the bikes amazed Kayla, but the noise was overwhelming. There had to be over a hundred bikes moving over the winding roads leading from the rural park area to the highway intersection. Kayla had never seen anything like it. And when the different chapters of the club separated to go their separate ways, it was done in such an organized fashion that she assumed it had been practiced. Kayla wondered just how often they rode together like this, and was already looking forward to the next time she would ride with them.

The ride home was peaceful once she and Marley broke off from the rest of the group. It surprised her when he turned off the highway at least two miles before their exit. Kayla had no idea where he was going or why he broke off. She decided to just enjoy the ride.

On the back road, Marley slowed the bike down considerably, so Kayla was able to sit up on the bike and loosen her hold on him. It was a beautiful, starlit night, and she could finally look around and enjoy the scenery.

The road was curvy and hilly, and Marley took his time. On these roads, you never knew when a car would come around the next bend. When he was younger, he and his older brothers would tear around the corners like daredevils. They were young and dumb, never expecting that the next car could be the last car any of them would ever see. He still took the curve hard himself every now and then. He knew the road like the back of his hand, but he didn't want to take those kinds of chances with Kayla on the back of his bike.

He slowed down near a paved road. Kayla thought he was going to turn down the lane, but at the last moment he revved the bike back up and continued on. She thought that perhaps he was stopping to visit someone who wasn't home. The lights were off. After his next turn, she knew where they were. This road would take them back to the highway and closer to their development.

Marley kept his bike moving until he was back at his house. In a moment of weakness, he had decided to take Kayla to the spot for a little make-out session. The spot was a roadway on his family's property that he and his brothers had paved. The road led to the softest, grassiest area on their property. There was a small elm tree and a little shed that his oldest brother, Robert, had bought. By the time Marley was in his later teens, he knew what the shed was used for.

Robert and Nester had taught Marley the rules of the shed and had made him promise to keep its existence a secret from their mother. It was doubtful that she ever knew about the shed. Their mother hadn't been the outdoorsy type. She hardly ever walked around the property unless it was for a romantic stroll with their father. Marley wanted to be so much like his older brothers that he listened to every word they said, hung onto every piece of advice as if written on stone.

For the last seven years, he believed he was the only one still using the old shed. Nester had moved to another state, and Robert had settled down, married, and now had five kids. After their parents died, Robert moved his family into the house, but he left the shed.

Even though the shed was still in perfect shape, Marley didn't feel it was the right place to take Kayla. She was not a bike-club groupie that he was hitting on for the night. He used to take Vanessa there all the time rather than spend money on a hotel room. But Kayla would expect more; her standards were obviously high. And he wanted better for her than he had been used to giving.

Kayla held on tight as he pulled onto the sidewalk and slowly drove around the back of the townhouses, slowly coming to a stop under his high deck. After a moment, the bike went silent, and he turned the headlight off. It was just the two of them alone in the darkness. Her arms were still around his waist.

Marley sat still and wondered why she wasn't getting off the bike.

Kayla didn't want to move. She wanted to stay right there on his bike, next to him. The day had been so wonderful. Whether it was the high from finally starting to get out of the house and enjoying herself or from riding on the back of his Harley all day, she didn't know, but something had her giddy and intoxicated. And it wasn't alcohol this time. It had to be Marley.

"You going to get off?" he asked.

"Only if you want me to," she replied. Kayla stood on the footrests on each side of the bike. Just as she was about to swing her leg over to get off, he stood up to his full height and grabbed her by her waist. Instead of landing on the ground, Kayla found herself sitting in front of him on the motorcycle.

"Whoa," she said. She was caught off guard by his strength and her predicament.

"Nah, I don't want you off the bike. I want you right here." He positioned her on the gas tank, but she kept sliding down toward him. He finally lifted her legs over his and kept her in place. "Yeah, that's better."

At any other time, Kayla would have been embarrassed by the position she was in, her legs spread over his, her center directly opposite his. But she liked it. A lot.

Marley thought at any moment she would balk and run for her house, but she didn't. She stayed with him in the darkness.

"Thank you for a wonderful day," she said. "I'm glad I decided to go with you."

"That's what I'm here for—to make sure you have a good time." He pulled her closer to him. The feel of firm breasts against his chest turned him on. Even though he couldn't see her too clearly in the darkness, in his head he could see everything. He had watched her so many times that her body was permanently etched in his mind.

Kayla kissed him first. It took her a second to get her nerve up, but it was something that she wanted to do, something she wondered about. How would his lips feel against hers? How would he respond to her?

Marley responded immediately to her kiss, holding the back of her head in a fit of urgency. All day long he had been wanting, longing to have her in his arms, and here she was giving it all to him. As he deepened the kiss, his arms went around her body. Marley pulled her as close to him as possible. She was straddled on his lap, but she still wasn't close enough for him.

Kayla returned his kisses eagerly. Her arms were around his neck and she used all her strength to pull herself onto his lap so that their bodies meshed together. Marley's hand spread down her back, gently kneading along her spine.

"Ow," she sighed into his mouth when his big strong hands clasped onto her ass cheeks. She loved the feel of a man massaging her behind. A small tremor ran down her spine. Kayla deepened the kiss.

Marley pulled her even closer, grinding into her through the tight fabric of their jeans. He couldn't get close enough. He needed to change their positions.

Kayla let him push her back onto the black gas tank. Her bottom was resting on the padded leather seat. He stood over her and took off the leather vest that he wore over his jacket and hung it on one of the metal hangers he had put under his desk to hang tools and other odds and ends.

"Hold on a sec," he said, removing his leather jacket and placing it under her back. "I don't want you to be uncomfortable." The hard gas tank cover was probably pressed into her back.

Kayla wasn't complaining. As Marley slowly lowered her back onto his jacket, his hand pressed against her lower stomach to steady her on the motorcycle. She felt her juices flowing. She wasn't falling.

Marley stood tall between Kayla's legs, which he had pulled up around his waist. The bike was between his legs. He bent forward to kiss her. The bike wobbled just a little, but he was able to stop it from moving too much, keeping it from swaying side to side.

Kayla enjoyed his kisses. She held onto him with her legs wrapped securely around his midsection. His hands were holding onto her shoulders.

"Umm," he sighed as her tongue twined deep into his mouth. His hands moved to her sides. "Kayla, you feel so good." Marley pulled away from her. He lifted her shirt up from the bottom and began to pull at it until the black bra was exposed.

Kayla shivered when he caressed her stomach. She had forgotten to be self-conscious about her tummy's little pudge. Her shyness was replaced by the urgency of desire. And she was so glad she had worn the bra with the front snaps when his large hand lifted and spread over her breasts. The snap gave easily.

Marley used his hands to gently knead her large, soft breasts as if they were dough. He felt himself jolt forward, a warning that it was nearly time for release. He uncomfortably shifted his weight to his other leg to give himself a little more room in his jeans. For now, he was only interested in making sure that she was comfortable.

Kayla leaned forward until her shirt was completely over her head. Dropping her arms down behind her made it easy for her bra straps to slide off her arms. Finally, from the waist up, she was completely nude. She was glad that they were secluded in absolute darkness under his deck. What little light the moon had provided was blocked out when he hung his vest.

She didn't need to see. She could feel everything he was doing to her. Kayla felt his fingers finding their way to her breasts, which were not perky from the warm night air. He squeezed them, not too hard, just enough to excite her. Then, she felt the wetness of his tongue when he bent down to suckle each nipple leisurely. Slowly, he traded one breast for the other until she was moaning from sheer pleasure.

Marley continued to concentrate on the bike between his legs. When she scooted close to him, he had to be careful that they did not both end up on the ground with the heavy bike atop them. But he wasn't going to stop. He couldn't do that. She seemed freer tonight than before. He wasn't sure if it was because they were on his bike. Maybe it was because he was able to participate more. Whatever the reason, he could tell Kayla was having fun.

"Kayla," he whispered close to the skin over her belly. His fingers were working to get her jeans unbuttoned. "Baby, unhook your legs." When she did as she was told,

Marley put her legs in front of him straight in the air. Her boots came off with no problem. He quickly stood and pulled both pant legs over her hips and off her.

Kayla tried to put her legs back down when the jeans were off. He stopped her.

"Wait. We might as well get rid of these now, too." Marley reached down to pull her panties off. Instead of cotton or silk, he felt skin, smooth, silky skin. Marley gently slapped her bottom. He reached further up until he could feel the thin stretchy material of her thong. His blood boiled, and he wished he could see her. He loved thong panties.

With one hard tug, he had the panties to her kneecaps, then over her feet. He brought her legs back down around him. Marley put his hand on her belly to hold her in place. He could feel the beginnings of her sprouting hairs against his palm.

This was exactly how he wanted her. He inhaled strongly and got a whiff of her intoxicating essence. *Oh, my goodness.*

CHAPTER 6

Kayla lay still, completely nude, spread eagle against the leather jacket and seat. She could feel him looking down at her. Even knowing that he couldn't possibly see anything didn't stop the heat from rising to her face. It penetrated her whole body, heated her from her face down to her center. And she wasn't sure how damp his bike seat had gotten while she waited for him to make his next move.

It didn't take him long. The hand on her belly turned until Marley's thumb was traveling between her curly locks and reaching between the folds of her center.

Kayla jumped up from the bike in one big convulsion.

"Whoa, girl. You better be careful before you end up on the ground." Marley laughed softly, placing his hand on her hip to keep her in place. "Come on, I think it's time for us to go inside." He searched for her hand.

She was silent for a moment. "I don't want to go inside."

"You don't?"

"No, I want to stay out here."

"Out here?" Marley asked, different sexual positions running through his mind. "Come on, I want to be with you, Kayla. God only knows what is on this ground. Want me to run up and get a blanket or something?"

"No. Don't leave me. Join me here, on the bike."

She couldn't see it, but Marley's eyebrow rose, but he hesitated for only a second. "You sure about this?" he asked as he moved toward the back of the bike.

Kayla giggled when he stumbled over the back pedal.

"You're going to fall," Marley laughed. The bike leaned sideways as soon as he wasn't supporting it between his legs.

Kayla let the slant of the bike guide her right off. She was standing totally nude beside his bike, watching as he removed his t-shirt. She couldn't see him clearly in the dark, only the outline of his body as he moved. Kayla waited as he bent over and pulled off his boots, then pushed his jeans down and stepped out of them. Damn, she wished she had a flashlight. But it didn't matter; Kayla was so excited she willingly let her imagination take over where her eyes failed. In her head, she saw Marley's body from head to toe.

Marley moved toward her and grasped her around the waist. He pulled her to him, fitting her body to his.

Kayla loved the feel of him standing next to her. As her arms went around him, she let out a stream of air. This was more than she had imagined.

He knelt down slightly until their lips met. His tongue softly traced the corners before pushing its way into her mouth. Before he deepened the kiss, his hands ran down her back. Then he gently squeezed her bottom.

"Get on," he whispered.

"Huh?"

"Go, get on it," he repeated.

Kayla wasn't sure what he was suggesting, but she was game. She followed his directions, went to the bike, and swung her leg over it. When she turned back to him, Marley was pulling something out of his pants pocket. The sound of ripping told her it was a condom. As he turned to apply it, she got a quick glimpse of the hardness he covered. That glimpse excited her even more.

He then got on the bike behind her. "Lean on the gas tank," he told her as he moved closer. Once she had done this, Marley grabbed her hips and guided her back onto him.

The breath Kayla had been holding rushed out with her loud moan as he filled her. Smoothly, she fell into his slow rhythm, using her forearms for support against the metal tank. Kayla closed her eyes and enjoyed the lazy strokes he guided her through.

Her moans made Marley want to take his time making love to her. He had to make sure she was thoroughly pleased. He leaned forward and licked her back as he deepened his strokes.

"You feel good, Kayla," he said in a husky voice. Reaching around, he kneaded her breast.

Kayla didn't reply. Each thrust drove her deeper and deeper into madness. Each time he withdrew, she greedily opened herself up to receive more. Kayla moaned louder with each pump of her hips.

"Are you close?" he asked. Marley was fast approaching his climax. He wanted to take it slow, but the more she moaned and squealed the more excited and hotter he got. Finally, Marley couldn't take it longer. He was too close, and he knew she had to be close, too.

Kayla didn't answer; she mumbled something incoherently.

Marley stood up and plunged deeply into her.

Kayla gasped at the unexpected pain.

Marley reached up and put both his hands on the handlebars, giving himself more leverage from that angle.

Kayla's moaning became louder. She felt the stirrings of her own release swirling at the pit of her stomach.

Marley hit the switch, and the motorcycle roared to life, settling to a low hum. The vibrations blasted through their bodies.

Immediately, the tremors shot through her. Kayla felt her body tightened as Marley sat back on the bike once again changing his strokes. She closed her eyes as she felt her release course through her.

When he sat back on the bike, the trembling hit his scrotum. Marley knew it wouldn't be long. When Kayla tightened up the walls surrounding him, he knew it was over. He held her hips still as he groaned out in relief.

First to break the silence, Kayla said, "Well, that was definitely a first." They were walking hand in hand across the two backyards between her house and his.

"Look, Kayla," Marley said, his tone pensive, "I'm sorry for this. I really wanted it to be more romantic."

"Are you kidding? That was better than romantic; it was spontaneous. Besides, you tried to get me to go into the house. I wanted it to be just like that. Just like that."

"Then I'm glad you enjoyed yourself. I know I did."

When they reached her back door, he offered to walk her around to the front.

"No," Kayla told him, "this is probably best. We don't need all the neighbors in our business."

"This is true. So when am I going to see you again?"

"I don't know," Kayla replied. She knew for sure that she wanted to see him again, but she had to stay focused. Kayla realized that she couldn't let a couple moments of weakness destroy what she had worked on so long. Just because she and Marley just had amazing sex was no reason to start thinking she could trust him. He was a man. As much as she enjoyed her time with Marley, Kayla knew that it couldn't happen again. She was supposed to be setting an example for the girls. Marley had plenty of women. She'd be a fool to believe otherwise. No, falling for Marley would be like setting herself up for failure.

Kayla had been hurt once, and no matter how much she had just enjoyed herself, she wasn't going to get all emotional and rush headlong into his arms. It would have felt good to have his arms around her, whispering sweet nothings in her ear, but she didn't need that. She didn't want that. She just wanted him to leave before she gave in to her feelings.

"Kayla—"

"Marley, look. Let's not make this out to be more than it is. I really enjoyed our evening, but that's all it was, an evening. It shouldn't have gone as far as it did, and I apologize if—"

"Don't do this," Marley interrupted. He took her by the arms and looked down at her. "Don't stand there and lie to me. You know there was more to what we did than that."

"All I know is that I need to get into the house," Kayla replied, rushing up her porch steps.

Marley followed her. "Wait! Kayla, we need to talk about this."

"I don't want to think about it. I just want to go inside."

"Kayla, don't leave like this. I thought we were doing great."

Now at the sliding glass door, Kayla she turned and faced him, "We were, Marley, but it's not what I want."

"You're lying, Kayla. I'm not going to believe you."

She knocked on the sliding door. "Just let it go, Marley." Kayla waited for one of the girls to open the door; it could only be unlocked from the inside.

"Mom? Is that you?"

"It's me, baby," she answered Kamry. Her heart was beating furiously.

Marley backed down the steps, and, from the bottom, he watched her until she entered the house. The sudden change in her surprised him. How could a perfect evening end so badly?

"What were you doing out back, in the dark?" Kamry asked, looking her up and down.

"Oh, I-I, um, was just sitting out here getting some fresh air," she replied, quickly coming up with a little white lie. "Um, come on, let's get inside. What are you doing up? You got to get up early in the morning," she said, changing the subject and practically pushing her daughter into the house.

Turning off the lights as she went, Kayla followed her daughter up the stairs. Safely behind her closed bedroom door, she collapsed on the bed and let out a long and frustrated breath.

Marley stood on his deck and watched as the patch of light in Kayla's back yard flickered out. Feeling a mix of anger, frustration, and disappointment, he slowly made his way into his house. If only she hadn't started analyzing the situation, maybe they could have sat outside and talked a little. Now she was talking as if she regretted the time they had spent together.

While she had never actually agreed to the idea of them being together, he had hoped she had at least entertained the possibility after the wonderful time they'd had. Under his porch, she had acted as if she had—and liked the idea.

Okay, maybe he was reading too much into the situation. But she wanted him tonight; the response of her body told him so. She probably thought he only wanted her body. That was not the case. Sure, when he first saw her, sex was the first and only thing on his mind. He didn't know her then. But he had gotten to know her better, had spent time with her, and he was now certain that she was exactly what he wanted.

Kayla lay still on her bed until her heart beat returned to normal, then she roused herself and went into shower.

She could still smell him on her, all around her. Before his scent became embedded in her memory, she had to get rid of it.

The water wasn't hot enough to erase his touch. Every spot the water hit was one that he had touched. Kayla couldn't scrub her body hard enough. When she had dried herself off, she was exhausted and clean, but his presence was still all around her.

And that is when Kayla realized for the first time that she might be in trouble.

"Hey, girl," Wanda called, walking toward Kayla's desk. It was only 10:15, but she had stayed away as long as she could.

"Hello, Wanda. What's going on?" Kayla asked. She kept her eyes focused on the pile of paperwork in front of her. Wanda was visiting this early for a reason, and Kayla didn't want to give her false impressions. If Marley's name came up, she was sure Wanda would know right away that she had been thinking about him all morning. And she wouldn't be able to lie about that.

"That's what I was going to ask you." Wanda had never been one to pull punches, but she did lower her voice to keep from arousing their coworkers' curiosity. "I saw y'all turn off yesterday. Did you go to his brother's house?"

Kayla looked up, puzzled by the question. "His brother's house?"

"Yeah, one of Smooch's older brothers lives back on that road. He's a member, too, but he doesn't ride that much anymore. Another cutie, of course. I thought that maybe he was stopping by there to introduce you to his family."

"Girl, you're crazy. Wasn't any need for him to be introducing me to his family."

"Are you sure?" Wanda looked at her friend long and hard.

Kayla returned to her paperwork. "Of course I'm sure."

"Well, it just seemed like the two of you were getting along really well yesterday."

"We were. Marley's a nice enough guy."

"But?"

Kayla looked up and tried to arrange her face in a stern expression. "But I've told you time and time again I'm not looking to be in a relationship. Marley and I are friends, and that's all. I went with him yesterday as a favor."

"Kayla, I'm only going to say this once, then I'm out of it."

"You are always saying something once," Kayla laughed.

"That's right," Wanda laughed. "But this is serious. I know. It's about you being afraid to trust, scared to open yourself up, and using that little promise of yours to hide from the world. And from what I can tell, you've hidden for far too long. Honey, you can't run from love. Love is strong, and when it decides to find you, all the promises in the world are not going to be able to stop it. Believe me."

"Well, then, I guess I'm just going to have to be strong enough to stop it. If I'm not looking for it, then it shouldn't be looking for me."

"Girl, that doesn't even sound right. You heard the old saying 'Love waits for no one.' That means you, too."

"Well, do the girls agree with all of this nonsense? I'm sure they realize that you're keeping them locked up, too."

"What do you mean? Of course they do."

"Kayla, I don't know a teenaged girl alive who wants to hear that they can't start socializing with boys, especially ones as pretty as your girls. I bet you those girls aren't happy about that pact of yours one bit. For goodness sakes, Kayla, they're what, fifteen and sixteen?"

"They are sixteen and seventeen, and no, they haven't said anything of the sort."

"And they're not going to. Kayla, look at what you're doing. This should be the best time of their lives. They're in high school. They should be dating, getting ready for homecoming and the prom. Come on, girl. You got them locked up so tight that when they do get out, they're not going to know how to act. And you know what that can lead to."

Kayla didn't reply. She could always count on Wanda for putting something in her head that she had never thought about before. She was always making her look at things from a different angle.

"You're so stuck on yourself that you're not thinking about the girls. You already know everything that I've said, and you know it's the truth. Just think about what I said. I'll talk to you at lunch, okay?"

"Okay." Kayla didn't want her friend to see her turmoil, her indecisiveness. She was upset with herself, not Wanda. She acknowledged that she was a little strict on her girls, but that was because she didn't want them making the same mistakes she had made. She was trying to protect them.

They were only sixteen and seventeen. At their age, she was making a lot of mistakes, because her mother and father hadn't been attentive enough. She dreaded making the same mistake with her own kids. Kayla sat back in her chair and thought about her situation for a moment. She realized that after she left their father, she had become a little more protective—maybe even overprotective—of them. But it was for a good reason; she didn't want anything to happen to them. Kayla didn't want for them the same kind of heartache she had experienced at the hands of their father.

She was so deep in thought she failed to notice two young women approaching her desk. Kayla was surprised when she looked up and saw Magie and Paula, who hardly ever spoke to her, standing in front of her.

"Hey, Kayla," Magie said, a tad too sweetly.

"Hello, Magie, Paula," Kayla responded cautiously. She didn't know what they were up to, but she knew to put her guard up.

Magie leaned over her desk and put her hands on her hips. "Kayla, I heard you were at the Zulu party Saturday night. We usually go to all of their parties, but I had family business to take care of that night."

"Did you?" Kayla looked at her, not willing to satisfy their obvious craving for scuttlebutt.

"We heard you were with Smooch." The two stood there waiting for a reply.

Kayla was determined not to give them one. She was too old to play the games these girls were trying to play. Instead of opening her mouth, she just leaned back in her chair. Her business was her business, and she wasn't in the habit of letting nosy-body women into her business.

"Well, were you?" Paula asked, growing impatient.

"Where I was and whom I was with aren't any of your business," she finally said, looking from one girl to the other. Since starting there, she had witnessed the pair being the source of more than a little bit of drama in the small department.

"I just didn't think you were Smooch's type, that's all," Magie smiled, rising to her full five-foot, eleven-inch height. "After all, you're nothing like Vanessa, and definitely nothing like me." Then she strutted away in her tight pinstriped navy shirt and black stretch pants.

Kayla visualized stretching her leg out far enough to knock the heel of Magie's three-inch boots from under her. But she didn't; instead, she smiled wickedly and kept working. She refused to allow herself to even think of how they knew Marley, not to mention what Magie had meant by that smartass remark of hers. But she wasn't going to give them the satisfaction of thinking they had rattled her. Not right now, anyway.

But she did have to think about what she was going to say to Wanda when she came back at noon. Kayla knew she wouldn't be late. There were way too many questions hanging for Wanda's taste. So Kayla spent the rest of her morning preparing for the inquisition she was bound to undergo.

"I don't want to talk about it, Wanda," Kayla said as soon as they sat down at the small wooden table for two in the far-off corner of the café. She hoped that would be the end it, but she knew better. This was Wanda she was talking to.

"I wasn't going to say anything," Wanda said. But after a few moments, she did anyway. "Fine. I was only going to say that Smooch is a really decent guy. I like him a lot, and I think you two would make a good couple. I just don't see the problem with you getting to know each other. The least you could do is make a new friend. What harm would it do?"

Kayla looked at her, her head titled to the side. "Is that *all* you were going to say?"

Wanda shrugged. "Excuse me for being concerned about your happiness."

"I am happy."

"No, you're not. And even if you are, I bet he could make you a lot happier."

"Just let it go, Wanda, please," Kayla pleaded.

"Well, you can't deny that the brother is fine."

"I never said he wasn't fine."

"And you can't deny that you like him."

"He's nice enough. I suppose from the limited amount of time I've spent with him I could say he's all right."

"All right? Girl, please, that brother's got it going on."

"Well, I don't know all about his personal life," Kayla laughed.

"And it is not for me to tell you, but—"

"But you will?"

"Exactly. He's the youngest of three fine-ass brothers, and I do mean fine. They own the land on that back road you turned off on yesterday. Their parents left them pretty well off. His house is paid for; his cars are paid for. Marley's an A.C.E."

"A.C.E.?"

"Available, credit-worthy, and educated. And any woman with half a brain would be trying to break down his door."

"Probably already is," Kayla mumbled before biting into her sandwich.

Wanda pretended not to hear the remark. "At any rate, I guess if you're not smart enough to—"

"Wanda," Kayla interrupted, putting her fork down and looking straight at her friend. "If you mention Marley's name one more time, I'm going to eat at my desk."

"Whatever, then." Wanda made a point of staying quiet for the next three minutes. It was hard, but she was mum until Kayla spoke.

Kayla finished her food and moved her plate away and then looked up at her. "So you can't say anything to me without talking about him? That kind of hurts."

"Well, it kind of hurts that you're not willing to take advice from your best friend."

"Wanda?"

Wanda glanced down at her watch. "Look, I gotta get back to my desk. I'll talk at you later. I'll just stop by your desk before I leave work for the day. Maybe then you'll want to talk."

"You better not leave. Wanda?"

But Wanda did leave. And kept right on walking.

"Kaitlyn, I just think this is a bad idea, that's all."

"Well, we don't have too much more time. The party is this weekend." They were walking home from the school bus with their friend Talisha, who agreed with Kamry.

"I think it's a good idea, too," she said, pushing back a strand of her perfectly straight, shoulder-length hair from her forehead. "Mr. Marley is fine. My mom says that all the ladies in the neighborhood are cackling like a bunch of hens over him."

"Yeah, but he actually likes our mom," Kaitlyn said proudly.

Kamry had run out of patience. Kaitlyn never saw the underlying problems. All she was worried about was winning. The girl was flaky. Already she had forgotten that their mother had sworn off men, and practically had them swear off boys. She had also forgotten that her main goal was to be able to date her boyfriend publicly. But at this exact moment, all that mattered was that Mr. Marley had chosen their mom to like over all the other women in the development. She was stupid.

"Kaitlyn, can we please stay focused? Regardless of what Mr. Marley thinks, we both know that Mom doesn't like him."

"Yes, she does. I saw it in her eyes when he came to pick her up for their date."

"Don't read too much into it. Mom said it was just a favor," Kamry corrected her.

Still backing Kaitlyn, Talisha raised the ante: "Wouldn't it be great if they started dating and fell in love?"

"I think you're too much of a romantic. I'm not hoping for all that," Kaitlyn said. "All I want is for them to start dating so Mom can relax a little and get off our backs about this no-boys thing."

"Don't you want her to be happy, too?" Kamry asked in a smart tone.

"Of course I want her to be happy. Besides, he said he would help us out. Why would he volunteer to help us if he didn't already like her?"

"I just don't want her to be mad at us when this blows up in your face."

Kaitlyn shot her sister an annoyed look. Kamry got on her nerves sometimes. She was always scared to do anything new. It didn't matter if her mother got mad. At least they were trying to make her happy, and she should appreciate that. Regardless of what her sister thought, she wasn't just thinking about herself.

"Are you with me or what, Kamry?" Kaitlyn asked as they rounded the corner to their street.

Kamry realized she had a decision to make, especially since Mr. Marley's car was in front of his house and the front door was open. She knew Kaitlyn better than anyone. Once her sister had an idea in her head, it was a go, and as much as she wished her sister would take a step back and think before she acted, she knew she was in a no-win position.

"I'm with you," she said softly. She and Talisha silently followed Kaitlyn to Mr. Marley's house.

Kaitlyn walked up the steps without hesitation. She was sure she was doing the right thing and confident that everything would turn out fine.

Hearing the doorbell ring, Marley welcomed the interruption. He hadn't stopped thinking about Kayla since he walked into his house thirty minutes earlier. At least when he was at work he was too busy to think about her for any extended time, but on the drive home, he couldn't get her out of his mind.

The fact that she didn't want anything to do with him didn't make him mad so much as it hurt his feelings. This was something new for him. He wanted her to want him, and he believed that she did. Their time together might have been spur of the moment, but it was also extraordinary and magical.

On his way to the living room, he tried to clear his head. *Listen to me,* he mused, *thinking like some lovesick pup.* When he saw Kaitlyn standing at the door, his curiosity was piqued. He knew Kayla hadn't sent her to him; she wasn't even off work yet. He knew the exact time Kayla pulled into her drive every day. So what was Miss Kaitlyn up to now?

"Hey, Kaitlyn," he said, opening up his screen door and stepping outside. He was conscious of the fact that she was a young lady and that it wouldn't be proper for her to come into his home. He didn't want to put either of them in the position of having to answer the questions that might arise should she be seen entering his house.

"Hi, Mr. Marley," Kaitlyn replied.

"Hello, ladies," he said to the other two girls.

"Hi, Mr. Marley," Kamry answered.

Talisha giggled.

Kamry looked at her. She was just as silly as Kaitlyn was. *Way to go, Talisha,* she thought. *Just fall all over the man's feet.* Girls acted so stupid when they had crushes. She doubted she would ever act like that.

"What can I do for you?"

"Well," Kaitlyn said, "remember yesterday you said that you would help us with our mom?"

"Yes, I do," Marley answered, crossing his arms.

"We were hoping that you would come to dinner tonight." Kaitlyn's hopeful expression let him know this was going to be a big surprise to Kayla.

"Dinner? Does your mother know about this?"

"Um," Kaitlyn looked around to her sister for help.

Kamry moved up the steps to stand behind her sister. She looked at Kaitlyn only briefly, but long enough to make her aggravation clear. She was always bailing Kaitlyn out. "Mr. Marley, we're actually trying to surprise her with a nice dinner. On Mondays, she usually has a hard day at work, and we thought we would hurry home, clean up the house, cook dinner, and wash the dishes so that she wouldn't have to do anything this evening. And since the two of you had such a good time yesterday at the picnic, we figured she wouldn't mind if you came to dinner."

"Is that so? She said that she had a good time yesterday?" Marley studied the three girls intently. He could tell they were lying.

"Well, she didn't exactly say that in so many words, but she was all smiling and whistling this morning before she left for work."

"Really?" he asked. Marley liked what he was hearing, but an inner voice warned him to not show just how happy their little report made him. Either he liked Kayla a lot more than even he thought, or these girls were very good storytellers.

"Yeah," Kaitlyn joined in. "We've never seen Mom in that good a mood in the morning. Usually, she's rushing to get out and hollering at us to get ready."

"Okay," Marley said, nodding, "I guess if you think it's going to be okay, I can come to dinner. What time do you want me there?"

The girls looked at each other. "I'd say around six—" Kaitlyn started to say.

"No," Kamry almost yelled out before catching herself. "Why don't you just come on over as soon as you see Mom come in?"

Marley looked at the girls with a lifted brow. "What gives, ladies?"

They remained silent.

"Come clean," he demanded.

Kamry spoke first. She knew Kaitlyn was stumped. "I just think that Mom would be more acceptable to having company if you, like, come over for something, anything, and we'll already have dinner ready and the house clean, then when you come over, we'll invite you to dinner again in front of her. She won't say no if that's the case."

Marley smiled. "You two really frighten me, you know that? What am I supposed to ask for?"

Both girls looked at him, then Kaitlyn answered.

"How are we supposed to know? You're the man. Ask her out on another date. Tell her how good a time you had yesterday. Just come over after you see Mom come into the house."

Turning to Kamry, she said, "Come on. We got a lot of work to do now that we have to clean up, too. Talisha, you helping?"

"We got to make sure she's happy, don't we?" Kamry asked.

"I guess," Kaitlyn answered.

"Am I allowed in your house, Kaitlyn?" Talisha trailed behind the two girls.

"Just go home, put your stuff up, and come on back. You'll be done way before Mom comes home."

The girls went to work as soon as they got into the house. They vacuumed and dusted the living room, which was never dirty because it was seldom used. Because there was no television in the living room, they girls barely set foot in it, and Kayla only entertained in there when they had company. The dining room wasn't so bad. Kamry swept and scrubbed the floor, and then set the table.

Kaitlyn took out hamburger and spaghetti noodles. She washed her dishes as she cooked, just as her mom did, and then started scrubbing down the kitchen counters and appliances.

By the time they heard Kayla pulling into the driveway, they had just about finished. Talisha left through the patio door. The spaghetti was made, and Kaitlyn was mixing iced tea.

"What she doing?" Kaitlyn asked.

"I don't know," Kamry answered, peeping out the window. "She's just sitting there."

On the ride home, Kayla mulled over what Wanda had said. She knew that Marley was a good guy, but because of what had happened the night before, she didn't want to talk about Marley. She was already having a hard time accepting the fact that she felt herself starting to like him more than she wanted to. And then there was the fact that she had made love to him on a motorcycle, outside, underneath his deck. It was all a little unnerving.

It had been three years since she had been with anyone besides Adam. Three years. She was so uninhibited with him, so unlike herself, but she had wanted Marley so damn bad. And as much as she wanted to deny it, she wanted him again.

But this went against everything she had forced herself to believe over the last three years. It was against everything she was trying to tell her girls.

To ease her mind, she started rationalizing her situation. She was a grown-ass woman. She didn't have to explain herself to anybody. It was only one night, one occurrence, and she was going to make sure that it never happened again. That wouldn't be hard. She had willpower, and if that failed her, she would just stay away from him.

Kayla didn't want to be involved. She didn't want a relationship. She didn't want to be dependent on a man for her happiness. You make your own happiness. That is what she was doing, and that is what she was teaching her girls to do. So from this moment forward, she didn't want to think of Marley. She didn't want to talk about him with Wanda, and she didn't want to see him anymore.

By the time she got everything out of her system, Kayla figured she had lied to herself long enough. She recognized it as such and even admitted it. That was half the battle, right?

She sat in her car for a few minutes just to get herself together before she went into the house. All that thinking had put her right back in the same place she had started—still in lust with Marley. And that's all it was. She didn't know him well enough for it to be anything more than that.

In normal situations, women tend to get emotional after having sex. It had something to do with their hormones. She would just give herself a couple of days away from him and things would return too normal. Hell, it made sense that she would be a little caught up—not whipped—by the first man she was with after such a long time. But she'd get over it soon enough.

Her feeling had nothing to do with Marley. This was all on her. The way he put his hands on her hips to steady her when he climbed behind her on the bike didn't matter. It was just her emotions. The kisses he placed on her neck and back as he slowly moved in and out of her weren't special. It was her emotions. When he told her how good she felt and mumbled his satisfaction just before his release, those weren't endearments. It was all her emotions.

Kayla pounded her hand against the steering wheel as if beating his name out of her head. Things were not going as she had planned. She should have known that she wouldn't be able to act so casually about their relationship. Maybe if she had given herself time to think about what she was doing, she might have thought twice before having sex with him. But as it was, she had put herself into a predicament.

She was behaving just like other females, head-over-heels crazy over some man. All day long, Kayla couldn't seem to get him out of her mind. She had to have replayed their lovemaking over and over in her head about twenty times, watching from different angles in the dark and letting her imagination take over. This was exactly how she didn't want her life to be. She didn't want to like or need him. But she did.

Now she had to spend the rest of her energy staying focused on two teenagers who didn't need her nitpicking over them all evening in an effort to keep Marley off her mind.

She slammed her car door then stomped up the front steps, trying to release the remnants of her anger. As soon as she walked in the front door, she put a fake smile on her face.

"Girls, I'm home," she said softly. She was already exhausted.

"Hey, Mom," Kamry said, coming out of the kitchen first to stall her. Kaitlyn had broken a glass jar on the counter and was picking up the last bit of glass. "You look tired."

"I'm okay. Just had a long day."

"Hi, Mom," Kaitlyn yelled from the kitchen.

"Hey, baby," Kayla replied.

"Well, don't worry about a thing. Kaitlyn and I have already cooked dinner, and we even cleaned up the house for you. All the dishes are washed, and we made enough spaghetti to last until tomorrow."

"Thank you, girls. I really appreciate it."

"Here, let me take your purse upstairs. You sit down here on the couch and rest."

"I think I will do just that." Kayla sat down on the couch and looked out the large bay window. At first, she wondered what had gotten into the girls, but then she decided to enjoy it, not to question it. The sun was still shining, and a few of the neighborhood kids were outside skateboarding. When she heard the sound of footsteps, she paid it no mind, assuming it was the next-door neighbor's house. The doorbell caught her off guard.

"I'll get it," Kaitlyn yelled, rushing into the living room.

Kayla remained where she was. Often Kaitlyn's school friends knocked on the door as soon as she pulled into the driveway. They watched like hawks for her to get home from work. The girls could then come outside.

"Hi, Kaitlyn, right?" His baritone voice was unmistakable. "Is your mother home?"

Kaitlyn smiled back at him. "Hi, Mr. Marley. She's here. Come on in."

"Thanks," he said, moving through the living room. He took a seat on the couch next to her.

Kayla made as much room for him as possible. *Damn if he didn't have some nerve,* she thought. Kayla looked at him, dumbfounded. "What do you want, Marley?"

"Now, is that any way to greet your company?"

"You know better than to come over here out of the blue like we're the best of friends, especially with my girls here." She kept her voice low.

"Oh, calm down. After last night, I would think that we were," he hissed. Marley raised his voice to normal and said, "I just came over to ask a favor of you."

"Um, another favor?"

"Yeah, this weekend, I—"

"Hi, Mr. Marley," Kamry said cheerfully when she saw him sitting in the living room. "Are you staying for dinner?"

"Um, well, sure," Marley replied. These girls were so damn good at what they did when they put their heads together. It hit him that they were in training to be women, not just physically, but mentally. His dad used to always say that women were better liars, connivers, and manipulators than men. Now he believed it.

"Good, I'll set another plate." Kamry quickly moved to the dining room and retrieved the stack of dishes she had already put out.

"Wait a minute," Kayla said, "what are you doing?"

"What do you mean? I'm accepting a dinner invitation, and might I add, your girls are very well mannered. I bet you weren't going to invite me to join you."

"You're damned right I wasn't."

"Why you treating me like this? I'm not your enemy." He lowered his voice again.

"You're not?"

"No, I'm trying to be your friend, and you're making it impossibly hard for me. Why is that?"

"Maybe it's because I don't want to be your friend. I don't need a new friend," Kayla said, turning to look him right in his handsome face.

"You can lie to yourself all you want, Kayla, but you can't lie to me."

"Look, what did you come over here for in the first place?"

"I came over here to ask you to go to my brother's anniversary party this weekend. I need a date."

"A date," Kayla smacked her lips. He could have asked any one of the women beating down his door to go, and they both knew it. So why was he bothering her?

"Yes, a date."

"Why me? I'm sure you got plenty of options."

"I have fun with you. Also good conversation. We talk about more than the party last week. So you going with me or not?"

"Dinner's ready," Kaitlyn called from the dinning room table. "Come and get it."

Without replying, Kayla stood up and walked to the dining room.

Marley followed closely behind.

CHAPTER 7

Marley wore a big smile. He hadn't expected the evening to be a complete waste of time, but he was surprised he'd had a good time.

Kayla's girls were fun and energetic. Good girls. Marley couldn't remember the last time he had such a good time at a dinner table. Living alone, eating alone—that was the lifestyle he wanted. But he now realized what he might be missing by not having settled down and having a family.

After a few uncomfortable minutes, even Kayla started to relax and enjoy herself. And the girls again amazed him by helping him keep the conversation moving along. Hopping from one topic to another, they kept everything light and entertaining. When they asked him the reason for his visit, he told them it was to ask Kayla to accompany him to his brother's anniversary party.

Kaitlyn was sharp enough to inform him that Kayla didn't date, as if he didn't already know. Then they methodically recited the reasons she should go—if she wanted to, of course. Kamry even suggested a mother-and-daughter evening on Thursday to eat out and then shop for a dress. Their performance so impressed him that he decided they were good partners in his quest to capture Kayla's heart.

He had first thought it was perhaps improper to try to manipulate the girls into helping him. But the situation was the complete opposite. They were the ones who had enlisted *his* help from the very beginning. Although he and the girls had totally different reasons, they all hoped for the same outcome: Kayla agreeing to date Marley.

Kayla collapsed on her bed. It was ten o'clock. The girls had just turned off their bedroom lights. In the last hour before her own eleven o'clock bedtime, her routine was to wind down, think about her day, read or watch television. But tonight, she didn't want to do anything. She lay on the bed for an hour, Marley on her mind, before hopping into the shower.

As she toweled herself off, Kayla swore she could hear Adam calling for her. She had been so horny and so hot and bothered by Marley's presence at her dinner table; everything about him turned her on. And he had fit so comfortably, so naturally, into their evening routine. He had joked with her girls at the dinner table as if he had known them for years. It was easy to imagine him as part of their family. *Whoa, girl! Not so fast.*

Kayla vigorously rubbed her legs, trying hard to concentrate on this simple task. She didn't want to start thinking silly thoughts. That would be very foolish, very premature.

She got into bed, Marley still on her mind. She now wished she hadn't agreed to go to the party with him. It could only be for the worst. But she knew she would be lying if she said she wasn't a little excited about the prospect of spending time with him again.

Kayla muddled through the week as best she could. Tuesday, after she told Wanda about her invitation to his brother's anniversary party, Wanda's mood seemed to improve.

"Kayla, I wasn't mad because you said you didn't want to date Marley. I was upset because you seemed to be closing yourself off from the world. From where I'm sitting, it seemed that you were letting your ex have too much power over your happiness. I don't like to see any woman stop living because of one man. So I especially don't like seeing it happen to one of my friends. Honey, there are so many good men out there. It just so happens that I know a good one who is after you right now."

"Wanda, I really appreciate you caring enough to feel that you need to get involved in this, but please believe me you don't have to. I'm going to be all right. Okay, I admit it has taken me a while to truly get over all the hurt and anger that I had held on to. Girl, I'm fine. I told Marley I would go, and I'm going. Honestly, I'm even looking forward to it."

"Good. I'll be there. Robert, Marley's oldest brother, and Pooh are really good friends. And I talk to LaToya a lot. That's Robert's wife. Robert and Marley look a lot alike. And Nester, the middle brother, girl, wait until you see him. He's got to be the most beautiful man in the world, not that the other two aren't handsome. But Nester, girl, good Lord," Wanda enthused, outrageously fanning herself to get her point across.

"Well, I guess I'll see Saturday."

"Yes, you will. This is a big step—introducing you to the family and whatnot."

Kayla looked at her intently. "Why do you suppose he asked me to go with him? I'm sure there is somebody he's been tooling around with he could ask."

"Maybe you are the one he wanted to ask. Why do you have to doubt the fact that he wants you?"

Kayla still looked doubtful.

"Kayla, don't you think you deserve some happiness? I don't know what else Quincy did to you, but he sure did bring down your self-esteem. I don't know why women give men the power to do that. You haven't been with this guy for years, but he still can make you stop loving yourself, let alone someone else."

"No, he doesn't," Kayla snapped defiantly.

"You're damn right he doesn't. So stop letting him. Honey, can't nobody make you happy if you don't let him. As much as Marley wants to be with you, unless you want to be with him, it doesn't even matter. You do want to be with Marley, don't you?"

Kayla didn't respond. Many thoughts ran through her head. Was she ready to admit her feelings out loud? To someone else? Willing to admit that her little "pact" was simply an idea spurred to life by a broken heart? Could she finally let the hurt and pain of the past go and look to the future?

"Wanda, I do. I do want to be with Marley," Kayla replied in a rush before she lost her nerve. "God knows I want that man, but—"

"No buts. If you want him, you get him." Wanda was happy that Kayla had finally made a decision, finally admitted the truth. "I gotta get back to work before we both get fired. Call me later."

"I will," Kayla answered. She let out a long breath. Having voiced her feelings to someone, her shoulders seemed a little lighter. But telling Wanda how she felt was a lot different from telling the girls or even Marley himself.

Kayla decided that she wouldn't say anything to the girls until they were at dinner on Thursday. That would give her a day to figure out what she wanted to say and how she was going to say it.

Luckily, she didn't see Marley at all on Tuesday or Wednesday. But he was still on her mind. At first, she wondered when she would see him, and then she wondered why she hadn't seen him.

Thursday evening, she rushed home from work to get the girls. They were going to the mall, and after dinner at Ruby Tuesday they would visit a few department stores in search of the perfect dress for her to wear to the anniversary party.

She was pulling out of her driveway when Marley came rushing out of his house, looking good in blue jeans and a black-and-white striped button-down shirt.

"Hey, ladies," he said, coming up to the car when it reached his house.

"Hi, Mr. Marley," the girls sang in unison.

"Marley," Kayla said softly.

"On your way to mother and daughter night?"

"Yeah," Kaitlyn said brightly, "want to join us?"

"Oh, no. This is your night. I know better than to go shopping with a bunch of ladies. I just wanted to let your mother know that is not going to be too fancy a party. Don't get carried away with your choice. Just a nice cocktail dress will do. I'll let you ladies get on with your outing. Have a good time."

"We'll see you later, Marley." Kayla said it so nicely Marley did a double take on his way back into his house.

"Girls, I want to talk to you about something." Kayla was nervous. She didn't know what reaction to expect when she made her announcement, but she knew she had to talk to her children. All their lives she had been preaching to them the importance of communication, especially with her. It was time to practice what she preached, because in the end, all they had to count on was each other.

Kaitlyn put her fork down immediately. Her fully loaded baked potato wasn't really holding her attention. She had ordered it only to please her mother, who would have disapproved of a salad. They didn't understand that it was important that she watch her weight.

Kamry didn't stop eating, the New Orleans seafood platter being her favorite. She was popping another piece of Cajun grilled fish into her mouth when Kaitlyn's elbow connected with her side.

"What's going on, Mom?" Kamry asked.

Kayla looked from one daughter to the other. Each was special in her own way; both were beautiful, intelligent, and popular. Kaitlyn was always concerned with beauty and clothing, while Kamry was more athletic and tomboyish. She loved them so much. Seventeen and sixteen now; the time had gone by so fast. Wanda was right. She was keeping too tight a rein on them. They should be having fun and hanging out with their friends. She was doing that and more when she was their age. Instead of letting her mistakes be some self-styled parenting guide, she should be thanking her lucky stars that she had gotten herself together and was able to raise two beautiful girls. They hadn't really caused her a moment's trouble. And they weren't dumb. They knew right from wrong. And they should be able to recognize when someone was taking advantage of them.

It was time for Kayla to trust herself and trust in what she had taught her girls. She had to loosen up the reins for all their sakes. Her parents had never let her do anything, and that was one reason she had been into so much. When she was old enough and finally had the chance, she did too much.

"Here's the deal," Kayla began. "I realize there might be some confusion here lately about the way things are going at home."

"What you talking about, Mom? Everything is fine at home," Kamry replied.

"Well, I mean with Mr. Marley coming to the house, asking me to go places with him—"

"They are called dates, Mom," Kaitlyn interrupted.

"Well, whatever. I just wanted to clear the air about some things."

"Mom," Kamry quickly interjected, "we think it's neat that you and Mr. Marley are going places together. We think he's pretty cool."

"Yeah," Kaitlyn added, "and he's fine, too."

"Okay. Look, I know that I've been riding you guys pretty hard over the last few years about not getting yourselves all crazy about any of these little boys who are running around behind you."

"Actually, Mom, you've basically been like, 'NO BOYS, PERIOD.' "

Kayla nodded her head, "You're right, and I apologize."

The girls looked at her, then at each other.

"I should have never been so strict with you two. I apologize, but I just didn't want you to find yourselves in the same predicament I found myself. You know, your father and I went through a lot of terrible times, both before and after you were born. You girls know. You aren't children, and I am sure that you remember that things were not as good as they might have seemed. I was beaten, abused both mentally and physically. He cheated on me numerous times, but I can't blame him for everything that happened. Most of it, yes, but not everything. And I sure can't blame every man in the world for what your father did to me. That's exactly what I've been doing these last few years."

"Mom, we don't think you were too strict," Kaitlyn interjected, trying to make her feel better.

"Yes, you do, but I appreciate the lie. I've done a good job with you two. You're smart girls, and it's time for me to trust you. And it's time for me to trust myself."

"Mom, do you think you might really like Mr. Marley?" Kamry asked.

Kayla didn't know how to answer, or she didn't want to answer.

"We hope you do," Kaitlyn answered. "You seem a little happier since you went out with him last week. You had fun at the picnic, right?"

Kayla didn't want to think about the picnic. She still couldn't get what happened after the picnic out of her mind.

"You know what? I think that I might like him a little, but we're really just friends. And you're right. He is fine." All three giggled. Even though she took her girls out often, this was the first time Kayla tried to be more than their mom. She was talking to the girls like a friend and found that was what they all needed.

"Now I'm not giving you permission to go buck wild, and I'm still not totally comfortable with the idea of boys coming into your lives, but that is something that I'm going to have to get used to. Boys, men, are always going to be around. I will be a little more lenient with the rules as long as you don't try to take advantage. I think that you should be going to the school dances and such. I trust you."

"So we can date?" Kaitlyn asked anxiously.

Kamry looked at Kaitlyn, annoyed. She was about to ruin everything. It was so obvious what was on her mind.

Kayla looked at her, too. She was sure that Kaitlyn already had someone in mind and that by tomorrow, she'll know that Kaitlyn has a boyfriend. That thought alone had her wanting to change her mind about the whole thing. She needed to test the waters, though.

"Make no mistake about it. This is going to be a test run. I don't expect anyone to come to me talking crazy about being in love. I expect your grades to stay as they are. I don't expect to get bombarded by phone calls at all times of the night, and I don't expect to see a bunch of boys knocking at my door. If any of that happens, then we'll chalk mark this experiment up as a failure, and things will go back to how they used to be."

"Mom, you can trust us."

"Uh huh. Well, I guess I'll see. Another thing. This is not permission to go have sex with the first boy who tells you that he loves you. I think I've raised you to be smarter than that. Boys your age tend to use the 'L' word a lot to get into your panties. So don't be fools."

"Mom, you don't have to worry about us," Kaitlyn smiled. "We know what you're trying to say."

Kayla looked at her girls and wished it were that easy. They said not to worry, but she knew she would. They were young girls, beautiful young ladies. And regardless of how much she tried not to blame all men for her misfortune, the fact remained that men who were dogs started out as boys who were dogs. That was just her life's experience.

"So does this mean that we can go to Christian Samuels's birthday party this weekend?" Kaitlyn asked. "Talisha said her mother could take us and pick us up."

"Why am I just hearing about this party?" Kayla sensed that she herself was being tested.

"Because we didn't think we would be able to go," Kamry answered. "We haven't told you about half the parties we were invited to because we didn't think you would let us go."

"Well, where is this party?"

"They're having it at the American Legion. It's from eight to twelve and—"

"Nine to two?" Kayla started shaking her head.

"Mom, you just said you trusted us. And there are going to be plenty of adults there." Kaitlyn was whining. She desperately wanted, needed, to be at this party.

"Now I don't know about that. I'm going to have to talk to this boy's parents before I agree to anything like that. And I want to talk to Talisha's mom also. I don't know of too many parents who are going to get up at twelve in the morning to pick their children up from a party."

"All our friends' parents do it," Kamry said, speaking truthfully. "Either that or they take turns carpooling. That way everyone can go to the parties and get home safely."

"It does make sense, but why can't we start out with something small like a ball game or something after school?" Kayla took a bite of her food. "Y'all hurry so we can go looking for this dress and get out of here."

"Mom, if you're going to trust us, you might as well start with something big. We'll show you that you can trust us." Kaitlyn was not going to let this chance pass her by.

Kayla didn't answer. This was harder than she thought it was going to be. She wasn't even aware that high-school kids were having parties until twelve in the morning. It shouldn't have come as that much of a surprise. The more things changed, the more they stayed the same.

At nine-thirty they left the mall, all three carrying bags. Kayla hadn't expected to spend so much money, but these mother-daughter moments were special. Soon both girls would be going off to college, and their mother-daughter days would cease altogether.

It had taken most of the evening, but Kayla finally found the right dress for the party. Kaitlyn was the one who spotted it on a clearance rack. Leave it to her to find something that looked like a million bucks but only cost fifty. The periwinkle slip-dress with rhinestone spaghetti straps and trimming had been a steal at seventy-five percent off, with an additional fifteen percent off on top of that. It was the only dress of its kind on the rack, and it just happened to be in her size.

The girls stood outside the dressing room while she tried the dress on and cheered when she walked out in it. But Kayla was very self-conscious about the form-fitting creation.

"Kaitlyn, I need a slip for this thing."

"Mom, it looks good. Of course, you can't wear that underwear. You're going to need a thong."

Kayla looked at the girls. That was another place where they differed. Kayla loved thongs; Kamry wanted sports briefs. She argued with them every school year that they needed real underwear for more than their personal days. They said they detested bloomers. But since she was the one with the money, she got her way.

Her mother's expression made Kamry laugh. "I don't like thongs either, Mom, but your panty lines are going to show."

"That's what the slip is for."

"Fine Mom, we will go with this slip. It will hold you in, and you can wear whatever you want." Kaitlyn picked up a beautiful strapless full slip.

"This isn't a slip, it's a girdle," Kayla replied, taking it from Kaitlyn.

"Yeah, one that will give you an hourglass figure. You're going to be so sexy, it's going to make Mr. Marley sick."

"What do you know about making a man sick? See, I'm starting to reconsider my decision already."

"Oh, Mom, cut it out. By the time I'm done with you, you're going to be the finest, sexiest woman at that party. You're even going to look better than the bride or whoever."

"I don't want to look that good, baby." But Kayla gave in and let Kaitlyn dress her. At the end, she had her complete outfit—shoes, earrings, and a necklace. She had to admit her daughter had style and taste; best of all, she was thrifty. Since she had saved so much on her purchases, she decided to treat each of them to outfits for their big party debut as well. She made sure they purchased conservative clothing, but they made sure they were still fashionably dressed.

Kayla didn't have to call anybody about the girls going to the party after all. On Friday, Christian Samuels's mother called to reassure Kayla that she and her husband both would be at the hall where her son's party was being held Saturday night. Although still not absolutely certain she was making the right decision, Kayla had to admit she felt more comfortable with the idea of the girls going to the party after the phone conversation.

Twenty minutes later, Talisha's mother called to offer to take the girls to the party with Talisha and to pick them up afterwards. She also said it would be okay if the girls wanted to stay the night at her house. Each time the phone rang, Kayla caught the girls watching her on the sly as they quietly washed and dried dishes. They had obviously been very busy at school. The enthusiasm they showed for their housework was duly noted, too.

"Why do I feel like I've just been played like a violin?" Kayla asked, walking over to them. Even Kamry, she noticed, whom she thought was not into parties, seemed interested in attending.

"What's wrong, Mom?" Kaitlyn asked innocently.

"Nothing, nothing at all. That was Talisha's mom. She said you two could stay the night with them on Saturday after she picks you up if you want to."

"Great. We have a lot of fun over there," Kaitlyn replied, perhaps too eagerly.

"Really?" Kayla responded.

Kaitlyn ignored her sister, who was softly kicking the side of her foot. "Yeah, you know, we sit up and gossip and stuff. Hey, now you can stay out late with Mr. Marley if you want to. I bet he'll like that." Kaitlyn was trying to get her mother to think more pleasant thoughts. Any thoughts except changing her mind and not letting them go.

Kayla turned away and started for the stairs. She didn't want to think about Marley in front of them. Her body was tingling, and she knew her face would display her every emotion. But she was smiling by the time she reached the top. She was going to be okay; they all were. Kayla was determined to keep her doubts in check and her trust unshaken. It was the only way for them to progress as a family. She had to start trusting them and herself.

Of course, she knew what the girls were up to. She had been a teenager once, and she didn't mind their plotting as long as it didn't put them in harm's way. Of course, they preferred hanging with their friends and people their own age instead of with her. She was just their mother, after all. It was funny how a parent went from being the most important person in your life as an infant, toddler, and young child to being the most important and least popular just a few years later.

Talisha's mother would take them and pick them up from the party. All she had to do was hope they were smart enough not to do anything stupid while they were there. And although Kaitlyn was a little boy crazy, she knew that Kamry was levelheaded enough for both of them.

Later that night, Kayla tried on her new outfit. She put on the entire ensemble for Kaitlyn's approval.

"Kamry, come look at Mom," Kaitlyn screamed. "She's hot."

"Hot? Hot to be your mom or hot for a thirty-seven-year-old?" Kayla laughed. "You guys act as if you've never seen me dressed up."

"Both," Kamry answered, walking into the room. "We haven't seen you look like this in a long time. Mr. Marley is going to lose his mind."

"Well, we don't want that."

"Why not?" Kaitlyn asked. "We want him running behind you like a little puppy."

"No, we don't," Kamry disagreed. "That's what boys do. Mr. Marley is a man. Men don't run behind women. They go crazy with lust."

"Well, I don't want Marley doing that, either," Kayla said, briefly turning away from them. She was lying through her teeth.

"You don't want Mr. Marley crazy with lust over you, Mom?" Kaitlyn looked at her sister, worried that their plans were going up in flames.

"No. What good is he going to be to me then?" Kayla laughed, and the girls joined in. This, she realized, was how she should be relating to teenaged daughters. She was their mother, but it was also time for her to start being their friend. "Listen, it's almost eleven. I'm going to take this stuff off, and y'all need to get to bed. The faster we get this house cleaned in the morning, the faster y'all can get to Talisha's house. I know she is going to be here as early as she can."

"I'm already packed," Kaitlyn yelled, walking into her bedroom.

"Me, too," Kamry said. Knowing they wouldn't be getting to sleep anytime soon, she followed her sister. Kaitlyn would keep her up for at least another hour talking excitedly about the party and, of course, David. This was going to be their first real dance.

Realizing the ringing she heard wasn't a dream, Kayla reached over and knocked the phone on her dresser from its cradle.

"Damn," she groaned, glancing at the radio clock. Twelve-thirty. "Hello," she said huskily into the phone.

"Hello, lady," the husky male voice on the other end answered.

Immediately, she became fully awake; all of her senses were suddenly alive. Marley's voice seemed to wash over her and make her whole body tingle.

"Mar-Marley, is everything okay?" She meant to ask herself that question.

He chuckled lightly. "Everything's lovely, my dear. I just couldn't sleep thinking of you lying so close to me."

"Close?" She smiled when she thought she had finally understood what he was talking about. "I'm not that close. There are two houses between us, you know."

"I'm not talking about the houses. I'm talking about your smell, your scent that still lingers on my jacket. I have it here next to me. I can still smell you as if you were right next to me. I can't bear to wash it off until I absolutely have to." He knew tomorrow would be that day. Some of the guys were riding in the morning. He was expected to join them. What he didn't tell her was that he had already used the jacket as a pillow cover.

"Marley, you're crazy, you know that?"

"My family has been telling me that my whole life. I thought they were just joking with me, though."

"No, they weren't joking. I think they were pretty serious."

They both laughed.

"Are you ready for tomorrow?" he asked, curious to see if she was going to try to bail out.

"As a matter of fact, I am. Me and the girls got everything we need to wear Saturday."

"Oh? They convinced you to buy them something?"

"No, I wanted to buy them something. I think I've been kind of hard on them lately. And I got some good girls. They're staying over at their girlfriend's house tomorrow night. The mother is going to take them to a dance and pick them up afterwards."

"You're actually letting them go?" Disbelief could be heard in his voice.

"Yes, I am," she snapped. "What are you saying, Marley?"

"Whoa, whoa, easy, baby. I'm not saying anything. I think that it's a good thing that you're letting them go. They should be out with people their own age every once in a while. That is how they'll learn to socialize with other people and how to carry themselves like young ladies." Marley was quiet for a second. "You know you got my head spinning right now, don't you?"

Kayla smiled. She needed to get the chip off her shoulder and allow herself to enjoy the rest of their conversation. "Spinning with what?"

"Ideas, honey, just a lot of ideas. I'll see you tomorrow evening, seven."

"Seven it is." Kayla couldn't sleep. The promises in his voice made her know that Saturday was going to be a good day. As horny as she was, she forced herself not to go into the closet and bring Adam out to play. She wanted to save herself for Marley.

"Come on, Kamry, put some elbow into it," Kaitlyn complained. "You're moving so dang slow. I'm trying to get done and get out of here."

Kamry snapped her eyes at her. They were in the kitchen, with Kaitlyn scrubbing the counters and wiping down the refrigerator. "Maybe if you hadn't kept me up all night talking about how you think the party is going to be, I would have more energy."

"You were talking to me, too," Kaitlyn argued back. "Look, let's just get the kitchen done so we can do the bathroom and be done."

"Fine." Kamry didn't want to ruin their day by arguing, but she was tired, and it *was* Kaitlyn's fault. Her freshly made bed was all she could think about for the next thirty minutes. She was going to have to mess up her bedclothes and lie down until Talisha came to get them. Until she rested, Kamry knew she wouldn't be excited about going to the party.

By six o'clock, Kayla was a bundle of raw nerves. The girls had left over two hours earlier. Putting on her dress was all she had left to do. She slid the thin material over her shoulders and goose bumps popped on her arms.

Come on, girl, she encouraged herself, *get it together.* She was a grown woman, and this wasn't her first date with a man. Not even with him. You would think they had done enough for her not to be this nervous about the evening, but she was nervous, anyway. She knew that when she saw him, he was going to charm her and make her feel so good that she was going to want to practically jump on him.

She nervously paced the length of her bedroom. Each time she passed the large wall mirror, Kayla would stare at her image until she found something wrong with her outfit. After the fourth time, she decided she was going crazy. The outfit was perfect. She had taken extra care to make sure she looked exactly as Kaitlyn would expect. And she had applied only a dab of makeup, just as Kaitlyn had insisted.

It was only her nerves. She was gorgeous, and she wasn't being vain to think so. It was the truth. But this didn't stop her palms from perspiring or her hands from shaking. All she wanted was to get it over with. She felt like an expectant father. The waiting was killing her.

Determined not to wear a permanent path in her carpet, she forced herself to go down to the living room. It was five minutes to seven. So what was taking him so long? It wasn't as if he lived far away. He was only three doors down. Maybe she should just walk to his house instead of driving herself insane. If she didn't leave the house, she was going to have to make herself a drink just to calm her nerves.

Kayla grabbed her purse off the couch and walked self-assuredly to the front door before her courage left her. She would rather waste the next few minutes walking down the street than sitting in her house like a caged mouse. There was nothing wrong with a woman going to a man's door. She yanked the doorknob hard; the doorbell rang at the same time.

The sudden opening of the door startled Marley, and he took a step back. He didn't know what he expected to come flying out, but he was certainly pleased to see the beauty standing before him. He had been right to give her time to prepare instead of rushing down to her house thirty minutes early as he had considered doing.

Kayla took his breath away. She was beautiful in the long, slim-fitting periwinkle. The dress, which fit her to perfection, emphasizing her hips and the swell of her shapely bottom.

He loved the way her hair lay smoothly against the nape of her neck, growing a little longer with every inch toward the top of her head until it was perfectly curled at the top. Even at the peak it was still no more than two inches long.

"Wow," Marley managed to squeeze through his tightening throat.

With that one word, he had managed to both boost her confidence and moisten her insides. She felt good.

"Thank you," she replied, smiling back at him. "You don't look half bad yourself." Looking him up and down, she knew she was lying. He looked damn good.

"Were you going somewhere?" he asked. He stood in the doorway, waiting for her reply, wanting to run his hands over her hips.

"I was on my way down to your house."

"Really?" Marley openly inspected her entire body again. "Well, we can still go down there if you want to."

Kayla's smile quickly turned into a smirk. "No, thank you. I was just wondering what was taking you so long."

"You sure? You look so good that I'm not sure if I want to go to this thing." Finally, he moved to the side and allowed her to step on to the porch. "We don't have—"

"*Thing*? This is your brother's anniversary party, correct?"

"Yeah, but he would understand if I told him that I was distracted by a beautiful, sexy lady who wanted my attention focused only on her."

Kayla's smile reappeared. "Flattery won't get you anywhere," she responded, feeling her stomach flutter.

"That's not flattery. It's the truth." He led her down the front steps and toward his car, which was still parked in front of his house. The hand on the small of her back created a hot spot that instantly radiated up and down her back.

"Well, thank you, again," she replied. Kayla looked around and realized for the first time that letting Marley escort her from her door was attracting unwanted attention.

Her neighbors all seemed to be occupied with some outside activity. Any other time, the street would be empty. She saw people watching them and knew it would be the beginning of something. Rumors were sure to start swirling.

"Hi, Mrs. Everett," Marley called to a woman kneeling at her flower garden and pulling weeds. Mrs. Everett lived two doors down from Kayla and next door to Marley. She smiled broadly as she watched them walk towards her.

"Hello, Marley," she replied. "Oh, don't you make a lovely couple? And that dress." She stopped her weeding and stood up to chat. "I remember when I was your age, dear. I would have loved to have a dress like that. It shows off your figure so well. You look beautiful. Going out for a night on the town?"

"No, Mrs. Everett. We're just on our way to a little gathering."

"Well, that's a beautiful dress," the older woman said.

"Thank you, ma'am," Kayla replied. She regretted not really knowing her neighbors. She made a mental note to rectify that. She had spoken to Mrs. Everett numerous times, but had never taken the time to ask her name. Her husband had passed the year before, and she now lived in the house alone. It must be lonely for her. Kayla went over to offer her condolences, but she never had the chance to speak to her personally. There were so many people there that day. And she never went back; it made her feel bad. She vowed to fix that, too.

"She's right," Marley whispered in her ear as he opened the door to his creamy white Cadillac. "You look real good, Kayla." Marley slid his hand down the length of her side, his touch having just enough pressure to let her know that she was on his mind.

Her goose bumps returned in full force. She slid down in the car and relaxed against the smooth, cool leather of the beige interior. Just like that, her breathing became irregular, her heart pounded, her insides tightened. She waited until they were pulling out of the parking space before she spoke.

"You know we've started something, right?" she asked.

"Something like what?" he smiled. Either he didn't know or he didn't care that the neighborhood would be talking about them.

"You know just as well as I do that by tomorrow everyone in the neighborhood will probably think we're having a relationship."

"No, they won't." His smile broadened.

"Yes, they will, and you know it."

"Well, would that be so bad? Most of them probably already think it, anyway. I don't have anything to hide. And we are kind of in some sort of a relationship, aren't we?"

"It doesn't really matter what we may or may not be in the middle of. I'm just trying to think of the girls."

"Kayla, calm down. Your girls want us together. If they didn't, they wouldn't have invited me to dinner or been happy about us going out tonight, right? Come on now, all you have to do is enjoy yourself and want to be with me."

"I know. You're right. I'm just a little nervous about this, that's all. Marley, you have to understand. It's been a long time for me. It's going to take some time. Plus, you got me going out here to meet your family."

"There's nothing to be nervous about. You're with me. Wanda will be there, and you look gorgeous. True, it has been a long time since you've dated. But, Kayla, you're a very beautiful, loving woman, and you already know how I feel about you. I'm here willing to give you all the time that you need for you to get comfortable with me. Maybe I should be nervous about taking you. I'm sure Wanda has already given my family her version of things between us, and I'm sure they'll be able to see how much I want you. Oh, and just so you know, my brother, Nester, will be there tonight. You look so good that he'll probably try to steal you away from me. He's a very good judge of character. He might notice what a good woman you are, and think that you would be better off with him."

She smiled.

"You think that's funny? I'm serious." Marley looked at her. "There might be a fight tonight. I might have to break my brother down to keep you for myself."

"Yeah, right," she smiled. "You know I'm not goin—"

"What was that?"

"Nothing."

"No, you were about to say something."

"No, I wasn't."

"Okay, I'll let you slide this time. But, Kayla, don't worry. You'll enjoy my family; they're good folks. And my sister-in-law is the best. A lot of the guys from the bike club will be there, too. You remember Jaybird and Danger."

"Yeah, I'm not really nervous *per se.* It's just been a long time for me." It had been a long time since she was out on an official date, let alone on the way to an important family gathering. What if they didn't like her? According to Wanda, he and his brothers were really close-knit.

"Well, don't worry. They know all about you and can't wait to meet you."

"They know all about me?" Kayla looked at him suspiciously. "What do they know about me? What have you told them?"

Marley smiled at her. "I told them the truth. I told them that I met a nice lady, and I wanted to start spending time with her. And I told them that they would like you and that I liked you a lot. What more do they need to know?"

"Well, you haven't told me anything about them. Why am I left out in the dark?"

"Look, I didn't intentionally not tell you about them. Fine, I'll tell you about them now before we get there. What do you want to know?"

"I don't know. Tell me something so I don't go in there looking like a fool."

Marley glanced down at the long, bronze legs stretched out on the passenger side of the car. Her skin seemed to glow. Her calf muscles were petite and curvy. He briefly wondered what she smoothed on them after a long, hot shower. He quickly pushed the thought aside, as the stirring in his loins was becoming intense. Talking about his family would probably be the best way to go at the moment. In his head, the alternative was to turn the car around and go back to his house.

"Robert is my oldest brother. He's a few years older than me. He lives in the house my parents built, the house we're going to. He works in Smyrna at the Delaware Correctional Center. LaToya is his wife. They've been married ten years. They have two kids together, Sean and Chandler. He has two daughters from previous relationships, NyJae and Justine. LaToya has a son named Christopher from a previous relationship. So they got five kids altogether.

"They are a very tight-knit family. Bobby and Toya are great parents. Toya is a teacher, and Bobby is a correctional officer. They were made for each other, and you can tell—well, you'll see for yourself. Anyway, Nester is the middle son. He's a couple years older than me, the pretty boy of the family. He's a confirmed bachelor and makes no bones about it. He doesn't want to settle down, can't stand the idea of being with just one woman for the rest of his life, and he'll let it be known. Fortunately for him, there are so many women out there who agree that he shouldn't settle down. You should see the way they flock to him."

"I've heard that women flock to the whole lot of you." Kayla waited for a response.

She didn't get one she expected.

Marley pulled the car over and came to a complete stop on the shoulder of the two-lane highway. Then he looked directly into her eyes. "Kayla, I have one thing to ask of you. Only one. Please forget about what you might have heard about me. I will be completely honest with you. All you have to do is ask me what you want to know. But nobody knows me better than I know myself. So don't listen to the gossip. Ask me, and I will tell you. And regardless of what you hear, I want to get to know you. I'm interested in knowing all about you. You, and no one else."

She got goosebumps again, and this time it wasn't because of the wind or his gaze on her body; it was because of the words he had just spoken. It was the sincerity she heard in his voice that had her inner muscles convulsing and twitching excitedly in anticipation of the evening ahead.

Either she was truly starting to fall for this man or he was very good at the game he was running on her, because she believed every word he said. He didn't have any reason to lie to her except that he wanted her. But Marley was smart enough to know that he wasn't going to get to Kayla with lies. She was too mature for that approach. Plus, she knew game when she heard it. She had been through enough to know the difference between game and truth. Because she didn't trust easily, Kayla was always on the lookout for game, but she didn't feel it with Marley.

Kayla was glad she didn't believe Marley was telling her lies. She would hate for their time together to be all for naught, as she truly enjoyed being with him. And if she was honest with herself, she didn't want it to be over anytime soon. She wanted to get to know him better, and wanted him to get to know her.

CHAPTER 8

A wide, concrete driveway led up to a two-story, colonial-style home with white siding and maroon shutters before curving back toward the road. Lanterns as tall as lampposts lined the driveway. Each sent rays of light through trees just as tall. The landscaping closer to the front of the house was even more immaculately cultivated than the landscaping on either side of the driveway. As the glow of the darkening sky surrounded it, the beauty of the house took Kayla's breath away.

She grew more anxious and nervous as she watched the other guests walk from the parking area toward the steps of the front porch leading to the foyer. Marley soon found a parking space in the wide yard.

She got out of the car and took a closer look around. "Marley, this is where you grew up? It's so beautiful. The house looks newly built." Her excitement was palpable.

"Yeah. It's always been big, but Robert is a carpenter by trade so he keeps the place looking great," he said, placing his hand on her lower back and guiding her to the front entrance.

Once inside, Kayla was struck by the cathedral ceilings and the spiral staircase running along the wall in the foyer. Off from the foyer, glass doors opened into a huge room that had been cleared of furniture. Waiters floated among the carrying trays laden with champagne and hors d'oeuvres. As a waiter passed, Marley reached for two glasses.

"Here you go, baby," he said, putting his hand at the small of her back after she had taken her glass. "This will help you settle down."

"I don't need to se-settle down," Kayla protested.

His thumb moved lazily, familiarly over the bare skin of her lower back, causing her skin to tingle and making her stutter. She tried hard to focus on the large silver trays the waiters paraded in front of her—crab balls, toasted baguettes and artichoke dip, caviar on crackers, and petit fours—Kayla found the seductive movements and pressure being applied to her bare flesh to be too unsettling. She was unable to focus on anything except Marley's hypnotic attentions.

"Okay, you're going to have to keep your hands off me if you expect me to make it through the night." Kayla said this jokingly, but she was as serious as a heart attack.

Marley moved closer and in a low voice replied, "Maybe I don't want you to make it through the night. Maybe I don't want either of us to make it. I was ready to not even come as soon as I saw you in that sexy dress," emphasizing his point by squeezing her waist just a little.

"You need to behave," she giggled, already feeling the effects of the champagne she had drunk too quickly. Hot anticipation flowed through her body, landing in the crotch of her panties.

Marley laughed with her. He liked the way she smiled when she didn't have her guard up and was just being her natural self. She was relaxed and confident, and most important, comfortable.

"Ah, there he is," Marley said, seeing Robert walk through the crowd and make his way over to them. On his way, he had to constantly stop to accept congratulations.

When he finally reached them, Kayla saw his resemblance to Marley immediately. He was only an inch or two shorter, and he sported a thicker mustache and beard. But his eyes had the same dark sparkle that Marley's had. Their noses were identical, and they had the same smile.

"Hey, little brother," Robert said extending his hand and smiling brightly. "I expected you to be on time tonight, but I see that you have a good excuse." His smile brightened as he turned it on Kayla.

She returned his smile, well aware that he was giving the once-over, but not in a casual or disrespectful way.

Kayla was doing her own appraising, equally thorough. As she looked him up and down, he examined her just as intently. She figured he needed to be reassured that she was right for his brother. But nobody—nobody—judged her. Especially not so intently; he wasn't God. Just as she was becoming uncomfortable under his gaze and was about to say as much, Robert turned to Marley.

"You not going to introduce me to your lady friend?"

"Of course. Robert, this is Kayla. Kayla, this is my oldest brother, Robert."

Robert bowed and took her hand. Raising it to his mouth, he kissed its back. "It's a pleasure to finally meet you, Kayla. I've heard a lot about you."

Kayla's lifted eyebrow said, *Oh?* but she couldn't resist smiling at his gesture.

"All from my brother and wife, of course, and all good. I might add that you look exceptionally wonderful tonight."

"Thank you, Robert. It's nice to meet you, too. And you look quite spiffy yourself," she said, giving him another once-over. And indeed he was in his double-breasted black suit. "But I have never met your wife."

"No, you haven't. But she is dying to meet you. She and Wanda talk every day, so she's heard all about you, and she has been passing the occasional tidbit on to me. I know it seems a little immature, but I hope you don't mind."

Kayla smiled sweetly. "I don't mind. Not at all. My life's an open book . . . well, almost."

"I like her," he said simply, smiling at his brother.

Marley laughed. His brother was a riot, was always trying to see how far he could go with the women his brothers brought around him, claiming that was how he tested how strong they were. But Kayla remained calm. She did not become upset when he said they had talked about her, and she stared at him just as hard as he stared at her. Kayla seemed to be the kind of woman Robert wanted his brothers to build relationships with, and he was already putting his money on her.

"Hey, y'all," Wanda said, joining the group. She hugged everyone and then stood next to Kayla. "Girl, you look good. I love that dress."

"Thanks. Kaitlyn helped me with it. I love your dress, too."

Wanda swirled around in her strapless black gown. A sequined pattern ran down the front side and it had a matching jacket. The gown grabbed her hips tightly. "I had to show that some of us white girls got back, too."

"Wanda, couldn't nobody ever deny or ignore that fact that you got back. God knows, you got enough back to—"

"Shut the hell up, Robert. I don't give a damn if it is your anniversary. I see we will always have to go at it. I was trying to be good today. That would have been your anniversary present, but I'm glad I bought you something instead."

"I'd rather just have the gift, because if you start being nice to me, I would have to be nice to you, and I don't think I'm up for that right now."

Marley laughed at the two. They had been going at it for years. It was no wonder that the two couples were the best of friends. Kayla enjoyed the good-natured bantering and laughed along with them.

"Kayla, I'm going to steal you away from Marley for a moment. You don't need to be standing next to this old goat, anyway," Wanda said, taking her arm and pulling her away.

"Wanda, you're three years older than me, you know?" Robert said to her departing back. He turned to Marley, looking amused. "She's too damn smart. I don't see how Pooh stands being with her all this time. She's lucky that he's such a good friend of mine, or I would have taken her out a long time ago."

"Cut it out. You know you love Wanda. If you couldn't jaw with her every once in a while, you would go crazy."

"Let's just keep that between us. Your friend is mighty attractive, little brother. Very beautiful, for sure, and a very strong woman. I would keep her close to my side if

I were you. There are a lot of single brothers here tonight, including your own brother, who might not realize that she is with you."

"I'll keep that in mind, but something tells me that I really don't have to worry about that. She's respectful—not of me, but of herself. So, he got here, huh? I wasn't sure if his flight was going to be in on time from what he said yesterday on the phone. He had some last-minute running around to do before getting to the airport and couldn't change his plans." Marley watched Kayla walk through the crowd. Almost as if she knew he was watching, Kayla turned around. "Yeah, brother, I'm getting the feeling that this one might be a keeper."

"I hope so. It would be nice to see both you and Nester finally settled down with good women. A good man needs a good woman by his side. And if she's anything like LaToya and Wanda say, I think this girl might be perfect for you. Besides, look at that ass."

"Hey, easy, man. Don't be looking at her ass," Marley laughed, lightly elbowing his brother in the side.

"I'm sorry, bro, but I couldn't help it," Robert joked. "When she turned to walk away, it was just there."

"Hey, I don't look at LaToya's ass. Come on, give me some respect."

"You got all the respect in the world," Robert laughed. "I got to respect a man who can handle all that." He held his hands up. "Okay, I'm joking, I'm joking. You better not look at LaToya like that. She would whip your ass."

"From now on, I'm looking at her like that, big sis or not."

"Oh, stop it. You couldn't look at her sexually if your life depended on it. You better stop before you mess around and make yourself sick."

Robert was right. There was no way he would be looking at LaToya's ass. He loved her too much like a sister to even try. That would be just nasty.

"I didn't really want anything, Kayla. I just haven't been able to talk to you lately. We haven't had a good talk at work since Tuesday. So, how are things going with you and Marley? Everything appears to be going well."

"Things are moving along nice and slow, just the way we want them to. We get along very well, and he's not too pushy. I enjoy the time that we've spent together, and he's fun to have around. I mean, we talk and joke together."

"And the girls?"

"They're doing well. They really like Marley, practically trying to push us together. I'm trying to give them a little more freedom. We had a nice long talk, and I've agreed to let them date a little. They need to get out and mingle with their friends. They're actually at a party tonight. Then they're staying over at their girlfriend's house."

Wanda's eyes lit up. "Good for them. I know this will probably be a good thing for all of you. Sooo, tonight might be the night for you and Marley, huh?"

Kayla watched her friend acting like a schoolgirl. "You're crazy. You know that, right? No, tonight might not be the night."

"I'm just happy for you. You need this. Every once in a while, it's okay to drop the ball and let loose for a bit. Girl, it's been a while for you. You sure you're ready?"

"Ready for what?"

"For Marley. Kayla, don't play games with me. I know you're a little slow, but your ass ain't stupid. You better take that man and enjoy him."

Kayla smiled. She hadn't told Wanda about the time she and Marley had spent together under the deck or in the car. Thinking of those times, she had to fan herself.

"I know just thinking about it has gotten you all hot and bothered, huh?" Wanda asked, happy for her friend.

"Uh, yeah. It could lead to an interesting night." Kayla wanted to drop the subject. The last thing she needed to think about was Marley between her legs filling her to capacity and driving her wild. Now wasn't the time for that. Not while she was in a houseful of people.

"Hey," Wanda said, tapping her on her hand, "did you hear me?" Wanda looked into her eyes. "You still thinking about tonight?"

"No," she lied. "What's up?" Kayla stopped a passing waiter and took a small paper plate and filled it with cocktail shrimp and crab balls.

"I wanted you to see that." Wanda pointed to a tall, cinnamon-complexioned man with a shaved head and a diamond earring in each ear. His mustache was neatly trimmed, his beard thinly lined. Even through the navy double-breasted suit that seemed tailored for his body alone, it was obvious that Nester was a well-built specimen. But as spectacular as his physical presence was, it could not compete with the aura of his stance, the confidence he exuded, the self-possession he wore like a cloak.

The shrimp Kayla held was suspended midway to her mouth as she paused to take a closer look. It wasn't like her to stare, but every woman appreciated a good-looking man when she saw one. The man was fine. He didn't make her stomach do somersaults, but he was fine. Apparently, a few other women in the room thought so, too.

Kayla noticed many of them openingly watching the man standing near the bar, Wanda included.

"You better get a grip, girl," Kayla warned jokingly, laughing. "If Pooh sees you looking at that man like that, he's going to have a fit."

"I am not worried about Pooh. He knows that I like looking at Nester. I told him once that even when I look at Nester, I'm thinking about what I want to do to him."

Kayla laughed harder. "And he believed that? Girl, you are crazy."

"Nah, Pooh loves these boys, and so do I. He knows I would never try to cross a line like that, but if I were about thirteen years younger, I would be all over that one."

"So that's Nester. Well, he does have a certain sex appeal."

"Girl, please. That boy *is* sex appeal. And he doesn't run after a lot of women like most men do, and that just makes him that much sexier. You know, women want you more when they don't think they'll be able to get you."

"Well, I doubt that he actually has to run anywhere. Looks like all he has to do is stand there and they come running to him." Kayla watched a tall, pretty girl in a light yellow lacy gown walk over to him and kissed him on the cheek. She began talking as if they were old friends, but Kayla could tell that he had no idea who the girl was. Still, he was polite and talked with her briefly before excusing himself.

"Yeah, I think you're right about that," Wanda laughed. "Oh, here he comes."

Kayla couldn't help but watch as he smoothly walked away with a slight jaunt in his step. Female eyes tracked his movements, but he acted as if he were oblivious to the attention as he maneuvered through the crowd. He had focused on his target and was heading their way.

"Hello, Wanda," he said, kissing her lightly on the cheek. "It's been a long time. How are you doing?"

"I'm doing very well, thank you, Nester. You've been away for a few years. I almost thought you wouldn't make it back tonight. Did you come alone this visit?"

He smiled. "Yes, in fact I did. Sorry to disappoint you, but I'm still a single man. And I wasn't about to miss my brother's big night. I know it's been a while, but you know me better than that, Wanda."

"Well, I guess disappointing little old me is nothing compared to disappointing your several admirers. I see, as usual, you have a fair share in attendance tonight." Wanda waved her hand to encompass the whole room.

"I'm sure that I don't know what you're speaking of, Wanda," Nester said, smiling at her, the sparkle in his eyes becoming brighter. "But besides all of that, how have you and Pooh been?"

"We're doing quite well, thank you. Just glad to be around friends and family."

Kayla wasn't surprised to see the sparkle. She had actually been looking for it. The tallest of the three brothers, Nester's strong physical appeal, as stunning as it was, didn't compare to his sensual and sexual appeal. He practically forced one's attention onto him.

"Speaking of friends, aren't you going to introduce me to your friend, Wanda? Or do I have to stand here and wonder who she is?" Nester moved closer to Kayla's side. He gave her the once-over, finding what he saw appealing.

"I'd love to. Kayla, this is Nester. He is Marley and Robert's brother. The middle child. Nester, this is Kayla. Kayla is *dating* Marley."

Kayla wondered why Wanda felt the need to emphasize the word dating? Was she making a point of some kind, or just letting him know that Kayla was off limits?

Nester took her hand and briefly held it. He looked at Wanda, then back at Kayla. "Is that so? Well, it is very nice to meet you, Miss Kayla. Being in California, I guess I missed out on all pertinent information."

"Yes, you did." Wanda smiled at him brightly, smartly. She had guessed the thoughts that ran through his mind as soon as he approached them. Nester rarely set his sights on a woman, but when he did, he didn't hide it. "Maybe next time you'll listen to me when I tell you that I have a nice young lady that I want you to meet.

The girl I tried to introduce you to last time would have been perfect for you, but what did you do? You up and moved over 3,000 miles away just to avoid settling down."

"That's because I wasn't ready to settle down," he countered.

"Are you ready to settle down now?" Wanda retorted.

"I'm seriously thinking about it," he answered honestly, giving Kayla another look. Then he felt a big hand on his back. Without turning around, he knew it was Marley. "Hello, little brother," he said, still looking at Kayla.

Marley walked around and stood beside Nester. "Brother, it's good to see that you haven't changed one bit. You're not trying your God-given charms out on my lady, are you?"

"Come on, man, you know me better than that," Nester replied, his arms going around Marley easily, familiarly.

"Yes, I know you," Marley laughed, returning the hug. "That's why I made my way over here as soon as I saw you talking to her."

"Hey, now that hurts. You don't trust your own brother?"

"Hell, no, I don't trust you. Luckily, I trust Kayla," Marley smiled, putting his arm around her waist. The thumb began its slow, erotic rotation automatically.

As soon as Kayla saw the two men together—side by side—she spotted the resemblance. The three brothers all looked alike. But Nester was the one with the most charisma. And he was the most debonair. Yet as appealing as Nester clearly was, it was Marley who had her blood boiling with anticipation of the things his hands would do to her. He definitely had a few charms of his own.

"Come on, baby," Marley said, "let's go dance in the other room. Besides, I need to get you away from my brother before his charm becomes his undoing," Marley said, squeezing her around the waist. "Brother, I will talk to you later. Wanda."

"Marley, I think I'll be in there later to ask for a dance myself," Nester said, watching them walk off. Turning to Wanda, he said, "Nice couple they make, huh?"

"Very nice and very compatible."

"That's good for him." A hint of envy flashed through him.

As brief as it was, Wanda saw it. "Don't you want that, too? A nice woman, maybe even a family one day?"

"I'll talk to you later, Wanda. Tell my brothers that I'm taking a walk around the property if they ask." With that, Nester took his leave; he had a lot on his mind. He needed a quiet place to think about his plans, his future. Once again, he was oblivious to the attention he attracted as he walked through the room. Only two women were bold enough to stop his march to the door, but he kindly but firmly forestalled conversation.

Robert and LaToya stood hand in hand on the sidelines of the spacious dance floor and saw Marley and Kayla come into the room and join the other dancers.

"Is that her?" LaToya asked.

"Yes. Nice girl. I get the feeling that she is very independent and doesn't take too much shit."

"And very beautiful. Very shapely. I love her haircut."

"Yeah, let's just hope she's everything Wanda says and not a trickster like that Vanessa was."

"I doubt that very seriously. She's not looking for someone to take care of her. Don't tell Wanda, but the fact that she approves carries a lot of weight with me."

LaToya smiled at her husband. "I agree, sweetheart."

Marley pulled Kayla closer. He loved having her in his arms. Her body melted with his to the slow rhythms of Luther Vandross. The yearnings within him began to swell as he traced the form of her body with his hands. For some reason, he always seemed to be on the brink of controlling his body, his emotions when he was around her. He wanted her so damn bad that it was driving him crazy. He knew that it wouldn't be socially correct for him to just drag her out of the party, but he damn sure wanted to.

"I can't wait to get some alone time with you tonight, Kayla. I love the way you feel in my hands. I want to taste you in my mouth."

His whispered words caused Kayla to almost lose sight of where they were. She was so engulfed in the sensations circling around her that for a moment it was just the two of them. All of her focus was on the pattern of his hands on her back and hips and the words that he continued to say to her. When the song ended, they continued to hold on to each other. So absorbed were they in the sway of the dance, the way their bodies blended together, the applause of the crowd startled them. Kayla was slightly embarrassed when she realized they were being watched.

Marley was also aware but not in the least bit embarrassed. He walked her off the dance floor and over to Robert and LaToya.

"That was pretty entertaining, Marley," LaToya said. "It was almost more romantic than those two people hanging off the edge of the *Titanic.*" She turned to Kayla. "Hello, you must be Kayla."

"Yes, and you must be LaToya," Kayla answered, extending her hand.

LaToya accepted her hand easily. "I've heard a lot about you, Kayla. Wanda and Marley do nothing but sing your praises. Welcome to the family."

"Uh, thank you?" Kayla responded, shifting her eyes to Marley, who averted his.

Robert usually enjoyed awkward situations, but this time he came to the rescue and suggested that Marley find Nester so that the anniversary toast could be made.

"Honey, don't you think it's too early for that?" LaToya asked, taking her husband's arm. "It's not even ten o'clock yet."

"Not at all. Besides, the sooner the toasts are done, the sooner the dancing can be over, and the sooner everyone can leave. I really want to have you to myself." He gave his wife a brilliantly seductive smile.

"Oh, you never change," she giggled as his hand went down to grace her bottom.

Kayla pretended she didn't notice. They apparently didn't notice that she was still standing there or they just didn't care.

"Kayla, she's lucky I don't throw her over my shoulder and head on upstairs," Robert continued.

"You wouldn't want to disappoint all your guests would you, Robert?" Kayla asked. So they did know that she was there.

"You don't know me very well yet, Kayla. Believe me, it's been done before."

The expression on LaToya's face said he was telling the truth. They were all laughing when Wanda and Pooh Bear joined them.

"What's going on over here? Or shouldn't I ask?" Pooh asked.

"Oh, Robert is just trying to get the night over with so he can rush LaToya upstairs," Kayla volunteered.

"Well, why don't you just throw her over your shoulder like you used to?" Pooh joked. "Hell, everybody here has seen that a time or two."

"Because Robert's not twenty-five any more, and LaToya doesn't weigh 115 pounds anymore," Wanda answered realistically. "But I wish you would try it. I think everybody would love to see you pull off that feat, Robert."

"Thank you, Wanda, for pointing that out," LaToya replied smartly.

"There she goes again with that smart mouth of hers. Pooh, man, do you want a drink? I know that dealing with her makes you want to drink all the time," Robert laughed, pulling his long-time friend away from the ladies.

Nester was in the gazebo in the back gardens that LaToya loved so much. She spent hours there tending to the flowers and bushes. He was happy that Robert had found her so long ago. His mother couldn't have found a better woman for Robert if she had picked her herself. He smiled, remembering how his mother tried tirelessly to fix Robert up with the right woman.

Being the oldest, Robert had endured the bulk of their mother's matchmaking. Her pleasure was immense when he returned from the service hitched to LaToya. LaToya was everything she had ever wanted in a daughter-in-law, and much more. They had the same and likes and dislikes. Robert had, in effect, married his mother. And it looked as if Marley was probably on his way to doing the same—from what little he knew of Kayla. He could tell just by looking at the two of them together that Marley was smitten.

Nester's mind was cluttered with decisions he needed to make. His plans included moving back to the East Coast. It wouldn't be hard to find work or to start his physical-training business. He had worked for Hollywood bigwigs for years, so he had made some good contacts and a very good reputation. But now it was time to come—

"So you're Nester? Marley's older brother, huh?" The low, husky voice was surprisingly sexual and caught him off guard.

Nester, his concentration broken, watched the beauty walking up the gazebo steps toward him. Her short purple dress glistened with each step she took. The four-inch heels accentuated her long, bronze legs. Immediately, he was interested. The woman was beautiful, but something in her look told him she was trouble. Nester had been with enough women to know trouble when he saw it. She must have followed him outside. And that was not a good thing in his eyes. Nobody knew where he was except Wanda.

"Yes, I am. And you are?"

She moved up to stand directly in front of him. Her body rubbed against his, her legs against his legs.

Trouble. Trouble. Trouble.

"My name is Vanessa. I've heard a lot about you, Nester. And might I say that you're as handsome and as sexy as everyone says you are. I don't think I've ever seen a more handsome man in my life."

"Is that so? You have obviously met my brothers. They look just like me, just as handsome, just as sexy."

"Yes, but it's something about you that—"

"That turns you on? Makes you horny? Gives you goose bumps? Which one is it? I've heard them all, honey." He didn't mean to be intentionally cruel, but it was what it was. So many women had used the same exact lines on him over the years that Nester could tell from the first words spoken that she didn't want anything but a good lay. That and to be able to say that he gave it to her.

Unfazed, Vanessa tried to catch him off guard. "That gives me the urge to screw you right here and right now."

Nester smiled and simply raised an eyebrow. "Talk like that makes me wonder how often you get this urge of yours. Urges like that can be pretty dangerous."

She smiled up at him, her lips inches from his, but he wouldn't take the bait. When she moved closer, he turned his face away.

Vanessa moved back a little, surprised that he would reject her. Nobody resisted her except Marley, now that he had his little friend. But every man wanted her, at least in her mind. She was irresistible.

"Huh, you don't want me? I find that very hard to believe. Most men would love to have the opportunity that I'm trying to give to you."

Nester realized that she was a little too full of herself. It had taken him a few years to understand women, but now that he did, he wasn't too easily fooled. This girl obviously had some lessons to learn herself. She really thought that she was God's gift to man. That was very naive of her. Surely she didn't think that she was the most beautiful woman he had ever seen.

"Vanessa, is it? I think I need to tell you something. First of all, I'm not like most men. I don't particularly give a damn how good you look. I mean, you're okay looking. I've seen worse, but believe me, I've also seen much better. I have had some very good relationships with women twice your size who may not have been as pretty as you on the outside, but they were beautiful on the inside."

"And where are they now?" she asked snippily.

"That is neither here nor there. They remain my friends because they have respect for themselves and for me. Now the fact that you came out here to me, a total stranger, and offered your body so easily tells me that you have very low regard for yourself. That's not attractive. I would presume that men don't treat you very well, or that you don't know what to do with a good man when you find one. And that's because you don't have enough respect for yourself to demand that others respect you. You look good, but most men recognize a trick when they see one."

She dropped her hands to her sides and looked at him as if he had just slapped her across the face. "I ain't no damn trick," she said tightly.

"Okay, well, I apologize for offending you. Maybe I shouldn't have said that. I don't know you at all. Again, I'm sorry. I just want to be left alone, please."

"You know what, Nester? I don't give a damn how good you look. An asshole is still an asshole." Vanessa was wounded. No one had dared talk to her so bluntly before, not even Marley. He had said some harsh things when he broke things off with her, but this was different. This was right in her face from someone who didn't know her at all, and it hurt for her to hear it from him.

She turned to go back into the party where she had left her date, another older member of the bike club. Vanessa always found a way to be at any function associated with the club.

"You're correct," he agreed, letting her comment roll off his shoulder. He had been called worse. Women seemed to take it kind of hard when he turned them down, especially the few women that he had to set straight. But he was only being honest. He didn't like loose women, he didn't care what size she wore or what she looked like. All he wanted was an honest, respectful woman.

"Hey, brother," Marley called out, just as Vanessa turned to walk away. When she got near Marley, she flashed her eyes at him. "I see you couldn't dig your nails into my brother, either. Nice try. Be careful going inside. I hear that Calendar just arrived with his wife." Marley laughed and she stomped off toward the house.

"What's up, man? You know that trick?" Nester asked, turning away from her and back to the gardens.

"Yeah. Don't sweat it. Nothing serious at all. That girl has a lot of issues to sort out. Thinks her shit don't stink."

"Yeah, I could tell by just looking at her. I wanted to talk to you about something," Nester said, changing the subject. No need worrying over spilled milk.

"What's up?"

"Don't tell Robert, but I'm seriously thinking about moving back home, for good."

"You sure? That's great." Marley hugged his brother briefly. "Why don't you want Robert to know?"

"Yeah, I think it's time to settle down and stay put in one place. I'm getting too old to be trotting the globe. Maybe I'll open up a gym or something around here. I just don't want Robert getting too excited until I've definitely made up my mind. I'll talk to him myself then. You know he's been riding me to come back home for a while now."

"Well, you know I'm with you. You can stay at my place if you don't want to stay here. It'll be a little like old times."

"It won't be anything like old times. You got a woman now. Won't be any more of those bachelor parties we used to have. Just keep things quiet for now. We'll see how it all works out."

"Yeah, I guess you're right about that. But you should come home, find yourself a nice girl, too. Either way, you can count on me. Robert wants us to come inside and do the toasts now. He's ready to get the party over with."

"Probably wants to get LaToya upstairs as fast as possible." Laughing, they headed back to the house.

"So, in conclusion, Marley and I would like to congratulate LaToya and Robert on ten wonderful years of marriage. We don't exactly know how LaToya stood being with him for this many years without going crazy, but we love her for putting up with the big lug anyway. And we thank her for taking care of us when we needed her as well. She is truly the big sister that Marley and I always needed."

"We love you both very much," they said together as they raised their hands in salute to the happy couple.

Everyone in the room raised glasses to toast Robert and LaToya before quieting down to allow them to speak.

"On behalf of my wife and myself, I'd like to thank you all for coming to celebrate this happy occasion with us. We ask that you eat, drink, and be merry, but don't drink too much because I'm not going to be responsible for your driving. Now, there are plenty of designated drivers here tonight. I want everybody to think before leaving. We've been to too many funerals in the past few years. No more brothers need pass because of a little over-indulgence."

"Now, band, please play my selection so I can swirl my wife around on this dance floor before taking her upstairs to ravish her body." The whole room erupted in cheers as the band began to play the Commodores' "Three Times a Lady".

Marley found Kayla and stood behind her with his arms around her waist. Slowly, he swayed to the rhythm of the music. Close to her ear, he whispered, "I'm ready to get out of here. I want you."

Kayla felt Marley's muscles clench. God, she was ready to leave, too. He had been on her mind all night.

Marley kissed her cheek.

She had to shut her eyes against the stirring inside her belly. He was turning her on just by standing behind her, rubbing his hands over her hips. She could feel his imprint against her thigh as he stepped closer behind her.

He didn't grind against her, but he wanted her to know that he was feeling it, too. "You feel that, baby?" he whispered. "I'm ready for you. Let's say our good-byes and go."

Kayla didn't trust herself to say anything. She simply nodded her head in agreement. It was just past 11 o'clock. They had been there less than four hours, but she was ready for the twenty-minute ride home so she could be alone with him.

CHAPTER 9

Marley and Kayla said their good-byes and headed for his car. He held the door for her and then quickly walked around to the driver-side door. He was glad to be getting away from the party. All he could think of was being alone with Kayla.

As soon as Marley turned onto the road leading home, Kayla slid across the front seat of the Cadillac. Marley was trying to concentrate on the road and was caught completely off guard when he felt Kayla's hand reach between his legs. "Whoa, girl," he said, jumping. "What you doing?"

"Having fun," she replied, massaging the flesh hanging loosely against his inner thighs. "You want to have fun?" she asked, feeling that same flesh harden immediately.

Marley twisted himself in his seat. "See what you've done? Now I got to sit here uncomfortably."

"No, you don't," she replied, unfastening his pants. "I'm sorry. Are you still uncomfortable?" she asked sweetly.

"Yeah," Marley replied. He slowed the car a little. A smile crept onto his face as he imagined what Kayla's next move would be.

Kayla smiled, too. She was glad to be away from the party. Now that they were alone, she was ready to enjoy the rest of her night.

Men were so obvious. Even in the darkness, she could tell that he actually thought he had come up with this solution on his own. He didn't comprehend that this had been her plan all along, not his.

As she lowered her head onto his lap, Marley moved his right hand off the steering wheel and rested it on her back. Her tongue lashed out, and he gripped the wheel tightly. Marley slowed the car more.

Marley moaned.

With her lips still around him, Kayla lowered her head again. She felt his hand rubbing her back.

"Damn," he whispered. Marley put his head back against the headrest, and then accidentally swerved off the road a little. He straightened the car, promising himself to stay focused. He had driven this road a million times before. But he couldn't concentrate with her mouth tightening over him, its wetness surrounding him.

Focus. Focus. Marley gripped the wheel with both hands. He couldn't allow himself to think about what she was doing, but it was feeling so good. So good, in fact, that he began to count the minutes it would take to get back to the house.

They were nearing the highway, which meant lights. From there it was only a six-minute drive to the house. Six minutes. He didn't want to wait that long. Down stroke after down stroke, Marley was taken deeper into pleasure.

Kayla hadn't thought about the ride home at all. She was totally engrossed in pleasing Marley. She loved it when she felt his hand on the back of her head. She loved hearing him moan deep in his throat. She wanted him so badly.

If it weren't for the fact that they would probably wreck his car and that her behind would be hitting the horn on the steering wheel repeatedly, she would have straddled him right then and there.

"Are we close to home, Marley?" she asked between suctions.

"Just a few more minutes, baby," he replied. "Don't stop."

Kayla had no intention of stopping. If she put her head up now, right under the four-corner lights of the highway, people were bound to see her and wonder what she was doing, or worse, know what she was doing. She was content to stay right where she was, doing what she was doing.

Applying a little more pressure with her lips, Kayla felt Marley's hand on the back of her head again.

"Ahhhh, Kayla," he moaned. "We're almost there."

Kayla could tell by the turns he was making that the house was only minutes away. When Marley pulled in front of the house, it was exactly 11:42 P.M.

And as soon as Marley put his car in park, he lifted Kayla's head and kissed her passionately on the lips.

"I want you so much right now," he whispered. There were no neighbors outside to worry about. There were no kids that he had to hide his feelings from. He could do whatever he wanted, except take her right there in the parking space. "Let's go." Marley grabbed the front of his pants with one hand, his keys with the other.

"Marley, aren't you going to fasten your pants first?" Kayla asked, following him out of the car and up the steps to the front house.

"I can't," he replied, in his haste, almost tripping on the third step. "Besides, as soon as I get into this house, they're coming off." He jiggled the key into the lock.

Kayla was close behind him. And true to his word, as soon as Marley crossed the threshold into his house, his shoes came off and his pants fell down. She barely had time to shut the front door.

He turned to Kayla, a tent raised in the front of his boxers and walked towards her.

Her excitement growing, her belly fluttering, Kayla didn't move; she wanted him to come to her.

Marley had to take only a couple of steps before he was standing right in front of her. "Come here, baby," he said softly, then pulled her hard to him. His mouth was already open and ready when she lifted her head to him.

Marley took her lips hard, his mouth moved across her face to her cheeks and then down to her neck. As his lips moved further down to her shoulders, his hands wrapped around her back and pulled in closer. He held onto her possessively, and Kayla could feel the imprint of his hands wherever he touched her. Urgently, he pulled at the spaghetti-straps that held the dress to her shoulders.

"Wait. Wait," she urged, still under the spell his lips had cast over her as they moved to the tops of her breasts. "The zipper."

His hands quickly went to the zipper and yanked it down. The dress loosened and fell.

Kayla stood before him in the body slip. The thing hugged her body so tightly that Marley thought she looked like a Tootsie Roll. Something inside urged him on, made him more determined to get under, inside, that damn slip. Like a kid at Christmas time, at tearing off the gift wrapper and ripping open the box just to get to the prize within, he pulled feverishly at the slip until it slid down, settling around her ankles.

She smiled, thinking that it had taken her almost five minutes to put it on, and it took him only five seconds to take it off.

Once the undergarment was off, Marley just stared at her. This was getting better and better. With each layer of clothing he had peeled away, his expectation of what was to come had grown. Kayla was sexy standing in the middle of the room wearing nothing but a black garter belt and thong, thigh-high stockings and her two-inch heel sandals. He grabbed eagerly at her bare breast, bending forward to place one nipple into his mouth.

"Awww," she yipped when he unexpectedly picked her up and carried her to the sofa. He literally let her drop. Kayla was about to respond to his foreplay, but then she turned and saw the look in his eye. A look of determination and urgency was plastered all over his face as he struggled out of his dress shirt and tie.

"Oh," she exhaled just before he fell to his knees and turned her toward him. Grabbing her hips, he pulled her forward until her back lay on the seat of the sofa, and his prize was right under his chin.

"This is what I want, right here," Marley said. He wasn't really talking to her. It was more to himself. He buried his face deep and inhaled her essence.

His tongue was long and wet as it glided over her, along the sides of her crotch and up to her center. Instead of taking the time to undo the garter belt and pull off her stockings and then the panties, Marley simply tugged at the crotch until the damn thing broke. He would buy her another thong if she insisted.

Once he had her completely free, he reached up her body until he had a firm breast in each hand and massaged them vigorously. With his head bent over her, he blew softly, then pleased her from one end of ecstasy to the other until his name was being called over and over and she was gripping onto the back of his head as if her life depended on it. Hearing her call to him was his undoing. It brought the urgency out of him, making him want to be a part of the strong orgasm ahead.

Kayla was too far along in her own erotic pleasures to be aware of what was going on around her. She was on the brink when his lips left her. In an instant, her eyes snapped open. *What the . . . ?* But in that same moment, she was being flipped over. Her knees were off the sofa. Marley was behind her.

"Marley, I wasn't finished." She could hear him ripping a condom wrapper and working to cover himself.

"That's all right. I got you," he replied. His breathing was ragged. Then he was right on her. He gripped her hips, pulling her up until she stood as he joined her. His hand was on her back, keeping her bent over.

"Marley?"

"Shhh," he answered, filling her deeply on the first thrust.

"Ahhh." Kayla struggled against the pain, but she loved the feel of him stretching her insides, completely filling her.

Marley didn't slow his thrusts or his pace as he tried to dig deeper and deeper into her soul with each jab.

"Damn, baby, you feel so good," he said between breaths.

Kayla could only moan her responses. She needed to save her breath, to concentrate on her buckling knees, to prepare for his every attack as he continued to drive into her.

Kayla thought that he was close to finishing because his grip on her became tighter and his breathing became harsh, but he didn't. In an effort to relieve them both, she began to rotate her hips, tightening and loosening the walls of her vagina with each rotation.

"Yes, baby," Marley moaned. "I love this."

He gave her incentive, a mission. She wanted to please him. So she worked it for him as he asked. Kayla knew she was going to be sore later, but she forgot that she was a thirty-eight-year-old woman and worked it like a video chick, driving Marley out of his mind.

When she looked back at him, his eyes were closed, his teeth were gritting, and a heavy sweat had worked its way across his forehead.

"Yeah, yeah, yeah," he mumbled, before letting out a low growl and clenching his stomach muscles together.

He gripped her hips again, this time to pull her as close to him as possible.

A long giggle escaped his throat as he pulled her with him to lie on the living room floor. He wrapped her in his arms and kissed her cheek.

Kayla willingly lay on his outstretched arm. They were both exhausted, too tired to move. She lay there until she realized that his heavy breathing had turned into snores.

"Marley." She shook his side a couple of times.

"Marley," she repeated, pushing harder until he stirred. "We need to go to bed. Come on."

Marley simply did as he was told. He got up and followed her up the steps. But by the time he reached the top, he was awake again with other thoughts on his mind besides sleep.

As soon as she reached the bed, his hands were all over her.

Kayla thought that it was the brightness of the sun shining through the window that woke her, but then she heard the pounding on the front door. Then she heard the doorbell ringing repeatedly.

"Marley," she said quietly, to no avail. His snoring became louder after she poked him in the side. "Marley," she repeated louder, "somebody's at the door."

"Hmmm." He slowly came awake. "What?"

"Somebody's at the damn door," she replied.

"They'll go away." Marley turned towards her. He was thick and heavy as he brushed against her thigh. Marley tried pulling her closer him, but Kayla resisted as the doorbell sounded again.

"Marley, go get it," she said, pushing him away.

"Damn. Whoever it is can wait."

Kayla was already sliding out of the bed. She didn't know who it was outside sitting on the doorbell, but whoever it was, they were adamant about getting in.

Vanessa. That was the name that her subconscious screamed out at her. And she would be damned if she would be found with her pants down, so to speak. She was going to be ready for whatever or whoever was on the other side of the door.

Before he could stop her, Kayla moved out of the way of his arm and jumped off the bed, stumbling a little. Then she stooped down and grabbed one of his t-shirts and pulled it over her head.

Marley stared at the sight before him. His t-shirt barely went past Kayla's waist. It was too small for her, but it turned him on to have a display of her legs so visible and her cheeks smacking as she went around the room looking for her underwear.

"Kayla," he smiled, "walk back past me again."

"No," she replied, lifting the bed skirt up to locate her underclothes and then realizing that they were downstairs on the living-room floor. "Damn," she mumbled. There was no need asking for a pair of his pants. They wouldn't fit over her big behind. "Go see who it is,

Marley." She stamped her foot impatiently, staring at him until he acceded to her demand.

"Okay, damn. I guess the sooner I get rid of them, the sooner I can dive back into you." Marley hopped off the bed, and strolled out the bedroom.

"Aren't you going to put something on?" she yelled.

"No," he replied, picking his boxers up off the living-room floor. He opened the front door, knowing full well who would be on the other side. He swung the door open. "What's up?"

"Don't 'what's up' me, man. Where you supposed to be?" He knew why his brother wasn't where he was supposed to be. He wouldn't have been there, either.

Marley rubbed his eye and tilted his head. "Come on, man. It's too early for this shit." He caught the hard-thrown basketball in his gut.

"You said, 'Meet me at the park first thing in the morning.' Well," Nester glanced down at his watch, "it's nine o'clock. And that's not even first thing in the morning. I gave you an hour because I knew that you weren't going to get up." He pushed Marley's door open wider, moving Marley out of the way, and walked inside.

On the couch were Kayla's dress and Marley's dress pants. His shirt was on the floor halfway across the room. Nester walked further into the room before turning around. When he did, Kayla's thong underwear was on the foot of his sneaker.

"I think you might want this," he chuckled, using his foot to toss the panties at Marley.

"Man, I'm sorry about this morning; I'm a little busy at the moment. But I can meet you later if you want."

"Nah, it's all good. I understand. I should have known it was a done deal when I saw you leave the party early last night. I'm going to see if I can get Wanda to make me breakfast. I'll holler at you later." Nester walked back toward the door. Before leaving, he turned toward the steps and yelled, "Good-bye, Kayla."

Kayla smiled when she heard his greeting. She stuck her head out the door. "Bye, Nester."

"All right, man," Nester said, walking out the door. He paused on the front step. It was good that Marley was involved with a good woman with the possibility of a strong relationship on the horizon. From what Robert had told him, she seemed to be everything that he needed.

Nester wanted that same thing. It wasn't even the fact that he was older now and more mature. This wasn't only what he needed, but it was also what he wanted. He wanted to know that someone had his back; someone was in this with him. A strong woman with her own mind, strength, and dreams, someone he could have dreams with. Maybe he was too deep in his thinking, but there was something missing in his life, and he knew that a good woman was it. He had made his decision to move back home in the wee hours of the morning. He didn't suspect he would have any trouble at all getting his gym built. The area was in desperate need of one, and he knew a few people who could help him.

The sound of Kayla and Marley playing upstairs came through the windows at the front of the house. He could imagine the fun that his brother was having with his lady. A tinge of envy ran through him, but he forced it aside. Bouncing the basketball hard against the concrete, he walked toward the rental car parked down the street and decided that instead of going to get a meal from Wanda and Bear, he really did need to go to the court and work off some of his frustration. Besides, Wanda would be throwing every single girlfriend she had up in his face.

He wasn't ready for a hook-up. The woman for him was out there somewhere, and he doubted very seriously if Wanda knew her. Although he wanted a special woman, he was willing to wait for God to bring her into his life.

Nester sat in the car quietly and thought about what he had been through the last few weeks. It wasn't as if he was running away from California, but he knew that it was definitely time for a change. Coming home seemed like the best decision at this point. It wasn't going to be a hard change to make. There was nothing keeping him there at this point. No woman, no real friends, and no job. It was a good thing he had wisely saved up his money over the years.

Coming home and starting over was almost his only choice. He started the car and pulled out, heading for the park to clear his troubled mind, if only for the length of the basketball court.

When the girls finally walked into the house, Kayla was standing in front of the stove in a long nightgown stirring noodles into her spaghetti sauce. Today, she had planned to have a lazy night with the girls. She couldn't wait for them to give her all the highlights of their weekend and especially the party. Kayla thought this was probably the most excited she had been with the girls in a long time. This was going to be the first time she and the girls ever had a mother-daughter talk after a night out.

A lazy night to her meant a quick spaghetti dinner and a movie. She had already gotten her clothes out for work on Monday and had told the girls to get their clothes out before they left Saturday afternoon. She had learned a long time ago that Sunday was actually the hardest day of the week because you had to prepare yourself mentally for Monday morning. The best remedy was to make Sunday as easy as possible by doing on Saturday morning everything you would usually do on Sunday.

"Hey, Mom," Kaitlyn cheerfully yelled as soon as she entered the house.

"Hello, girls. Did you have a good time?" She leaned back to receive a kiss on the cheek from each girl.

"We had a great time," Kaitlyn answered. She still had a glow of happiness on her face that made Kayla glad that she had made the decision to let them go.

"And you?" Kayla knew that Kamry wanted to go, but she didn't really see her tomboy daughter as the party-girl type.

"I had a good time, too." Kamry smiled.

"She did, Mom. You should have seen her. There were a lot of guys there asking Kamry to dance."

"Shut up," Kamry warned.

"What you getting upset for, Kamry?" Kayla turned to her daughter. "That's all a part of growing up. You're a beautiful young lady. Of course boys are going to be interested in you. You're athletic and in shape. Guys like that."

"I do not care what guys like. I don't have time for any boys. And they talk so dumb."

"Well, did you dance?" Kayla asked curiously.

"She danced all night long. Every time she stopped with one, another boy would come up and ask her to dance."

"But they talk so dumb. And they kept talking about themselves."

"Maybe they were trying to impress you, Kamry. Did you ever think of that?"

"No. Well, anyway, I had a good time."

"Well, that's good. That's what parties are for. You should be out dancing and meeting people. But none of that slow grinding and shaking what your momma gave you mess that I see those girls on the videos doing. That's a fast way to get an even faster name for yourself." Kayla felt really good about her decision to let the girls start socializing. At their ages, they needed to get out and enjoy life a little.

"Mom," Kaitlyn chimed in, "I'm going upstairs to unpack my clothes. Is dinner ready?"

"Not yet. Give me about another fifteen minutes, then we can eat and get that out of the way."

"Yeah, and you can tell us about your date with Mr. Marley," Kamry joked.

"Yeah, Mom. Where is he, anyway? Isn't he coming to dinner tonight?"

"No, I wanted this to be a ladies' night so y'all could tell me all about the party." She wondered if they really thought that Marley would be eating with them every night. Although she enjoyed her time with him, they were a long way from nightly family dinners.

The girls were headed up the stairs when Kamry came up behind her sister and joked, "I bet you won't be telling her *all* about your evening."

"Shut up, Kamry," Kaitlyn hissed. "You always saying something."

"Don't tell me to shut up." Kamry followed behind her sister closely. "I think it was stupid of you, anyway."

"Well, that's why you're you and I'm me."

"Yeah, and it's a good thing, too. I wouldn't have been dumb enough to fall for his lines."

"He wouldn't have said anything like that to you. He loves me."

"You know you sound just like one of those dumb teenage girls on the Lifetime channel. He loves me. He cares for me. He wants to spend the rest of his life with me. You do know that's a bunch of bull, right?"

"Kamry, you're just jealous because nobody wants to be with you."

"Whatever." Kamry shook her head and started heading to her own room. She paused. "For your sake, I hope you're right. I mean I hope he really does love you. What did Mom always tell us? Our bodies are the most valuable things we own."

"Kamry, get out." Kaitlyn walked to her bedroom door and shut it in her sister's face. She wasn't going to let Kamry spoil the best weekend of her life. She stood in front of the full-length mirror that was on the back of her bedroom door and turned her body from side to side. She didn't look any different. She didn't even feel different. She was happy and excited because she and David had finally made love. Talisha and her other girlfriends didn't think that she would go through with it, but she proved them all wrong.

Now she was a woman, and David was her man.

"Girls, come and eat," she heard her mother yell from downstairs. Kaitlyn forced the deep smile off her face. She had to play it cool when she went back downstairs. As she passed Kamry's room, her sister came out and the two girls just looked at each other. Kaitlyn knew Kamry wouldn't tell their mother on her, but she would be saying as many smart remarks as she could during dinner.

They were all sitting at the table when Kayla brought up the dance again. "So, tell me about the dance. Were there a lot of kids there?"

"Yeah," Kaitlyn said, "practically everybody from school was there. It was crowded."

"And was your little friend there? What is his name? David?"

"Yeah, he was there all right," Kamry chirped in, half under her breath. She didn't like David anyway. He thought he was all that. But as dumb as she thought Kaitlyn was for having sex with him in his father's car at the dance, she wasn't about to rat her sister out. Kamry wasn't a snitch. She just wanted Kaitlyn to sweat a little for her dumbness.

"Well, did y'all dance? Tell me all about it." Kayla grudgingly admitted that she was beginning to like the idea of watching her girls socialize. It was almost as if she was living vicariously through them. It was going to be fun watching them go out on dates, to the prom, falling in love for the first time.

"Gosh, Mom, there's really nothing to tell," Kaitlyn replied. She didn't want to say too much. "You seem more excited than we do. It was nice and hot, but they did have punch, which no one spiked, by the way. Kamry danced a lot. I danced with David a lot. Talisha danced, too. We had fun. Then when it was over, Talisha's mom came and got us, and we stayed up all night talking about the party."

"Okay, well, I'm just glad that I now believe I made the right decision by letting you guys spread your wings a little. I should apologize for my behavior before. I never meant to keep you locked up from the world. I was just trying to protect you. But now that you're going out and having fun, there are still some things that you have to uphold. The most important thing is that I want you to know that I trust you to carry yourselves like respectable young ladies when you're out. You don't have to let anyone take advantage of you to be popular. And no one should pressure you to do anything that you don't want to. I'm here for you no matter what happens. I know that I raised you right. And I love you. Okay, that's all I got to say."

Kaitlyn put her head down. She almost said it out loud, but her *Thank you, God* stayed in her mouth. Her mom was pouring it on a little too thick for her to handle. She was beginning to feel a little guilty, but she didn't feel that being with David was a mistake like Kamry said. He hadn't really pressured her. She had done it willingly because she didn't want to lose him. There were a lot of other girls at the school who wanted David. He was one of the most popular guys in school. If she didn't, he would have broken up with her. But she really liked David. Kaitlyn was determined not to lose him to a girl that wasn't as pretty or popular as she was. What would her friends say? What would the other kids at school think?

"So, Mom," she shook her head free of her thoughts and concentrated on her mother's face, "how was your party? Did Mr. Marley like the dress we picked out?"

"As a matter of fact, yes, he did. He gave both the dress and me plenty of compliments. The party was very nice. It was an older crowd, a sophisticated affair. The food was excellent, too. And we danced. I met his family."

"What's his family like?" Kamry asked. "Are they all as good-looking as Mr. Marley?"

"Well, he has two older brothers. Both of them are very good-looking, too. His brother Nester is especially gorgeous, though."

"Nester?" Kamry questioned. "Huh, what's the other brother's name? Robert?"

Kayla looked at Kamry and smiled. She would be the one to figure it out. "You guessed it, girlie. Robert,

Nester, and Marley. Their parents had to obviously be huge Bob Marley fans to name their children after him. And Robert's wife is so nice. They are really good people."

"Well, it sounds like you had a ball."

"I did. I guess that I've been missing out on a lot myself all this time staying cooped up in the house."

They finished their meal and cleared the dishes, and then tried to decide on a movie they all could agree on watching before going to bed. Then the phone rang.

"Hello. Mom! It's for you," Kamry yelled down to the family room. "It's Mr. Marley. No, that's okay, Mr. Marley. We aren't doing anything. Here she comes."

Kayla came up the steps and took the phone from her smiling daughter. She felt the warmth of a blush creeping up the side of her cheeks. The fact that she was standing across from her daughter stopped the blood from rushing to the little nub between her legs. But as soon as Kamry ran down the steps and she heard his voice, her panties moistened. Damn, she hadn't had enough of him.

"Hey, baby, what you up to?"

She allowed his voice to caress her, to give her body a little of the pleasure it craved. She gripped the phone a little tighter. "I'm just watching a movie with the girls. They were telling me about their evening."

"Oh, right, the dance. How was that? Did they have a good time?"

"They said they had a great time. I guess I was being a little too paranoid in my own thinking. I don't know what I was trying to do to them."

"Hey, don't be too hard on yourself. You were just being a good mother. A lot more mothers need to keep an eye on their daughters or at least talk to them a little more. Maybe then there wouldn't be so much teenage pregnancy, because they wouldn't be so ready to believe the first lies they hear. At any rate, I think you're doing a hell of a job, especially on your own. I miss you."

She was speechless. He had caught her off guard with the confession, especially since it was completely off the subject. "I-I miss you, too."

"So what we going to do about it?"

Kayla thought for a moment. As bad as she wanted to open the door and run down to his house, she realized that it was too soon for her to start making it that convenient for him to get to her. Besides, she didn't want to seem too desperate or caught up in him, either. *Games,* she thought.

"Marley, can I call you back later after we finish the movie and the girls are asleep?"

"Sure, baby. I'm not going anywhere." He said it very slowly, separating each syllable for her benefit. The meaning of his words was too obvious.

Kayla got the meaning, but she didn't reply. She just said goodnight and hung up. And she smiled.

The movie ended at 10:15. She couldn't have planned it better herself. That gave the girls fifteen minutes to wash their faces and brush their teeth, and then they could all go to bed. Kayla walked them to their rooms and kissed each of them on the cheek. She hadn't done that in such a long time. Truth be told, it was more for her benefit than theirs. They weren't babies anymore. Her girls were growing into women right before her eyes. Kayla wondered if her mother had gone through the same scary feelings when she was growing up.

It was hard. You protect them from harm for all these years, then you have to let them go out into the world and learn that it isn't as perfect as they think it is. You know that some rotten bastard is going to come into their lives and destroy the perfect world that you built around them. But its inevitable, and sadly, it's a lesson that they have to learn on their own. All you can do is be there for them when it happens and pray that they'll be stronger the next time around.

After she left their rooms, Kayla didn't feel much like talking to anyone. She had managed to put herself into a rut with worry about her girls. She lay across her bed and sent a silent prayer up asking for her babies to be looked after.

Kayla dragged herself down the steps, making sure all the lights were out and that the doors were locked. Rolling her neck to stretch her taut muscles, she walked back up to her room and called Marley as she had promised.

"Hello," he answered, obviously waking from a deep sleep.

"Hey, Marley. This is Kayla. I was just calling you back, but I can tell you're sleeping. I'll talk to you in the morning."

"Whoa, whoa, whoa—what's going on? What's wrong?" He could hear it in her voice. Something wasn't right.

"Nothing. Just got some things on my mind, but it's nothing important." She crawled onto the bed. "You go on to sleep. I'll see you tomorrow."

"Kayla, I'm up now. And I can hear it in your voice that something is not right with you. Talk to me, or at least let me take your mind off whatever is bothering you. I could come down there and give you a good rub down."

Kayla smiled again. She wished it were that simple. "You know we can't do that with the girls here."

"Well, you come down here then. I'll hold you for a little while."

"No, you won't. We'll end up doing the same thing we did this morning when you were supposed to be holding me for a little while."

They both laughed.

"Maybe, but I promise that I'll try not to." Neither of them believed that. They laughed harder.

"I think I'm just going to stay right where I am, thank you very much."

"That's cool, too. I can make you feel good from right here." His voice had grown deeper. "You going to help me do that—make you feel better."

"Just how you plan on doing that?" Kayla asked, anticipation coursing through her.

"All I got to do is talk to you, but you got to promise to do what I say. Can you do that? Do you trust me?"

CHAPTER 10

"Of course, I trust you, Marley."

"What are you doing? Where are you at?" he asked.

"I'm in the bedroom, lying down. Why?"

"What are you wearing?"

"My nightgown."

"Take it off."

He said it so simply she hesitated. Marley must have known because he repeated his command.

"Take it off, Kayla."

She did as she was told.

He could hear the rustling of the clothes through the phone line, but he asked her, anyway.

"Are you naked?"

"Yes," she whispered, her heart rate starting to accelerate.

"Are you lying on your back on the bed?"

"I am."

"Relax. Listen to the sound of my voice, and just relax. Kayla, I want to be with you so badly right now. Shut your eyes, and imagine that I'm lying next to you."

Kayla closed her eyes and let her head sink deeply into the soft pillow. She could have sworn that there was an indention in the empty space next to her. She concentrated on his words, concentrated on how he was making her feel.

"I'm right there with you, baby. Whatever you're worrying about, put that on me, let me carry that burden for you for a little while. Do you feel me lying next to you?"

"Yes."

"Baby, I can smell you. You smell so sweet. I just want to put my head on your shoulder and let the sweet scent of you float up into my nostrils. Mmm. Touch yourself for me, Kayla. I want to touch your neck. Nice, slender neck. I love your neck. Kissing you there lets me know that you're alive, and I feel your heartbeat quickening."

Kayla put her hand to her neck, and she could feel her heart racing—just as he said.

"Kayla, baby, move your hands to your arms. When you wrap them around me, I feel comfort and security. I love your arms. A real man needs that, too. Wrap your arms around yourself for me and squeeze tight. That's me loving the feel of you as you fit perfectly next to me."

Kayla hugged herself, held herself tightly. And she liked the feeling. It was not something that she needed someone else to do for her. She could learn to hug herself, lift herself up sometimes.

"So do you trust me yet, Kayla?" he asked.

"Of course, I trust you, Marley," she replied.

"Then just follow my lead."

Twenty minutes later, they were both breathing heavy. Marley was the first to speak.

"Baby?"

Kayla didn't respond. She was on her bed, drawn into a tight ball. The phone wasn't at her ear, and she couldn't hear a word he was saying until she picked it up off the bed, where it had fallen from her hand.

"Hello," she breathed.

"Yeah, you all right, baby?"

"Yes, thank you. I needed that," Kayla giggled.

"Hey, you don't have to thank me. That's what I'm here for. Now you go on to sleep, and I'll talk to you in the morning."

"Okay. Goodnight." Kayla had a peaceful night's sleep.

In the morning, she was relaxed and ready to start her day. The girls were on time and anxious to get to school to talk to their friends about the weekend. It was going to be a good day.

Around lunchtime, she had to make a run to another part of the hospital. Wanda was sitting at her desk when she returned.

"Good afternoon," she said, wondering what Wanda wanted to talk about, assuming it would be about the party.

"Good afternoon, dear. How are you doing?"

"Just fine, Wanda. What's going on?"

"Well, I'm here for two reasons. One, I didn't get to talk to you yesterday, and you left the party so early I figured you and Marley must have had plans for a late night." Wanda smiled, continuing, "Two, those tricks in my office saw Nester come in this morning and have been hounding me for a hookup ever since."

"I bet they have. He is even more handsome than you said he was. That man is fine as hell. I mean, I'm very happy with Marley, don't get me wrong, but Nester is fine. I can't take anything away from him. He looks good in a suit and even better in a pair of gym shorts and a tee."

"Well, then, you should have seen him this morning in blue jeans and a brown, white, and gold Timberland shirt and wheat Timberlands. Girl, he even had my mouth watering, and I'm old enough to be that boy's momma. These young girls didn't stand a chance against that boy's looks or charms. You know they love the 'thug' look. Too bad none of them is right for him. I would love to fix him up with a good woman."

"You're always trying to fix somebody up. You should be a marriage counselor instead of a recruitment supervisor. Leave that man alone, Wanda, and mind your own business. He might not want to be hooked up."

"That's what you thought at one time, too. Now look at ya. You got Marley written all over you." She was teasing Kayla, but her happiness for her friend was real.

"Shut up, girl," Kayla responded, shyly ducking her head. Wanda was right. At one time, a man was the last thing she thought she wanted or needed. But she was wrong, very wrong.

"What did Nester want?"

Wanda looked around, and then lowered her voice. "He's thinking about moving back, or he's basically decided to, and wanted my helping finding a place and getting settled. You know, he and Marley treat Pooh and me like we're their surrogate parents. And we love it."

"Well, y'all treat them like they're your kids, so what's the difference?"

"True that. At any rate, keep an eye out for him, or he'll be moving in with Marley. I know you don't want that."

"That's Marley's brother. If he needs a place to stay, I would assume that Marley would give him one. I would do the same for my sister, if I had one, at least for a few months. Why should I mind?"

"Because that would take away from your loud sex-capades," Wanda suggested.

"Ain't nobody having loud sex-capades, Wanda."

"Yeah, right. You can lie to some of the people some of the time, but don't ever try to lie to me. It's really a waste of time. Okay?"

Kayla didn't respond. For what? They both knew what the truth was. One of them just was not willing to admit it.

"So where's lunch?" Wanda asked.

"I brought in something. How about you?"

"Your future sister-in-law demanded that I take food for the both of us. She packed a bag of food and had Nester drop it off this morning. I'm sure they had a lot of leftovers from the party. She's just probably trying to get rid of some of it."

"Hey, that'll work for me. I'm starving either way. And I didn't really want tuna on wheat." Kayla intentionally chose to ignore the sister-in-law remark. She knew that would only result in another argument between them. "Give me ten minutes, and I'll meet you in the lunchroom."

The rest of the workday raced by. Marley called just before she left for the day inviting her and the girls over for dinner. She accepted, knowing the girls wouldn't mind. She called them and told them not to start dinner.

When she got home, Kamry was at the table doing her homework, and Kaitlyn was upstairs in her bedroom.

"You girls ready to go to Marley's for dinner?" she asked cheerfully.

"I'm ready," Kamry answered. "I only got one more math problem to do. I don't know if Kaitlyn wants to go. I don't think she's feeling well."

"Oh, no. What's wrong with her?"

Kamry just hunched her shoulders, but when her mother started up the stairs, she followed.

"Kaitlyn, honey? You feeling all right?" Kayla asked as she walked into her daughter's room.

Kaitlyn didn't answer, burying her head deeper into the pillow so that her mother wouldn't see her tears. But this didn't stop her body from shaking.

"Kaitlyn? Baby, what's the problem?" Kayla quickly walked over to her daughter and turned her over.

"I just don't feel well," Kaitlyn lied. She had to say something, anything to get her mother out of the room. "I think I'm about to come on."

"Baby, you just had your period two weeks ago." Kayla knew that wasn't it. She kept better track of her daughter's menstrual cycles than she did her own. "I can't help you if you don't tell me what the problem is, Kaitlyn."

Kaitlyn turned to her mother and tried to smile. She didn't want to worry her. It was her own fault, anyway. She was so stupid. "I'm all right, Mom. I just don't feel good. You and Kamry go on to Mr. Marley's. I don't feel like going, but if I start feeling better, I'll come down."

Kayla wiped her daughter's face. "You sure, baby?" She bent down and kissed her cheek.

"Yeah, I'm just going to sleep so I'll be ready for school tomorrow."

"Okay, if you say so." Kayla kissed her again. "I love you."

"I love you, too."

One look at Kaitlyn's face told Kayla it was more than an illness bugging Kaitlyn. The girl wasn't sick at all; not in her body, at least. Heartache is what she saw. Probably has something to do with that David boy. She had been through enough heartache herself to recognize it when she saw it. She wanted to stay there and probe Kaitlyn to death, but she knew that would get her nowhere. As a teenager she herself had kept plenty of secrets from her parents. That wasn't the kind of relationship she wanted with her girls. Kayla wished Kaitlyn would talk to her, but she knew it would take time.

This was when that trust and honesty stuff they had talked about had to kick in. Against her better judgment, she decided to have to wait until Kaitlyn was ready to come to her with her problems.

"Well, Kamry, I guess it's just the two of us," Kayla said, following Kamry down the hall and out the house. As soon as they got outside, she asked, "What's going on with her? Do you know?"

Kamry shook her head. At school, she had heard that David had cussed Kaitlyn out and had broken up with her. But she wasn't there to see it. That piece of information came from Talisha, who was supposedly there. She said a lot of their schoolmates had witnessed it. David was such an asshole. He always had been. She couldn't understand why Kaitlyn didn't see it from the start, but he was popular and good-looking. In Kamry's head, that didn't make him a nice person or good enough for her sister.

And for better or for worse, like a marriage, Kaitlyn was her sister. She wasn't going to rat her out to their mother. Nor was she going to tell their mother that Kaitlyn had sex in the first place. Not that their mom didn't need to know or have a right to know, for that matter, but she wasn't telling. That would be like breaking a secret code of sisterhood. Plus, it would make it easier on Kaitlyn if she told. That way, Kaitlyn could direct her anger about the whole situation onto Kamry. She wasn't falling for that. Kaitlyn was going to have to get up her courage and talk to their mom herself.

"Hey, Mr. Marley, what's going on?" Kamry asked as soon as she walked into the house. She loved Mr. Marley's place. It looked like a straight-up bachelor's pad. The carpeting was dark red through the house, and all the furniture was cream. A lot of bodybuilding magazines were on the coffee table, and a large, flat-screen television set was in the entertainment center. And, there was also the most handsome man she had ever seen in her life standing at the kitchen counter.

God, she thought Mr. Marley was a handsome man, but whoever this guy was . . . *Wow, Kaitlyn picked the wrong night to be mad at the world.*

Kamry was unaware she was staring until he winked at her. Her mouth fell open. She was embarrassed. So embarrassed.

"Hello, sweetheart, how you doing?" Nester asked, walking over to her with his hand outstretched.

He had said something because she saw his mouth move, but for the life of her, Kamry didn't know what.

"Hello?" Nester looked from Kamry to her mother. He was wondering if she was okay. Marley hadn't mentioned that Kayla's daughter was deaf. He had said they were both very nice, lovely girls.

Kayla came to her daughter's rescue. Placing her arm around Kamry's shoulders, she smiled. "Sorry about that, Nester. This is my youngest daughter, Kamry. Kamry, don't be rude. Say hello to Marley's older brother. This is Mr. Nester."

"Just Nester will do."

"No, it won't," Kayla replied. "This is Mr. Nester."

"Hi, um, Mr. Nester," Kamry said. Red seeped into her face as her embarrassment grew. She couldn't believe that she had acted just like a little schoolgirl. She turned to go back into the living room.

"No, come on, Kamry. Stay in here with us. Don't worry about it. My brother is used to it. In fact, if I were you, I'd feel good about myself. Most time girls your age fall out from his beauty," Marley said, an amused twinkle in his eyes.

"Okay, cut it out," Nester warned. He tended to be as embarrassed by the attention to his looks as those who react as Kamry just did. At least young girls were usually too afraid to do anything other than stare. Older girls tended to follow and stare, whispering and giggling. And grown women were the worst, often a little too bold for his taste. Wanting to ease the girl's discomfort, as well as his own, he redirected the conversation. "So you're the ballplayer, huh?"

"Uh, yeah," she said, quickly snapping her out of her shame-faced silence. "Yeah, shooting guard and small forward."

"Okay, I hear you. I see we're going to have to take you to the courts," Nester responded.

"I have to warn you that I play hard. You might want to make sure that I'm on your team."

"Aaah, and she talks shit, too," Nester laughed.

"Yeah, she gets that from her mother," Marley joked. "Hey, somebody's missing. Where's Kaitlyn?"

"Oh, she wasn't feeling well. I think she has an upset stomach or something."

"Really? Well, there is plenty of food, so you can take a plate home to her if you like."

"Thanks. She'll really appreciate that. What you cooking? It smells like—

"Barbecue spare ribs, mac and cheese, deviled eggs, seafood salad, green beans," Marley answered.

"Are more people coming?" Kayla asked, surveying the spread he had laid out in the kitchen.

"No, don't worry about it. Nester eats enough for three. And I'm no slouch, as you well know, Kayla. Everything will be ready in a minute. Say, can I talk to you?"

"Sure. I'll be right back, Kamry."

"She'll be right back, Kamry," Marley echoed. "She's all right, Kayla."

Kayla followed him up the stairs to his bedroom. "What's—"

Before she got her question out, Kayla found herself in his arms, his lips on hers, his tongue parting them and entwining with hers. One hand was on the back of her neck, doing what he had done by phone the night before. The other hand was kneading her breasts. The muscles of her vagina clenched instinctively. Oh, God, if it wasn't for the fact that her daughter was downstairs, she would beg him to take her right now.

"We can't," she protested, sighing. "I gotta go back downstairs." Her breathing was labored.

He, too, was breathing hard. "Come see me tonight."

"I can't; you know that. I got her downstairs, and Kaitlyn's not feeling too well at home."

"I want you so bad," he said, grinding into her. "You feel that?"

She did feel it, and Kayla would have loved nothing better than to let Marley bend her over and lift up her skirt. But she had to think, and to do that she really had to get away from him.

"Come on, don't put me in this situation. Let's go."

"I want you, Kayla," he growled into her ear as she was about to pull away. "I want you."

"I know you do, just please be a little patient. I'll come back down tonight, but only for a minute."

"I might need more than a minute," he replied.

"No, you won't," she said, moving out of his arms and going to the door. "Get yourself together." She left him there to calm down and went back down to Nester and Kamry, who were still talking basketball. Kamry seemed to have gotten over her initial shock, and it looked as if she and Nester had become fast friends. After dinner, he even gave her his new cellphone number and urged her to call him when she wanted to go to the park and play some ball. She had told him all about her summer-league games, including where they played and when.

Back at their house, Kayla could tell that Kamry was still in awe of Nester, but in a way unrelated to his looks. He had told her stories about basketball games he had played in and the celebrities he had played with thanks to the gym he ran in California. She now saw him as some kind of a celebrity himself. But the little crush was still there. It was kind of cute, Kayla thought, going upstairs to check on Kaitlyn.

Kamry came up behind her. "Mom, I know you're going back down to Mr. Marley's house. It's okay. I'll take care of Kaitlyn if she needs anything."

Kayla turned and just stared at her daughter.

"Go ahead, Mom. She's asleep, anyway. I'll see you in the morning."

Kayla continued staring at Kamry. *The youngest daughter.* For the first time, it dawned on her that her girls were not ignorant of things beyond their cozy and safe world. They were both more mature than she had even imagined. Their loss of innocence had caught her unawares.

"You go get ready for bed, baby. I'm not going anywhere for a little while." Kayla kissed her daughter goodnight then went to her room and began to get her clothes out for work the next day. Her eyes kept going to the alarm clock next to her bed. She told Marley she would be back by eleven o'clock, and she wanted to keep her word.

Before she leaving, Kayla freshened up and put on a short skirt and tank top, not bothering with underclothes. He only lived three doors down.

Kayla noticed that Nester's car was gone. She wondered if he had already moved in with Marley. According to Wanda, that was his next move, not a move that had already been made.

She boldly walked up his front steps. The fact that it was so late at night helped to make her less afraid. Kayla rang the doorbell, and the front door opened immediately.

Marley had been waiting for her for the past two hours. As soon as Kamry and Kayla were gone, he had talked to Nester for a second and then rushed him out of the house, unsure of exactly when she would be there. He was on edge by the time she got there. He wasn't sure if she would still be able to come, what with Kaitlyn not feeling well. When the doorbell rang, he was damn near ecstatic.

"Come in, baby," he said, pulling her through the front door and right into his arms. "I've missed you."

"I missed you, too." She eagerly returned his kisses. Only Sunday, she had been in his arms, but she was ready to be there again.

CHAPTER 11

Nester was awakened by the unfamiliar ringing of his new cellphone. It was 8:45 A.M. His first impulse was to ignore it and roll over, but because this was a new phone and only a few people had the number, he reasoned it was a call he should take. Probably Wanda with news about an apartment. It had been so long since he had been home that he really didn't know what was what as far as a good place to live. The area had changed a lot over the past three years. The once good places to live were now bad places, and there were so many new developments and apartment complexes he felt like being in a maze when he drove around. Even the Acme wasn't where he had left it.

Groggily, he said, "Morning."

"Hey, Uncle Nester?" a high, very young voice responded. "I need you to come pick me up from school. I had a little altercation, and they're holding me at the principal's office."

Nester looked at the phone and wondered which one of Robert's kids was calling him. And why? Robert's daughters didn't live close enough to call him to come get them from school. So who the hell—

"Uncle Nester? It's Kamry. Mom's at work, and I need somebody to come pick me up." Kamry shut her eyes and prayed that Nester wouldn't let her down. The school secretary was standing close by, probably listening to everything she said.

"Kamry?" He quickly ran the name through his mind before remembering who she was. "Hey, baby girl, what's going on? Uh, oh, what are you up to?" Nester wasn't born yesterday. He knew "game" when he heard it. He could also hear the desperation in her voice.

"Did you hear me? I really need you to come pick me up from school."

"You just got to school, didn't you? What did you do? What happened?" Nester tried to sound stern, but failed at it miserably. He wasn't father material at all. He sounded just like an uncle, questioning her with a hint of amusement in his tone.

"I'll explain when you get here. Are you coming?" She moved a little farther away from curious ears and lowered her voice. "I got into a fight. I'm sorry, but—"

"A fight? I'm on my way," Nester interrupted. "What school?"

"The high school, duh?"

"Don't be a smartass. You need me, remember?"

"Yes, sir," Kamry laughed. It was hard for her to act like he was really an uncle who would be disciplining her. He was so funny.

Nester got out of bed, mumbling that she was lucky she was his girl, or he would have said hell no and hung the phone up. It was too early in the morning for him to be up running to the school after some unruly teenager. He wasn't used to these early-morning start-ups. His days usually didn't start until after noon.

"Damn, why didn't she call her mom?" Nester had to admit that he liked Kayla very much and that she was perfect for his brother, but he didn't honestly know how this uncle thing was going to work for him. Especially with a teenage girl. With him being away from Robert's girls, he wasn't used to being called for anything, really. When the girls were younger, he would send them a gift with a tag on it reading 'Love, Uncle Nester'. And that seemed to be good enough.

The school looked just as it did when he was a student there. Nothing seemed to have changed too much around town except for the people and the new buildings that were attached to the outside. Yep, everything was exactly the same; even the principal's office was in the same location. He had spent a lot of time in there himself.

As he entered the office, a woman—a teacher he presumed—was leaving. He held the door open for her, but she was so busy staring at him that she missed her exit mark and walked into the glass window.

He reached out to assist her. "You all right?" Out of respect, he held in his laughter, unlike Kamry. He cut her a look that silenced her.

"Yes, I'm fine," the woman answered, deeply embarrassed. "Excuse me." She never looked him in the face again; she just scurried out the office holding her nose.

Poor woman, he thought. She was attractive, too. Could have been a prospect if she hadn't concentrated so much on his appearance.

"Hey, Uncle Nester," Kamry called to him. Now she saw firsthand what Marley was talking about. The entire office staff seemed to have stopped working to stare at him. Kamry laughed to herself. She had never met anyone around whom the world actually revolved. But at the same time, he was so modest about it all that he seemed to take little or no notice. That must have come from years of working at being unaffected by other people's reactions. Kamry couldn't imagine him not knowing that he had this kind of effect on people. Kaitlyn would love to have the power that Nester possessed.

"Girl, what did you do?" Nester asked as soon as he got to her. He could see the guilt written all over her face, but at the same time she was ready to defend herself to the death. Whatever went down, she felt she was justified in doing it. Okay, Nester had to think. This was all new to him. First of all, he was here for her and on her side. Although he wasn't her legal guardian in this instant, he was all she had.

He remembered how he felt when his father had come to the school for him and had defended him furiously. Most of Nester's fights were due to jealousy on the part of others. His father understood that. Unfortunately, when their father came to school, it was usually to pick up at least two of them, because they usually fought together.

Nester didn't even wait for her to answer. Instead, he turned to the counter and waited for someone to approach. That didn't take long. When three women came forward, he hesitated, waiting to see which two would step back and let the third handle his situation. No one moved. It was obvious that they would not try to listen to a word he had to say if it wasn't *let's screw*.

"Um, excuse me, miss." He intentionally ignored the girls at the counter, even though they were all young, perky, and beautiful in their own way. He wasn't here for that. "Excuse me, miss," he repeated, and then the elderly lady sitting at the desk furthest to the back of the room looked up. "Can you help me, please?"

"Sure, son, what can I do for you?" She passed by the other office workers and smiled at the handsome man standing in front of her. Instantly, she liked Nester. He wasn't as shallow as she had first suspected when he walked into the office. Most of the fathers that came into the office fell for the charms of the flirtatious women she had the misfortune of having to working with.

Miss Sheri had told her granddaughter on several occasions that she needed to replace the girls in the main office. They caused too much drama and commotion to be effective office workers. And they didn't take too much pride in their work. She had worked in an office for over forty years, and that is why it was so hard for her to let it go when retirement age befell her. But God bless her grandbaby for offering her a couple of hours a day to come in and help in the school's office. She would have gone crazy sitting at home all day long doing nothing.

"Thank you, ma'am," Nester said. The other women walked away with a lot of attitude, murmuring under their breath that he wasn't all that, but continuing to give him their attention anyway.

"Call me, Sheri, son."

"Miss Sheri, I'm here to pick up my niece." He motioned to Kamry. Damn, he didn't even know the girl's last name. He had only been formally introduced to Kayla once and couldn't remember her last name.

Kamry came forward. "Hi, Miss Sheri."

"Kamry, what's going on? I didn't even know you were in here. Chil', what happened?"

"I, um, got into a fight." Kamry kept her eyes down.

"Got into a fight? That doesn't seem like you. Who did you fight?"

"David Thomas."

Nester's head turned so fast to look at her he got dizzy. "A boy?"

"What were you doing fighting David?" Miss Sheri asked. She had never particularly liked the boy. Popularity made some kids mean; besides, he was a spoiled jock from a very well-off family.

"He hurt my sister. That's all I'm going to say." Kamry stood her ground. That's all she could say without telling them that her sister had given that dumbass boy her virginity.

Miss Sheri could see that Kamry was becoming upset. "Kamry, dear, why don't you just have a seat? I'll get your uncle in to Dr. English so you can be on your way. Okay, baby?"

Kamry did as she was told. Nester sat beside her to wait until they called him into the office.

"So you were taking up for big sis, huh?" he asked, trying to break the ice and get her out of the bad mood.

"Yeah."

"Where's the boy? Did he hit you first?"

"No, I hit him first and last." She smiled to herself. "He's in the nurse's office."

"You know you're scaring me, right?" He patted her on her knee. "It's all good. But why did you call me? Your mother isn't going to be mad at you taking up for your sister. She seemed pretty reasonable to me. All you have to do is explain things to her."

"I don't know. I tried to call her first, but I was glad that she didn't answer the phone. I can't tell Mom why I had to kick his a—I mean, butt." Kamry put her head down.

"And you're not going to tell me either, right?"

"Right. It's kind of personal."

"Sir, she'll see you now," Ms. Sheri said, opening the swinging halfdoor that led from the front of the counter to the back.

Nester followed her through the door that read 'Principal' on the front, wondering how he had gotten into this situation. Then he stopped in his tracks.

She stood in front of him in a soft green pantsuit that hugged her curves perfectly. She still wore her hair straight except the part was on the side instead of down the middle. She might have grown a few inches, but she was still only five feet, five inches with the help of the two-inch heels. And she was beautiful. Her skin still glowed like burnt almonds, and that little black mole over the right side of her mouth was sexier than ever.

"Well, if it isn't Nester Jarnette, as I live and breathe," she said. "I never thought I would see you again."

"Cyndi? Cyndi English?"

"That's right. How have you been?" She moved from around the desk and walked toward him.

"I've been good, real good. How are you?" he asked, moving toward her.

When they reached each other, it became a little awkward. She extended her hand; he put his arms out to hug her. They reversed positions. Then laughed. Finally, Nester took it upon himself to wrap his arms around her. He pulled her close and squeezed tight.

Cyndi had secretly had a crush on Nester all through high school, but she never told him. Why? Because that wouldn't have made her any different from any of the other girls in high school. So in order to be different, Cyndi decided that being one of his best friends would be better. But she was wrong.

Instead of being the object of his affection, she got to hear about all the objects of his affection or how the other girls who wanted to be objects offered themselves to him on a regular basis. Talk about killing yourself slowly. It was absolute torture. The day he left town Cyndi believed that she was just as relieved as he was. At least now, she could give her heart a break and focus on other things—like her career.

Nester held on to her a little longer than he intended. It was good to see her again, and she just felt good in his arms. He wasn't sure if it was because she was a familiar face or because she was beautiful and he was attracted to her.

"So when did you get back into town?" Cyndi asked, stepping back cautiously, afraid her equilibrium hadn't quite stabilized. Her heartbeat had accelerated too fast.

He was everything she remembered and more. If felt so good to be in his arms, even if it was just a friendly, glad-to-see-you-again hug. As a grown man, Nester was damn near perfect.

"I'm here for good. I've been tossing the idea around for a while. I'm contemplating opening a business over here, hoping that it is just as successful, if not more so, than the gym I have on the West Coast. I'll just have to do more traveling, but I'd rather be close to my family."

"And which of your brothers does Kamry belong to? I didn't know that either of them had kids her age."

"Actually, she will be Marley's stepdaughter soon." He decided that it might not be a white lie by the way things were looking. "She couldn't get in contact with her mother, so here I am. That's not a problem, is it?" He watched her closely as she walked back to her desk. The skirt fit snug enough around her hips for him to see her ass cheeks shake back and forth with every step.

Nester felt a response go through him that he hadn't experienced in a long while, and it surprised him. The fact that it was Cyndi didn't surprise him, either. He had always been attracted to her, but from the first time they met, she had made it absolutely clear to him that she wasn't interested in being anything but his friend. And they eventually became the best of friends. Even though he would have loved to have made their relationship more, Nester always respected her enough not to try to go there with her.

It had been a long time since his curiosity was piqued by a woman. He wasn't trying to brag, but there was so much being thrown at him that most of the time he ignored it. Back in the day, he was trying to catch everything he could; luckily, with age came wisdom.

"Well, usually, I wouldn't release a student to anyone not on her contact form; however, because I know you, I'll make an exception. You know, your, um, niece hurt that boy pretty bad—not physically so much as emotionally. It's going to take some time for him to work off the embarrassment of being beat up by a girl."

"Well, according to her, he had it coming."

"So she says, but I can't really make a decision until I find out the whole story. All I know, thus far, is that it had something to do with her sister, who, by the way, was David's girlfriend until yesterday."

"Well, then, there you have it." Nester simplified the matter for her. "She was defending her sister's honor, if you will. I guess I would have done the same thing if I had a sister. I can remember taking up for you once or twice."

Cyndi crossed her arms. Damn, the man was fine; standing in the middle of the room as if this was his office instead of hers. His legs were spread apart, one hand in the side pocket of his track pants. His clothes always fit him well.

"Somehow I knew you would get around to bringing that up. Look, nobody asked you to beat up Vaughn Davis for me. That was a long time ago, anyway. And it's not the same thing."

"It is the same thing. Even though I wanted so much more from you, you wanted to be my friend, my sister, if you will, and I had to protect you when Vaughn got a little too friendly with you."

"You wanted so much more?" Was she hearing him correctly? Cyndi's arms fell to her side. She was dumbfounded.

"Of course I did. You were my best friend, one of the only people I could talk to about things that—"

" 'Things' being other girls. I never wanted to hear about all of the girls running after you." Her voice rose a little with her admission. Cyndi stopped trying to hide her feelings a long time ago; right after he left, to be exact. Hiding her feelings in school had prevented her from getting the thing she wanted the most.

Now Nester was the one looking dumbfounded. "But you were always willing to listen. I don't—"

"Understand? Nester, I only listened because at least I was able to be close to you. And you beat up Vaughn Davis because you didn't want me to get close to him."

Her statement hit him smack-dab in the face, but it was hard to deny the truth. "True that, but I still think I deserve dinner or something for my gallantry."

She stood back and looked him up and down. Maybe he did deserve something, but dinner wasn't what she wanted to give to him.

"That is, if your significant other wouldn't mind," he said.

"Sorry to disappoint you, but there is no significant other. Just me and my daughter, Abby."

"I'm not disappointed at all, and I still want my dinner. How old is Abby?"

"Ten, going on twenty-five."

"Perfect. I can get my niece to babysit. I think she owes me one."

"Is that what you do for a living, Nester? Go around making people repay their debts?"

"Only if it gets me what I want. So Friday night?" He waited for her response, and for once, it felt good not knowing if the woman he was talking to was going to say yes. Cyndi wasn't trying to please him; she never had.

"Let me think about it. Besides, this doesn't have anything to do with Miss Kamry beating up David." She decided to switch back to her professional self before she became too sidetracked by Nester. "I gave Kamry a disciplinary notice to give to her mother for signature, but one will also be mailed to the home. You wouldn't believe how many students we have who try to forge—yeah, you would." She laughed, remembering some of the hijinks they had pulled off. "Just make sure her mother signs the paper. She's going to be suspended for three days; that's the standard."

"No problem. Thanks for everything. And it was really good seeing you again, Cyndi. Oh, my number." He walked to the desk and grabbed a pen and paper. "So you can call me when you're ready to take me to dinner."

"You're too much, Nester," she smiled.

"Not for you, Cyndi. You always knew how to handle me. I'll be waiting for your call, baby." Nester opened up the office door and walked out.

Cyndi let out a long breath. Nester was dangerous. She wondered if she should give him a call. What harm could it do? They were old friends, but that was childhood. Now the stakes were much higher. They weren't kids anymore, and grown-up games didn't consist of baseball mitts and jump ropes. Well, unless you were into that sort of thing.

"Girl, you owe me big time," Nester said to Kamry as they left the school building. "I could get into big trouble for this, you know. I'm not your guardian. Why didn't you try your mother again?"

"I'm sorry. I wasn't thinking, all right? I'll pay you back, I swear." Kamry thought Nester was really mad at her until his next words.

"I know you will. You're going to babysit for me Friday night."

"Friday night?"

"Yeah, I'm taking Miss Cyndi out Friday night. We need a babysitter."

Kamry's footsteps slowed. "Oh, you slickster. You done went in there and made a date with my principal. How could you? This is so embarrassing. She's about forty years old."

"I'm about forty years old, too, give or take a few years. We're the same age. We went to school together."

"You and Dr. English? That is so nasty."

"Shut up. I would think that you have enough problems on your hands."

"Yeah, I guess that I can babysit for you. When my mom finds out about this, I'm going to be grounded for a few months, at least."

"Well, if I were you, I'd call her as soon as I got home so that she won't be madder when she gets to you."

"That makes sense, I guess." Kamry knew that she was in for it. Kayla never did play when it came to discipline. But she had done the right thing, and she would do it again, especially for Kaitlyn.

As soon as Nester dropped her off, she went into the house and called her mother.

"Mom?"

"Kamry? What's going on? Why are you calling me from home?" Kayla asked, worry instantly evident in her voice.

"I-I got suspended from school today for fighting. I tried to call you earlier, but your voicemail came on."

"Fighting? Kamry, what have I told you about that?" Certain she was being watched, not by her supervisor but by her nosy little co-workers, Kayla was always careful not to raise her voice on the job. "Just stay in the house. I'll deal with you when I get home. Where's Kaitlyn?"

"She's still in school." Kamry's voice wavered, but she didn't cry. Her mother was disappointed in her, but she didn't know the whole story. This was one that she was just going to have to take for her sister.

Instead of sitting around, Kamry decided that she would at least wash the bowls they left in the sink after breakfast and make dinner. Maybe that would help her in the long run when she pleaded her case.

"Kamry! Kamry!" Kaitlyn called as soon as she and Talisha burst through the door.

"I'm in the kitchen," Kamry replied. She was shocked when Kaitlyn ran around the kitchen counter and threw her arms around her.

"What's that for?"

"Thank you," Kaitlyn replied.

"Yeah, Kamry. We heard what you did today," Talisha added admiringly. "That was cool. David is walking around school with a black eye and swollen balls. Now he's the one getting laughed at."

"Good. He deserves it. I told you he wasn't any good, Kaitlyn. Next time, listen to me, will you?"

"I promise. Next time, I will definitely listen. Does Mom know yet? And who was the fine man who picked you up? Everybody was talking about him."

"Yeah, that's what I want to know," Talisha chimed in.

"That was Mr. Nester. He's Mr. Marley's brother. You would have met him last night if you had come to dinner. He looks even better than Mr. Marley does. Mr. Nester had so many women looking at him it was ridiculous. Mrs. Ryan was so busy staring at him, she even ran into the glass door in the office."

"Better looking than Mr. Marley? That's hard to believe." Talisha still had a little crush on him.

"I'm telling you the truth," Kamry said, putting her hand up. "I can't wait for y'all to see him."

"And he just came and picked you up from school?" Talisha was clearly trying to read more into the situation than was necessary.

"Yeah, I called him and he came and got me. That's all, Talisha."

"Well, I wish I could stay, but I know your momma is going to be in some kind of a foul mood when she gets in. I don't want to make matters worse for y'all. But call me later."

Talisha left, and the girls waited for their mother to come home.

When the doorbell rang, they both jumped. They had been silently, intensely pondering the trouble they were in. Kamry had been thinking about the punishment she was about to get. Her mom would probably not let her play basketball this year, and basketball season was right around the corner. Kaitlyn was thinking of how she had ruined any opportunity she had to ever go out again. She could kiss what little popularity she had goodbye.

"Go get the door, Kaitlyn," Kamry said.

"You go get it," Kaitlyn replied. "It's not her. She has a key, duh?" Kaitlyn finally dragged herself to the front door, but only after glancing at the clock to see if it was close to the time their mother usually got home.

"Hey, Kaitlyn."

"Hi, Mr. Marley. And you must be Mr. Nester. How are you?" she said, extending her hand to Nester, who accepted it. *Wow, he is as good looking as they said.*

"Uh, fine, thanks," Nester replied.

"My mom's not home yet, Mr. Marley."

"I know. I just wanted to stop by to see if Kamry was all right. Nester was just telling me that she got into a fight with some boy at school. What's that about?"

"Kamry, Mr. Marley and his brother are here to see you."

Kamry came to the front door. "Hey, I'm all right, Mr. Marley."

"Come on out here on the porch, Kamry. I want to see for myself. Nester told me that you actually won the fight, but I really don't think there is any reason for a boy to put his hands on a girl. Did he hit you first?"

"No, I hit him first—in his stomach. Then he swung and I ducked, so I hit him in the eye real good. Then he pushed me down on the ground and was about to jump on me, because everybody was laughing at him, but I kicked him between his legs before he could. He fell to the ground. And that was it."

"Good girl," Marley laughed. "Well, we're going to go to the house. Your mom should be coming home soon. I don't want her to think that I'm trying to overstep my bounds or anything. We thought we were going to have to go rough this boy up." They all laughed. "No, I just wanted to make sure you were okay. Tell your mom to call me later."

"We will. Thanks, Mr. Marley. Bye, *Uncle* Nester," Kamry laughed.

"Kamry, Mr. Nester is fine," Kaitlyn said as soon as they got back into the house. "I wish I was older. There aren't any boys in our school that look that good."

Kamry turned and gave her sister a you-can't-be-serious look. "Aren't we in enough trouble already because of you and a good-looking boy at school?"

They both fell silent when they heard a car pulling into the driveway. Damn, they both thought, it's time to face the music.

Kayla was not in a good mood. It was bad enough that she was working at a job that didn't seem to appreciate her ideas or input, but she couldn't even count on her daughters to act like they had common sense at school. She hoped for Kamry's sake that the girl had a good reason for getting into a fight. The boy had better be the one who had thrown the first punch. That was the only time, she had stressed to her girls, it was all right to fight—because you had to protect yourself.

As soon as she walked into the house, she smelled the corn cooking on the stove. The smoky aroma of barbecued ribs filled the air. Her living room was spotless, and the dining-room floor was gleaming. For a second, she wanted to go easy on her daughter, but the fact was that Kamry was endangering her school record. That was something more serious than a clean house.

"Kamry," she yelled, heading for the stairs, "let's go." She didn't stop when she heard Kaitlyn say something to her. She continued walking, fully expecting to hear her daughter's footsteps right behind hers.

Downstairs, Kaitlyn held on to her sister's arm. "Kamry, I'm so sorry," she said, meaning what she said, but just not knowing how to make things right.

"Don't worry about it," Kamry said. "It's all right. I'm just going to go up there and tell her what happened."

"But—"

"I'm not going to tell her about that. I'll just tell her about the fight. That's all."

"Kamry—"

Kamry trudged up the stairs slowly. She knew that her mother didn't play when it came to discipline. Even at sixteen, she was scared to death of her mother. It had been a long time since she had actually gotten a beating, but she did remember how they felt. She was more afraid of disappointing her mother than anything. Kamry didn't know what awaited her upstairs.

"Mom? You call me?" Kamry asked softly as she entered her mother's bedroom.

"You know I did," Kayla said simply. She was sitting on the side of her bed holding a black leather belt resting across her lap.

Kamry averted her eyes from the strap. She swallowed hard, but straightened her back and looked directly at her mother.

Kayla saw the change in her. It was as if Kamry had made up her mind to accept a beating before she was even given one. Usually, the girls were so afraid of the strap they would come into the room ready to confess everything.

"Well, what do you have to say for yourself, Kamry?" Kayla asked.

"Nothing."

"Nothing?" Kayla looked her up and down. She had come so far with the girls. She had loosened a lot of the strings she had wound so tightly around them. Her life and that of the girls had seemed to change in the last few weeks, but now she was beginning to doubt her decision.

"No. Maybe I shouldn't have hit him, but I did."

"But why, Kamry? Do you realize how much trouble you could be in? What if his parents decide to press charges against you?"

Kamry doubted that would happen because David wasn't going to tell them that a girl had beaten him up. He would rather lie in the nurse's office for the rest of the school day. At any rate, she didn't have answers for her mother's questions. And she could tell that Kayla was getting madder by the minute.

"Well?"

Kamry could do little more than stand there. But she made the mistake of not displaying even a trace of remorse, and to Kayla that was inconceivable for one of her girls. Never had either of them stood in front of her and not been at least sorry for her actions, especially when caught red-handed.

A call from the principal's office was just about as wrong as you could get.

"Well?" Kayla decided to give her the benefit of the doubt. Maybe she didn't hear the first question.

Kamry remained completely silent.

Okay, Kayla resolved, if this was how it was going to be, then so be it. In her heart, she didn't really want to be so harsh with Kamry. They had come so close as a family in the past week, but the girl was leaving her no choice.

Kayla stood up from the bed with the black leather belt in her hand. She was waiting for Kamry to break down, but she didn't. Pointing to the bed, she waited until Kamry had assumed the position.

A long time ago, she had grown tired of chasing them around the room as if they were wild turkey. She started making them lie across the bed so, when she needed to keep them in place when they were younger, all she had to do was put a knee on one of their legs. And they were still getting a lot better treatment than she had when she was a child. Her mother would beat her with whatever was available at the time, belt, rope, switch, shoe, dishes, the broom. And if nothing was around, her foot did the job just as nicely.

Kamry lay on the bed and braced herself for the first blow. She knew it was going to hurt. Her mom was heavy-handed. For a split second, she had considered saying something to lighten her punishment, but short of telling on her sister, she really didn't have an excuse.

The first hit was quick and painful. Although Kamry knew it was coming, she still wasn't prepared for the tingling sting of the leather. Her eyes began to water.

"Do you have anything to say now?" Kayla asked.

Kamry kept her mouth closed and gritted her teeth, bracing for the second blow. She heard her mother rambling on about knowing right from wrong and thinking before acting, but she tried to shut it out of her head. It was bad enough that she had to endure the torture that was closely related to abuse in her mind; she shouldn't have to listen to a lecture, too.

She was determined not to cry, but it was getting harder as the silence lengthened. Wondering what was taking her mother so long, Kamry turned her head in her mother's direction. To her surprise, Kayla was standing behind her in tears.

"Mom?"

"Kamry, get up. I don't want to do this. You're too old for me to be giving you beatings."

Immediately, Kamry got off the bed and went to her mother. She hugged her. "I'm sorry, Mom. I'm sorry I disappointed you. I wouldn't have gotten in a fight if it weren't for a good reason."

Kaitlyn waited in the hallway outside to the closed door. She cringed when she heard the crack of the belt hit what she imagined was her sister's backside. Her hand was on the doorknob, and the guilt she felt for her sister's punishment doubled.

Tears slowly ran down her left cheek as she listened to her mother's stern words. Then there was silence.

"Stop! Stop! Please, stop, Mom. It's all my fault." Kaitlyn rushed into the room hysterically before she cowed and stopped herself.

Kayla had already thrown the belt down and was hugging Kamry when she felt Kaitlyn's weight against her leg. She looked down and saw her lying in a heap at her feet, in tears.

"Kaitlyn, girl, get the hell up. What's the matter with you?"

"Don't beat her any more, Mom. It's not her fault." Kaitlyn's words were hard to make out as she held her head down in shame. "Please."

Now, Kayla was pissed *and* confused. "What the hell?" This had never happened before. Never had one of her girls tried to save the other from getting her ass busted, and she never expected one to, especially Kaitlyn. She was too focused on herself. But this was something different. "Okay, what's going on?"

Kamry lifted her head to see what the commotion was about, but she didn't move from her position. Kaitlyn must have lost her mind.

"It's my fault," Kaitlyn blurted out again. "Kamry was fighting because of me."

"What?" Kayla put the belt down. "Look, everybody downstairs in the living room right now. And y'all better have your shit together by the time we get down there."

Kayla stood in the middle of the living room floor. Kaitlyn was sitting on the sofa, and Kamry sat across from her on the love seat. She walked back and forth between the two pieces of furniture. It was times like the present that she wished she smoked like those women in old movies so that even when she was going crazy on the inside, she could at least look sophisticated and together on the outside.

Kayla stopped in front of Kaitlyn and said, "Speak."

Kaitlyn took a deep breath and was about to say something when the doorbell rang.

Kayla raised her index finger to silence her daughter.

"Hello, Kayla," Marley said when she opened the door.

"Now is not a good time, Marley," Kayla replied, not opening the door too wide. She began to close it when he stopped her.

"Hey, is everything okay? Nester told me about today. You all right?" By the look on her face, he knew she wasn't. And he hoped that she would confide in him. Before she could answer, he added, "Look, if you need to talk later, I'll be home."

"Thanks," she replied, and without another word, she shut the door.

"Well?" she demanded, turning back to the girls but focusing on Kaitlyn. "What do you have to say for yourself?"

Kaitlyn hesitated. She had been ready to put it all out there, but she'd had a few minutes to think about it, and she wished now that she had kept her big mouth shut. She just felt so guilty, and she honestly didn't want Kamry to be punished for taking up for her.

"Um, I was just saying that Kamry was taking up for me. That's why she got suspended." She swallowed hard; the sound of her pounding heart flooded her ears.

"What do you have to do with this? Why was Kamry fighting a boy for you?"

"He was talking about her," Kamry chimed in. She was trying to protect her sister, stop her from saying too much.

"Oh yeah?" Kayla found that hard to believe. Kaitlyn was popular and beautiful; she prided herself on that.

Kaitlyn could tell Kamry's excuse wasn't working. It was time for her to come clean or they would both have to pay a heavy price in the end. "Mom, David was talking about me at school, and Kamry overheard him. He broke up with me the other day, and Kamry heard him joking about it with his friend."

"What was he saying?" she asked Kamry.

Kamry didn't know what to say. She didn't want to tell the truth, but she couldn't think of a lie. "He, um . . . he said—"

"He said," Kaitlyn interrupted, "that I was easy. And that we had sex in the back of his grandfather's car at the dance last weekend."

Kayla's whole facial expression changed, and Kaitlyn knew that she had made a mistake by telling it the way she had.

"What is that boy's number? I'm calling over there right now." Kayla quickly moved to the phone, but Kaitlyn stopped her from picking it up.

"Mom, don't, please."

"You think I'm just going to sit around and let some little piss-ant talk about you like that? Come on, we're going over to his house." She grabbed her car keys and was heading for the door. Kayla's anger upstairs was nothing compared to how she was feeling at that moment. She wanted to get her hands around that little motherfucker's throat and squeeze the life out of him. Talking about her baby like that.

"It's true, Mom," Kaitlyn said softly.

Kayla stumbled. She knew she hadn't heard what she just thought she had heard. *Her baby had sex.* Kaitlyn wasn't a virgin anymore.

When Kayla turned back to the girls, Kamry was sitting next to Kaitlyn, and they were holding hands. She was still mad, but tears were running down her cheeks. Kaitlyn was damn near hysterical, and Kamry was trying to console her.

"What do you mean, Kaitlyn, that it's true?" Kayla asked, dropping her keys and kneeling before her daughters. She ran her hands over Kaitlyn's hair and face.

Kaitlyn kept her head down as streams of tears flooded her face. She didn't want to face her mother. Didn't want to see the disappointment in her mother's eyes. She resisted when her mother tried to lift her head to face her.

"Kaitlyn? Baby?"

"I'm so sorry, Mommy," Kaitlyn whimpered between sobs. "I'm so stupid. I really thought that he liked me. We had been dating for a few months, but only during school and he said that if I didn't, we had to break up because there were a lot of other girls who wanted to go out with him and who would. And—"

"And you believed that? Oh, Kaitlyn, baby. I thought I had taught you better than that."

"You did, Mom. You did. I was just stupid. I thought that I needed to do this to stay popular. But when we got to school Monday, he broke up with me. That's why I was in a bad mood all week. I didn't understand why he would do that after we—but I couldn't do anything about it because he's David, Mr. Popular."

"Why didn't you tell me?"

"Tell you what? That I had sex with a guy that I wasn't even supposed to be dating in the back of a car that I wasn't supposed to be in?"

Kayla left the question hanging and turned to Kamry. "And what do you have to do with all of this?"

"I was walking behind Kaitlyn and Talisha this morning, and when we walked into the school, David and his friends were standing around talking. As soon as his friends saw Kaitlyn, they tapped David on the shoulder and started laughing. Then I heard David say something like he had laid Kaitlyn easier than a chicken laid an egg. So I went up to him and told him that he was a dog with a little wiener. He told me to get lost before he laid me next. When he walked towards me, I hit him in the stomach. Then he tried to hit me, but I ducked and punched him in the eye. He pushed me down, and I kicked him in the privates before he could jump on me."

Kaitlyn held her sister's hand a little tighter.

"And that's why you got suspended?"

"Yes."

Kayla sat on the love seat. She was quiet for a minute, struggling to digest everything that had been just revealed to her.

"Mom, please don't be mad at me," Kaitlyn begged, crying harder. "This is all my fault."

Kayla didn't reply right away, but she knew that she had to say something. First and foremost, she had to make sure that Kaitlyn was okay. A girl's first sexual experience was supposed to be a momentous event in her life. Her own had been a disaster, but she had hoped that her girls' first time would mean something. So although it wasn't what she wanted for Kaitlyn, at least it was what Kaitlyn wanted at the time. And although peer pressure played a huge part, she hadn't been forced or raped. It was her decision.

"Kaitlyn, I'm not going to lecture you about this," Kayla said plainly, her voice so calm that she surprised the girls and herself. They looked at her, confused. "I wish that you hadn't decided to lie down with that boy, but you made the decision. We can't change it, and we have to move on from here. The exact reason why you were so upset all week is the same reason I had hoped you two would wait to experience sex. You're not ready for it, and you are most certainly not mature enough to handle the consequences."

Kayla got up and went to the kitchen. She checked on the meat and returned carrying a glass of water. The girls were still sitting in the exact same spot.

"Did you at least use protection?"

"Yes, we used a condom."

"Well, be that as it may, I'm still going to make an appointment for you with the doctor so that you can get checked out."

"But I don't want to go to the doctor." Kaitlyn hated the thought of spreading her legs on a table and have some stranger look all up and between her legs. It was embarrassing.

"Oh, you're going to the doctor. See, this is one of those things that you're now going to have to be mature enough to handle. It's a whole 'nother ball game now, sweetie. And I'm not trying to be smart or hard, but that is why I always tell you to think before you act. There are a lot of things that come with having sex besides letting that little boy between your legs thinking he's doing something. And women have to take much more care of themselves than men do, so welcome to the big league. We're going to do this right from here on out. And I will be waiting for your period to come next week, and it had better come."

Kayla got up from the couch. She had said her say, and that was it. She paused on her way to the kitchen. "Kamry, I apologize for beating you earlier. If it had been me, I would have done the same thing—defend my sister. But you still need to think before you act, too. Because your sister wanted to play grown-up, you got your ass whopped. Kaitlyn, I think you need to start paying her back. A thank you and an apology would be nice."

Dinner seemed to last for hours. They ate silently, only the sound of their utensils hitting the plates a sign that anyone was conscious. Every so often, Kamry would see her sister wipe at the persistent tears streaming down her face. She wasn't mad at Kaitlyn. At this point, she actually felt sorry for her and what she was going through.

No child liked to think she has failed a parent. And the silence was making Kaitlyn feel as if she was alone in the room, in the house, in the world. She mentally berated herself for being so gullible and weak. Why did she think that having sex with David would mean anything to him? She was so stupid.

After washing the dishes in silence, they headed up to bed early. Their conversation seemed to have taken the energy out of them all.

CHAPTER 12

Kayla lay in bed and wondered where she had gone wrong. The questions swirling around in her head ranged from reasons to accusations to excuses. Maybe she was too hard on the girls for too long. Maybe that was why Kaitlyn felt a need to have sex so soon, the first time she let her out of the house. She had talked to her girls until she was blue in the face about boys and men. And even though she was strict, she made sure to show them that they were loved. She made sure that they had more than enough confidence so that their self-esteem didn't get low, even when she doubted her own.

What more could she have done? Kayla let one tear fall. A good mother would know the answers, all the answers, but this was one question she couldn't figure out.

If their father had stayed in their lives, this probably would never have happened. Girls needed their father. Unfortunately, she had made the mistake of picking the worst one out of the bunch to be their father. That was her burden to bear, but a no-good man was a no-good man was a no-good man. She couldn't change that.

After lying in bed for a while, Kayla came to terms with what had happened. She couldn't dwell in the past. It was time to move on. Time to make sure that this mistake or misjudgment didn't happen again. Regardless of how well Kaitlyn said she was doing, Kayla had to make sure. First thing in the morning, she was going to make a doctor's appointment and have her checked out. Then they would have to go back to the way things used to be. Obviously, neither she nor the girls were ready for a more relaxed lifestyle.

She had been enjoying herself so much with Marley for the past two weeks that her parenting skills had begun to suffer, and she couldn't risk that. As good as Marley made her feel and as much as she loved having his strong hands all over her body, she couldn't take the chance of losing herself in him. No matter that she could almost feel herself falling in love with him. It was time for her to take a step back from the fairytale and come back to the reality of her single-mother status. She couldn't have them both. He was a distraction that caused her to lose sight of what was going on in her daughters' lives.

She should have known that Kaitlyn was no longer a virgin. Why hadn't she seen that? She knew her girls almost as well as she knew herself, had prided herself on that fact. But because she couldn't stay focused on the important things, she had to let that part of her life go. It was her own fault. And she was going to miss him—spending time together, talking, and riding on the back of his bike. It was as if she had waited all this time for him only to have him for just a little while.

If you need me, I'll be home, he had said. The temptation to call him was strong, but she knew that if she went down to his house, she would end up in his arms. That would only make it harder for her to tell him that whatever they had was over.

Her ringing cellphone brought Kayla out of her reverie. She knew who it was by the playing of Carl Thomas' "I Wish I Never Met Her", and she didn't want to answer the call.

"Hello?" she said, attitude already in place in her voice.

"Hey, girlfriend," Quincy answered.

Kayla hated when he called her that. She wasn't his damn girlfriend. Not his girlfriend, his lover, or his wife. Not anymore.

"What do you want, Quincy?" Kayla asked, not even making a stab at being polite. *Unbelievable.* This would be the day that he would call of all days. They hadn't heard from him in months. Now, on the worst day of her life, when all hell had broken loose, he was calling.

"Damn, baby, what, you having a bad day? I was just calling to check up on my daughters. Can't a father be concerned?"

"Of course, a father can, but a father, a real father, wouldn't call to check on his daughters *every three months,*" she said bitingly.

"Oh, here we go. Look, Kayla, I've been busy."

"Yeah, I wonder what her name is." She regretted saying it as soon as it came out of her mouth.

"You're jealous?"

"Oh, please. Look, I don't have to be on this phone with you right now. The girls are in bed, but I'll let them know you called." She hung the phone up without waiting for his comeback. There was no way she was going to deal with listening to Quincy's bullshit.

As soon as she hung up, the phone rang. Kayla didn't answer it.

Two minutes later, it rang again. By now, Kayla was so upset she didn't notice that the ringtone was different. This time it was Ashanti's "Baby".

"I don't want to talk to you right now, Quincy," she answered, attitude still in place.

"Kayla? You all right?" Marley's voice was full of concern.

"Oh, hi, Marley," she replied quietly. "I'm sorry. Yeah, I'm all right. I just got a lot on my mind."

"Do you want to talk about it?" he asked.

Kayla put the phone to her head. Why did he have to be so nice to her right now? She didn't want him to be nice to her, not when she was going to have to tell him that it was over.

"I can come down, and we can sit outside and talk. I'm a good listener."

"Marley, look," she said softly, trying not to let the pain in her heart convey itself through her voice, "I, um, I can't do this anymore."

He fell silent, but Kayla could hear him breathing on the other end. "Kayla," he finally began, "what brought this on? Is it something I did? I mean—"

"No, Marley, no. It's not you. Believe me, I have enjoyed spending tine with you so much. I mean that, even though I tried to fight it off in the beginning. I-I'm just glad you came into my life. But I think that maybe

I've been enjoying myself a little too much. I mean, I think that I need to get my focus back on the girls. I kinda let myself enjoy—"

"Kayla, you have to enjoy yourself. That's what life is all about. You deserve to enjoy life. And as far as the girls are concerned, they're really good girls. I don't—is this because of the fight that Kamry got into at school today? Is that why you're doing this? Kayla, you can't stop little things like that from happening. Girls are going to get into scuffles, and from what I hear, Kamry handled it very well."

"It's not just that, Marley. There's more to it than that."

"Then talk to me. Make me understand it." Marley was not getting off the phone without an explanation. They had been getting along so well. He just knew that this was going to be the beginning of something great. And here she was trying to break it off as if it were nothing but a booty call.

"Marley, please. Look, I just need to be here for the girls. I need to focus on them."

"So you're going to just kick me to the curb? I thought that you cared for me, for what we were starting here."

"You know I do, but I have to protect my girls."

"Protect them from what? We can protect them together. You know I love your girls. We get along great, so I know that's not the reason you're pushing me away here, Kayla. What is it? Is it the Quincy guy, whoever that is?" Marley hated that he had brought up this guy's name as soon as he had done it. When she answered the phone the way she did, he had swallowed his pride and not questioned her, but now he had no other choice. Marley had to know what was going on.

"Quincy? Marley, please don't go there." It was just like a man to throw another man's name into the fray. "That was the girls' father. He had called just before you did and we got into a small argument." If it had been any other man, she wouldn't have explained, but she owed Marley at least that much. "Marley, look, I know I'm not doing a good job of explaining things to you, but I just realized that I lost my focus on my priorities. I need to get back on track."

"You're not making much sense to me. We were having a very good time together. And I realize you love your girls, and I know how devoted you are to them. But, Kayla, you have to live your life, too. I'm not going to harass you, but I believe I deserve a better reason for you doing this to us." Marley was angry. He knew that she loved him; she was just stubborn as hell. "Okay, this is what I'm going to do. I'm going to give you some time to get things straight in your head. And I think that I'm being pretty reasonable by doing so, because I'm going to miss you."

"Marley—"

"No, I'm going to miss holding you in my arms, kissing you all over your body, feeling your muscles tightened around me when I'm lying between your legs. I'm sacrificing a lot here, Kayla. But I'm willing to do that to have you be a part of my life."

Kayla didn't want to, but she couldn't help smiling. God knows she didn't want to let this man go. She enjoyed herself so much with him that she actually hated it when they were apart. After her divorce, Kayla never thought that she would find the man for her. And she had to admit she would have never guessed that man would be Marley. She was glad it was. But, now just wasn't the right time for him to be in her life. It was one of those cruel tricks God sometimes plays on you.

"Marley, I'm going to miss those things, too, but I have to do what's right for my girls. And right now, they need me to be here for them. I can't afford to make any more mistakes where they are concerned."

"So this was a mistake? Is that what you are saying?" Marley wanted to hang the phone up. She was talking crazy, not making any sense at all. It was as if the girls were four and five years old. These were teenagers. "You know what, Kayla, if you don't want to be with me, I can't make you."

"Marley."

"No. I'm just going to let you go. I'm starting to feel like I'm making a fool out of myself for nothing. And I'm not going to let even you make me feel that way."

"Marley, don't be like this."

"Well, how am I supposed to be, Kayla?"

He was silent for a few seconds, but when Kayla failed to answer his question, Marley simply hung up the phone.

Kayla let the tears flow. She was losing something, and she wasn't sure if she could ever find it again. She lay back on her bed and silently berated herself for allowing her feelings for him to grow so strong, but there was no way she could have stopped it from happening. She finally fell asleep, only to dream of him.

Wanda returned the phone to its home base. She closed her eyes briefly and exhaled deeply. Every day at the same time for the last two weeks she had received the same call. Frustrated and at the end of her rope, she decided to take an early break.

When she stopped at Kayla's desk, she saw exactly what she had expected: Kayla was sitting at her desk, her head bent low, a frown on her pretty face. She had looked that way for the past two weeks, and frankly, Wanda was sick and tired of it.

They hadn't talked in three days because, one day at lunch, Wanda had told her to stop being an asshole and go get Marley back. And here she was standing in front of her girl again today about to tell her the same thing.

Kayla didn't look up. She knew who there by the smell of the Victoria's Secret Pure Seduction body spray and lotion that Wanda drowned herself in daily.

For a minute, neither said anything, their stubbornness equally unbending. Then Wanda finally broke the silence, as she had to get back to her desk soon.

"Kayla, you need to make a phone call."

"Not now, Wanda. I'm busy." Kayla looked up at her, and then looked around to make sure no one was listening to their conversation. To her surprise, the room was empty.

"Now, Kayla," Wanda said, taking the seat beside her desk. "You and Marley are both driving me crazy with the way you're acting. He's calling me every day just to see how you're doing, what you're wearing, wondering if you've said anything today. And you are trying to sit here and act as if this doesn't affect you at all."

"That's because it doesn't."

"You're such a bad liar. I'm your girl, Kayla. I love you to death. And if you want to be miserable for the rest of your life, far be it for me to stop you, but I have to tell you that you're not the person that I thought you were."

Kayla sat back and crossed her arms. She gave Wanda a sour look.

"I don't care if you get mad. I'm going to tell you this, and then I'm staying out of your business from here on out. I don't even want to hear you and Marley's names mentioned in the same breath. Kayla, dear, you can't live your life this way. You're miserable, Marley's miserable, the girls are miserable, and I'm miserable. Kaitlyn called me the other day damn near in tears asking me to talk to you. You can't keep them locked up for the rest of their lives because of one mistake. Kamry is being punished for no reason at all."

Kayla just sat quietly. Wanda wasn't sure if she was even getting through to her.

"Kayla, you're going to lose them. Kaitlyn is seventeen. She's going to be a senior this year. What do you think is going to happen if you keep her locked up for this whole year? She's going to get away from you as soon as she can. That girl won't be able to find a school fast enough or a place to live quick enough. Then she'll make the same mistake you did and hook up with the first man that lies to her good enough. That is what you need to think about."

Kayla remained silent.

"Kayla, it's the fall. They want to go to the football games and school dances. You can't make them stay locked up in the house as if they're in prison. They're going to end up resenting you for it. You're the only one who can change it, Kayla, and you need to do it before it gets to be too late. Kaitlyn made a mistake, the same mistake we've all made. You did what you had to do to get past it. You and she talked. She went to the doctor, and he said she was fine. She promised to think first before it happened again, and she has clearly learned her lesson. And believe me, she will think twice next time. Kayla, you got to let it go, and put your trust back in her. Can't you see what this is doing to your family, and most important, to you? Have you taken a good look at yourself lately?"

Kayla propped her elbows on her desk. She didn't know what to do; she could admit that. The last two weeks had been horrible for her whole family. She knew that she had been in a foul mood because of both Kaitlyn and Marley. Kayla had honestly come to terms with Kaitlyn's actions. It was a teenage mistake, and Kaitlyn realized that. But she missed Marley so damn much, and she didn't know how to fix that problem.

During the day, she thought about him all day at work. His face was all she saw when she looked at her computer screen. If it hadn't happened to her, Kayla would never have believed that someone could fall in love so fast.

At night, she lay in bed thinking about how close three doors down actually was. She missed him holding her in his arms and making her feel as if she belonged there, making her feel wanted and desired. At her lowest points, when she thought she would go insane for wanting Marley, Adam's willingness to temporarily help her was tempting, but Kayla found it in herself to resist. She knew that once she cleaned Adam off and returned him to his little bag her misery would return full force. Kayla didn't think she could handle that.

Since their last talk, she had only seen Marley once. When she turned the corner to their block, he was pulling long slabs of lumber from the back of his truck. He watched her until she parked and went into the house. Kayla could feel his eyes on her the whole time, but she avoided looking his way. It would have been too painful. Since that day, she had hoped to see him, but never had. But one of his cars was always gone.

Kayla found herself wondering where he was, what he was doing, and whom he was doing it with. At night, she tried to watch for his car pulling into his parking spot, but when she fell asleep, it would be still missing. He said that he would give her time, but she didn't expect him to disappear.

Kayla looked at her friend helplessly. Even if she wanted him back—and she desperately did—she didn't know how to get him back. It couldn't be as easy and simple as to just walk up to his door and knock.

Wanda looked back at her, waiting for answers to her questions, but when she got none, she simply threw her hands up and said, "Well, I hope you know what you're doing. You know where I'll be if you need to talk."

After her friend left, Kayla wished that she had opened her mouth. Wanda did have her best interests at heart, even though she didn't come across like the most sympathetic person in the world.

Robert walked into the dining room and took a seat at the head of his table. It was laden with serving dishes piled high with fried chicken, spare ribs, greens, macaroni and potato salad. LaToya had done a wonderful job of preparing a huge meal for the extra company, although she had just finished grading a ton of papers less than two hours ago. It was Sunday afternoon, which was when she did most of her grading. He took her hand and squeezed it gently. His brothers settled themselves comfortably in their seats.

They said grace, holding hands around the table as their parents had taught them to do. Right after, Robert spoke up.

"Okay, I got a question."

Marley and Nester looked up at him.

"What the hell's going on with you two? Nester, why are you still at my house? And Marley, why are you here every night?"

Shocked, neither answered. They just stared at Robert.

"I mean, don't get me wrong. LaToya and I love you both to death, but what's going on? I haven't seen as much of you two in my life as I have in the last few weeks."

"Hey," Nester explained, "I'm just waiting for my apartment to become available, then I'm outta here."

"I thought I heard you talking to a woman the other night, Nester," LaToya said. "I wasn't trying to eavesdrop, but I could have sworn it was something about moving in with her."

"No, nosy. That was Cyndi. She asked me to help her remove her old bed. She had a new one delivered the other day." He gave her a look that said, *Well, anything else?*

"I apologize," LaToya said simply, and then turned to Marley. "And I suppose you're staying here every night so that you don't have to face Kayla."

"It's not that I don't want to face her. I don't want to see her. Not until she's ready to see me," Marley answered honestly.

"And when do you think that will be? If you're not over each other after two weeks, I doubt that you'll be over her in a month, two months."

"LaToya, look, Kayla said that she didn't want to be with me. What can I do about that?"

"Well, sitting here with us isn't going to make her change her mind, now is it?" LaToya looked at her husband. "If Robert told me that he didn't want to be with me, I would be like, okay, but I would be everywhere he could see me until he realized that he was missing out on a great thing."

Robert sat up in his seat. "She's right, Marley. Sometimes you can't take no for an answer, especially if she's the one. Take your ass home tomorrow and stay there."

"Damn, bro," Nester said, "talk about tough love."

"That's right," Robert agreed. "Because of you two knuckleheads, I can't get my freak on like I want to."

"What?" Marley laughed. "Rob, we hear y'all every night."

"I said like I want to. In the kitchen, living room, on this table," he said pointedly, looking at them both.

Everybody laughed when Nester and Marley both grabbed their plates and got up from the table.

"We'll eat outside on the porch," Nester said. Marley followed him outside.

Robert and LaToya held hands at the table.

"Should we tell them?" she asked.

"No. If we tell them everywhere we've had sex, including on the patio furniture, they'll never come back."

Monday and Tuesday, Marley did exactly what his sister-in-law had suggested. He made sure that he was in front of his house on both of those days when Kayla left to go to work and when she came home. In the morning, he waved at her and told her to have a good day. She didn't acknowledge him, but she saw him. In the evening, he stood on his front steps and watched her until she went into the house. Again, she looked his way, but then acted as if he wasn't there. Once he even thought that she was about to say something to him. Instead, she just went right into the house. It was going to be tougher than he thought.

Later that evening, he saw a green SUV pull into one of Kayla's parking spots. Marley told himself that he only came out on the front steps because he didn't recognize the vehicle. A tall, dark-skinned man wearing sunglasses got out of the car. He was dressed more like a thug than a businessman, so Marley assumed that he had to be family. And when Kamry opened the door and yelled the word 'Dad' at the top of her voice, Marley's assumption was verified.

So this was the ex-husband.

Marley stayed on his front steps until the ex-husband left, which was exactly forty-two minutes, twenty-seven seconds later. After the car pulled out with only one occupant, Marley headed into the house and took a shower.

That night, he lay in bed wondering what he would have done if Kayla had gotten into the car with that man. He would have snapped. Marley realized that he couldn't keep doing this. He couldn't live three doors down from her and not see and talk to her, not have her in his arms, not know that she was his.

"So what are we going to do about Mom?" Kamry whispered to her sister Thursday night while they were in the family room watching TV. Their mother was in the kitchen finishing up the dinner dishes.

"I've been thinking about that. Since we don't have school tomorrow, we're going to have to put things into action. And this weekend might be the only chance we're going to have to get things back the way they used to be."

"What do you mean?"

"Well, since we'll be with Dad this weekend, we're going to have to work fast. Listen, tomorrow after Mom leaves to go to work, we're going to go down and talk to Mr. Marley."

Kamry looked at her wide-eyed.

"Stop being so scared all the time. Once we think Mom is at work, we'll call Miss Wanda to be sure, then we'll walk down there together. I don't know about you, but I'm tired of seeing her like this. She's in love with him."

Kamry totally agreed. Their mother was driving them crazy with her bad mood. After what happened, they made sure to keep the house spotless and even did a quick cleanup every day when they knew she was on her way home, but Kayla still managed to find something to argue about. And both girls knew that it was because she and Mr. Marley had broken up.

"What are we going to tell him?" Kamry asked her.

"The truth. We're going to let him know that we are leaving this weekend and that Mom will be here by herself. Hopefully, he'll be smart enough to jump at the opportunity to get back with her."

"Yeah, if he's acting like her, it should be easy enough, but what if he's okay with them splitting up?"

"Not a chance. Remember, he was more than happy to help us out when we suggested it the first time. Besides, when you called Mr. Nester, didn't he tell you that Mr. Marley was going thro—"

Kaitlyn fell silent when she heard her mother take the first step down into the family room.

"But we don't know what time he leaves in the morning. What if we don't catch him before he goes to work?" Kamry asked.

Kaitlyn's head fell back. "I don't know. I didn't think of that. I guess we're just going to have to pray that we either catch him before he goes or before Mom comes home."

The next morning they both lay in bed, feigning sleep, until the sound of Kayla's car disappeared in the distance. The girls jumped out of bed at the same time and practically ran into each other in the hallway.

"Wait! Wait!" Kamry yelled. "We have to wait until we're sure she's at work. We'll call Miss Wanda in twenty minutes. I'm going to get something to eat."

"No, get dressed so we can go down to Mr. Marley's as soon as we find out Mom's at work."

"Kaitlyn, I doubt if ten minutes is going to make a difference. Once we're sure Mom is at work we have at least seven hours before she'll be home. Don't rush it. Your plan will work."

Forty minutes later, both girls were anxiously standing in front of Marley's door. Kaitlyn rang the doorbell and waited for Marley to answer.

When the door opened, they were surprised to see Nester. Dressed in a wife-beater t-shirt and pajama bottoms, he took their breath away a little.

"Hi, Uncle Nester," Kamry laughed, using her nickname for him. "What you doing here?"

Nester smiled back. "Hello, girls. I decided to stay over last night. What are you two up to?" He hadn't known them long, but he knew them well enough to know that something was up. They probably weren't even allowed to be out of the house.

"Um, hi, Mr. Nester." Kaitlyn smiled shyly. She still hadn't gotten over her little crush on the man. "We were wondering if Mr. Marley was around. We need to talk to him. It's important."

"Well, he's getting ready for work right now. Why don't y'all come back in a half hour?" Nester suggested that instead of asking them inside. Even though nothing was amiss, he wasn't about to invite trouble. "I'll tell Marley that y'all stopped by."

Disappointed, the girls' faces fell. "Okay, we'll come back," they said in unison and turned to leave.

But before they had gotten down the first two steps, Marley had pushed Nester aside and was trying to get out the door. He was out of breath. When he heard the doorbell ring, he looked out the window, but didn't see a car. He figured that it was the girls. He had just stepped out of the shower and had thrown his clothes on over his still-wet body and rushed down the steps as fast as he could.

"Hey, hey, girls. What's going on? Something wrong?" Nester came out on the front steps behind him.

Both girls were silent for a moment, but then Kaitlyn spoke up first, as usual.

"Mr. Marley, we came by to tell you that our father is coming to get us tonight. We're going to be staying with him for the weekend."

There was silence. Marley knew what they were trying to say to him, but he had no idea how to respond to two teenage girls who were trying to hook him up with their mother again.

Kamry's patience was running out. She didn't want to be out of the house for too long. And for some reason, she felt that her mother was going to be driving around the corner at any minute.

"Mr. Marley, if you want to get Mom back, you're going to have to do it this weekend," Kamry stated. "We'll be gone *all* weekend. It's now or never. We want you and Mom back together. She was happy then. Now all she does is sit around moping and complaining about everything. We want you to do whatever you have to do to get back with our mom."

"Girls," Marley sighed, "I don't think it's that easy."

Kaitlyn took her eyes off Nester for a minute to say, "You want her, don't you?"

"Of course, I do. I really care for your mom, Kaitlyn. But the question is, does she want me back?"

"Believe me, Mr. Marley, she does," Kamry answered.

"Mr. Marley," Kaitlyn said, "I messed up really bad. And I apologize. My mistakes have messed things up for everybody, Kamry, Mom, and me. But it's not their fault that I was stupid. Mom is punishing herself for my mistake. She won't admit it, but that's the bottom line. She thinks she has to watch over us like we're kids again. If I could go back and change things, I would, but I can't. So Kamry and I figured that talking to you would be the next best thing. We know that you love her, and she loves you, too. We just want her to be happy again."

"Besides," Kamry added, "in a couple of years, we'll both be gone to college. Then she'll hate this decision to stop seeing you. We don't want her to be lonely."

"Marley," Nester piped up, "they do make a lot of sense. Maybe this is something you better take into consideration." He winked at the girls.

Kaitlyn actually sighed.

Kamry looked at her like she was stupid. He was just Nester. Maybe she had better explain to Kaitlyn that, besides the fact that he was too old for her, he really *would* be Uncle Nester if Mr. Marley and their mom did get back together for good.

Marley stayed quiet, but his head was working a million miles a minute. He had to be careful how he handled Kayla. Right now, she was all emotional and unsure of herself. Or maybe he should just go at her hard and let her know exactly what he wanted.

He finally focused back on the girls. "Thanks for your suggestion. What time are you leaving?"

"We'll be gone by eight. But I'm sure you'll hear us leave in that great big truck our father drives. It's so loud, and the music will be loud, too," Kaitlyn said, looking back at Kamry, who looked shocked to hear what Kaitlyn was saying about their father.

"Okay, then, I will keep my eyes and ears open."

"Mr. Marley," Kaitlyn continued, "we wouldn't be doing this if we didn't know that you were the right man for our mother. And me and Kamry both believe that you guys will be happy together. At least that's what we saw before when you were spending time together."

Kamry agreed, but still gave Kaitlyn a confused look. She had never heard her sister talk about or be so concerned for anyone other than herself. Maybe she had learned a lesson from all the mess David had put her through. Maybe, Kamry thought, the beating she got on Kaitlyn's behalf was worth it after all.

"Well, thank you, Kaitlyn. I really appreciate your saying that. And I appreciate you two coming over here to help me out. I really do care for your mother."

"We know," Kamry said. "And she cares for you, too. She's just mad, that's all. But if you talk to her, maybe everything will get back to the way it should be." She looked around again. "We had better get back to the house."

"Yeah," Kaitlyn agreed. "We got to get home. We're going to clean the house and start dinner. Maybe that will put her in a good mood."

"No, don't make dinner. I'm going to come over and ask her out to eat. I'll be there before your father comes to pick her up. As a matter of fact, as soon as she comes home, I'll ask her. So don't be in the living room or the kitchen when she comes in. I'll be right behind her."

The girls looked at each other. They wondered what Marley was up to, but didn't ask. "Okay."

It was 5:30 P.M. when Kayla left work. Because it was early October and close to the end of the hospital's fiscal year, employees were often asked to work a little late if necessary to finish their workload. Luckily, her daydreaming about Marley had stopped and she had been producing more work than usual, so she was able to leave earlier than the other girls.

She was determined to get home before Quincy came to pick up the girls. She was already mad as hell that he just popped up out of the blue to visit them the night before. When the doorbell rang, somewhere in the back of her mind, in the bottom of her heart, she thought that it might have been Marley coming to see her.

Deep down, that was what she wanted. It had been three weeks since they had talked, since she was close enough to smell him, feel him. She missed him so much. But now she had to deal with Quincy trying to become a part of the girls' life after being an absentee father for the past two years.

Her first instinct was to tell him to go to hell. He wasn't taking her daughters for a whole weekend. God only knew what he was into right now. But the girls were so happy to see him. They had forgotten that they had seen him only three times in the past year. All he had to do was come in and promise a weekend filled with excitement and adventure and they were ready to go.

Kayla still wanted to say no, hell no, no. But they weren't little girls anymore. They were almost grown women. All she could do is talk to them; let them know that she was worried. This was their father. She had to let them form their own opinions of the man and not let her past experiences with him dictate their decisions concerning him.

Kayla had hoped that what he had told the girls the night before was more of his famous bull. She didn't expect him to come pick the girls up. She honestly didn't believe that he was serious about spending time getting to know them better.

But during her lunch hour, she made sure that she went out and added minutes to their cellphones. The night before, she told them not to let him know that they had the phones, but to keep them on their persons at all times, and to call her every night, every single night.

Now that she pulled up in front of her house and saw that Quincy was already there, Kayla's heart dropped a little. She was really going to have to let them go. God knows she didn't want to. But she did her motherly duty and walked into the house with a bright smile.

"Hello, girls," she yelled. Quincy was the only one in the room.

"They're upstairs getting ready," he said from the living room sofa.

Kayla tried to ignore him.

"Kayla, I have to hand it to you. You've done well for yourself. And you've done a great job with the girls."

She looked at him. "Quincy, you can keep that to yourself. I don't need any acknowledgment from you for being a mother."

"Well, you look good, real good. Even look like you might have finally lost a few pounds." He stood up to his full five-foot, ten-inch height. He was only an inch taller than she, but for some reason he thought he was a foot taller. And she did, too. After his actions had knocked him off that pedestal, Kayla realized he wasn't anyone to look up to. She began looking at him eye-to-eye and seeing all of his terrible faults.

She gave him a dark look before heading toward the stairs. There was really no need to continue the conversation. As soon as her foot hit the second step, the doorbell rang.

"Who in the—" Kayla began as she walked to the front door. She opened the door and Marley stood before her with a dozen red roses.

Before she could say anything else, he walked into the house, right up to her, took her into his arms and kissed her hard. The swift movement of his lips across hers took her breath away. When Marley finally released her, she was practically panting. Her breathing was so shallow that she couldn't introduce Quincy, who had moved closer to the couple, confused and curious. She simply stood next to Marley, weakly looking up into his face.

Kayla had almost forgotten that Quincy was even there. Marley was so handsome in his dark blue t-shirt that showed every bulging muscle on his torso. He hadn't shaven, and the five-o'clock shadow he sported was sexy with a capital 'S'.

"Oh, I'm sorry, love," he said to Kayla, passing her the flowers and putting his arm around her waist. "I didn't know that you had company. I was just missing you so much I couldn't wait another minute."

For a second, she wondered if what he was saying was prompted by Quincy being there or if he was serious about missing her for the past few weeks. It had to be the latter because she had never told him about Quincy. She had missed him, too.

"Hey, man, I'm Marley." Marley walked over to Quincy with his hand extended, a questioning look on his face.

"Um, what's up? Quincy, man. The girls' father."

As thugged-out and in control as Quincy always seemed to be in the past, at that moment, Kayla could see that he was uncomfortable having to look up at Marley.

"Oh, okay. Nice to meet you, man," Marley replied, then went back over to where Kayla was standing. "Well, I see that you're busy. I have to run out to Robert's for a quick second, so why don't I call you as soon as I finish."

At that moment, both girls came downstairs.

"Hi, Mr. Marley," they chimed. And to everyone's surprise, they both stopped to give him a quick hug.

"You and Mom doing something tonight?" Kaitlyn asked.

"Yeah, I heard that you two were going away."

"Yep. We gotta go stay with our dad for the weekend. So you got the whole house to yourselves. What you going to do?"

"Kamry!" Kayla interrupted. She didn't know what was going on, but Kamry knew better than to ask such a question, especially with its suggestive undertones.

"Well, we better get on the road. Y'all enjoy your weekend," Kaitlyn said brightly. "Come on, Dad."

"Yeah, let's get out of here," Quincy replied. He didn't like thinking about Kayla being in the arms of another man, especially when she seemed to enjoy it so much. Just because he didn't want her as he used to did not mean it was okay for someone else to want her. And this man wanted her passionately. He could see that.

Kayla stood at the door. Marley left first, but not without a quick kiss on the lips. After him, the girls each gave her a hug good-bye. Then Quincy walked past her. She noticed that he was looking at her strangely.

Kayla waited for Marley's call by changing her clothes and watching the news. When the phone rang, she waited for two rings before she answered.

"Hello."

"Hey, beautiful. What's for dinner?"

Kayla glanced at her alarm clock. It was 7:30 P.M. She hadn't even thought about food. "That's a good question. I wasn't thinking that I could have cooked us dinner. It's not too late for me to throw something together. What do you have a taste for?"

"You," he answered.

They were both silent, then he continued, "No, don't cook. I'm going to take you out to dinner. How about a real date? Would you do me the honor of going to dinner and a movie with me?"

Kayla laughed, "Of course I will. What time?"

"Now. Are you ready?"

"Yes. I'll be there in a second."

"I'm already here."

"Already here?" she asked. "Where's here?"

"Your front steps. Just come on out when you're ready. I'll be waiting."

"Marley, I owe you an apology," Kayla began as soon as the car pulled onto the highway. She wasn't sure exactly how to begin to explain what she had been going through the last few weeks.

"No, I understand."

"I don't think you really do. I should have never treated you the way I did. I've been trying hard to deal with some problems I had, but my way of dealing with them was by pushing them away instead of actually dealing with them."

"Kayla, you don't have to explain yourself to me if you're not ready. I'm just glad that you agreed to go with me tonight. At least you're letting me back into your life."

"But I want to explain, Marley. Talking about my feelings about the past is one way of dealing with it. I never wanted to talk about what happened. Even when Wanda tried convincing me to join one of those support groups, I ignored her advice because I wasn't ready. But now, I'm ready."

"I just want you to know that you don't have to rush to change anything because of me. I—"

"No. Marley, this has nothing to do with you. It has everything to do with me and where I want to be in my life. In order for me to move forward, I have to let go of the past, or at least learn to deal with it. My daughters taught me a very important lesson."

"Your daughters. Those girls are going to go very far in life. They are just as determined and headstrong as their mother."

"Yes, so I decided that Wanda was making a lot of sense. And I joined a support group so that I can come to terms with my past, which included a lot of abuse."

"Your ex-husband used to put his hands on you?" Marley had no idea Kayla had been abused.

"But I didn't join the group because of that. I joined for me because I refuse to let my husband continue to have power over the direction my life takes, and by cutting myself off from the world, I was doing that."

"It sounds as if you've already come to terms with a lot." He pulled into the Red Lobster parking lot and turned off the car. They walked to the restaurant hand in hand. The hopes of a new beginning rose in Kayla's heart.

"I also came to terms with the fact that I want you in my life. After the time we've spent together, Marley, I can honestly say that the time we spent apart was horrible. I want to take the time to get to know you better; one day at a time."

"That can be easily arranged. Kayla, I want you to take your time. I'm not going anywhere, and you know where I'll be."

"Yeah, three doors down," Kayla laughed.

Marley laughed, too. "That's right. Three doors down."

ABOUT THE AUTHOR

Michele Sudler lives in the small East Coast town of Smyrna, Delaware. Busy raising her three children, Gregory, Takira, and Kanika Lambert, she finds time for her second passion, writing, in the evenings and on weekends. After attending Delaware State College, majoring in Business Administration, she began and continues to work in the corporate banking industry. Recently, enrolling back in school, she is currently working hard on time management skills to balance family, work, and school.

Three Doors Down is her fourth novel. Her first, *Intentional Mistakes,* introduced the world to Tia Avery and Jeff Daniels and the lovable Avery Clan. In her second novel, *One of These Days*, Shelia Daniels and Charles Avery formed a memorable relationship. *Stolen Memories* introduced the Philips family, who promise to be an interesting lot. She is currently working on her next novels in the Avery and Philips family trees, along with a number of other projects.

Besides spending time with her children and writing, she enjoys playing and watching basketball, traveling, and reading. She would also love to hear from you. Please send any comments to her email address: micheleasudler@yahoo.com.

2008 Reprint Mass Market Titles

January

Cautious Heart
Cheris F. Hodges
ISBN-13: 978-1-58571-301-1
ISBN-10: 1-58571-301-5
$6.99

Suddenly You
Crystal Hubbard
ISBN-13: 978-1-58571-302-8
ISBN-10: 1-58571-302-3
$6.99

February

Passion
T. T. Henderson
ISBN-13: 978-1-58571-303-5
ISBN-10: 1-58571-303-1
$6.99

Whispers in the Sand
LaFlorya Gauthier
ISBN-13: 978-1-58571-304-2
ISBN-10: 1-58571-304-x
$6.99

March

Life Is Never As It Seems
J. J. Michael
ISBN-13: 978-1-58571-305-9
ISBN-10: 1-58571-305-8
$6.99

Beyond the Rapture
Beverly Clark
ISBN-13: 978-1-58571-306-6
ISBN-10: 1-58571-306-6
$6.99

April

A Heart's Awakening
Veronica Parker
ISBN-13: 978-1-58571-307-3
ISBN-10: 1-58571-307-4
$6.99

Breeze
Robin Lynette Hampton
ISBN-13: 978-1-58571-308-0
ISBN-10: 1-58571-308-2
$6.99

May

I'll Be Your Shelter
Giselle Carmichael
ISBN-13: 978-1-58571-309-7
ISBN-10: 1-58571-309-0
$6.99

Careless Whispers
Rochelle Alers
ISBN-13: 978-1-58571-310-3
ISBN-10: 1-58571-310-4
$6.99

June

Sin
Crystal Rhodes
ISBN-13: 978-1-58571-311-0
ISBN-10: 1-58571-311-2
$6.99

Dark Storm Rising
Chinelu Moore
ISBN-13: 978-1-58571-312-7
ISBN-10: 1-58571-312-0
$6.99

2008 Reprint Mass Market Titles (continued)

July

Object of His Desire
A.C. Arthur
ISBN-13: 978-1-58571-313-4
ISBN-10: 1-58571-313-9
$6.99

Angel's Paradise
Janice Angelique
ISBN-13: 978-1-58571-314-1
ISBN-10: 1-58571-314-7
$6.99

August

Unbreak My Heart
Dar Tomlinson
ISBN-13: 978-1-58571-315-8
ISBN-10: 1-58571-315-5
$6.99

All I Ask
Barbara Keaton
ISBN-13: 978-1-58571-316-5
ISBN-10: 1-58571-316-3
$6.99

September

Icie
Pamela Leigh Starr
ISBN-13: 978-1-58571-275-5
ISBN-10: 1-58571-275-2
$6.99

At Last
Lisa Riley
ISBN-13: 978-1-58571-276-2
ISBN-10: 1-58571-276-0
$6.99

October

Everlastin' Love
Gay G. Gunn
ISBN-13: 978-1-58571-277-9
ISBN-10: 1-58571-277-9
$6.99

Three Wishes
Seressia Glass
ISBN-13: 978-1-58571-278-6
ISBN-10: 1-58571-278-7
$6.99

November

Yesterday Is Gone
Beverly Clark
ISBN-13: 978-1-58571-279-3
ISBN-10: 1-58571-279-5
$6.99

Again My Love
Kayla Perrin
ISBN-13: 978-1-58571-280-9
ISBN-10: 1-58571-280-9
$6.99

December

Office Policy
A.C. Arthur
ISBN-13: 978-1-58571-281-6
ISBN-10: 1-58571-281-7
$6.99

Rendezvous With Fate
Jeanne Sumerix
ISBN-13: 978-1-58571-283-3
ISBN-10: 1-58571-283-3
$6.99

2008 New Mass Market Titles

January

Where I Want To Be
Maryam Diaab
ISBN-13: 978-1-58571-268-7
ISBN-10: 1-58571-268-X
$6.99

Never Say Never
Michele Cameron
ISBN-13: 978-1-58571-269-4
ISBN-10: 1-58571-269-8
$6.99

February

Stolen Memories
Michele Sudler
ISBN-13: 978-1-58571-270-0
ISBN-10: 1-58571-270-1
$6.99

Dawn's Harbor
Kymberly Hunt
ISBN-13: 978-1-58571-271-7
ISBN-10: 1-58571-271-X
$6.99

March

Undying Love
Renee Alexis
ISBN-13: 978-1-58571-272-4
ISBN-10: 1-58571-272-8
$6.99

Blame It On Paradise
Crystal Hubbard
ISBN-13: 978-1-58571-273-1
ISBN-10: 1-58571-273-6
$6.99

April

When A Man Loves A Woman
La Connie Taylor-Jones
ISBN-13: 978-1-58571-274-8
ISBN-10: 1-58571-274-4
$6.99

Choices
Tammy Williams
ISBN-13: 978-1-58571-300-4
ISBN-10: 1-58571-300-7
$6.99

May

Dream Runner
Gail McFarland
ISBN-13: 978-1-58571-317-2
ISBN-10: 1-58571-317-1
$6.99

Southern Fried Standards
S.R. Maddox
ISBN-13: 978-1-58571-318-9
ISBN-10: 1-58571-318-X
$6.99

June

Looking for Lily
Africa Fine
ISBN-13: 978-1-58571-319-6
ISBN-10: 1-58571-319-8
$6.99

Bliss, Inc.
Chamein Canton
ISBN-13: 978-1-58571-325-7
ISBN-10: 1-58571-325-2
$6.99

2008 New Mass Market Titles (continued)

July

Love's Secrets
Yolanda McVey
ISBN-13: 978-1-58571-321-9
ISBN-10: 1-58571-321-X
$6.99

Things Forbidden
Maryam Diaab
ISBN-13: 978-1-58571-327-1
ISBN-10: 1-58571-327-9
$6.99

August

Storm
Pamela Leigh Starr
ISBN-13: 978-1-58571-323-3
ISBN-10: 1-58571-323-6
$6.99

Passion's Furies
AlTonya Washington
ISBN-13: 978-1-58571-324-0
ISBN-10: 1-58571-324-4
$6.99

September

Three Doors Down
Michele Sudler
ISBN-13: 978-1-58571-332-5
ISBN-10: 1-58571-332-5
$6.99

Mr Fix-It
Crystal Hubbard
ISBN-13: 978-1-58571-326-4
ISBN-10: 1-58571-326-0
$6.99

October

Moments of Clarity
Michele Cameron
ISBN-13: 978-1-58571-330-1
ISBN-10: 1-58571-330-9
$6.99

Lady Preacher
K.T. Richey
ISBN-13: 978-1-58571-333-2
ISBN-10: 1-58571-333-3
$6.99

November

This Life Isn't Perfect Holla
Sandra Foy
ISBN: 978-1-58571-331-8
ISBN-10: 1-58571-331-7
$6.99

Promises Made
Bernice Layton
ISBN-13: 978-1-58571-334-9
ISBN-10: 1-58571-334-1
$6.99

December

A Voice Behind Thunder
Carrie Elizabeth Greene
ISBN-13: 978-1-58571-329-5
ISBN-10: 1-58571-329-5
$6.99

The More Things Change
Chamein Canton
ISBN-13: 978-1-58571-328-8
ISBN-10: 1-58571-328-7
$6.99

Other Genesis Press, Inc. Titles

A Dangerous Deception	J.M. Jeffries	$8.95
A Dangerous Love	J.M. Jeffries	$8.95
A Dangerous Obsession	J.M. Jeffries	$8.95
A Drummer's Beat to Mend	Kei Swanson	$9.95
A Happy Life	Charlotte Harris	$9.95
A Heart's Awakening	Veronica Parker	$9.95
A Lark on the Wing	Phyliss Hamilton	$9.95
A Love of Her Own	Cheris F. Hodges	$9.95
A Love to Cherish	Beverly Clark	$8.95
A Risk of Rain	Dar Tomlinson	$8.95
A Taste of Temptation	Reneé Alexis	$9.95
A Twist of Fate	Beverly Clark	$8.95
A Will to Love	Angie Daniels	$9.95
Acquisitions	Kimberley White	$8.95
Across	Carol Payne	$12.95
After the Vows	Leslie Esdaile	$10.95
(Summer Anthology)	T.T. Henderson	
	Jacqueline Thomas	
Again My Love	Kayla Perrin	$10.95
Against the Wind	Gwynne Forster	$8.95
All I Ask	Barbara Keaton	$8.95
Always You	Crystal Hubbard	$6.99
Ambrosia	T.T. Henderson	$8.95
An Unfinished Love Affair	Barbara Keaton	$8.95
And Then Came You	Dorothy Elizabeth Love	$8.95
Angel's Paradise	Janice Angelique	$9.95
At Last	Lisa G. Riley	$8.95
Best of Friends	Natalie Dunbar	$8.95
Beyond the Rapture	Beverly Clark	$9.95

Other Genesis Press, Inc. Titles (continued)

Blaze	Barbara Keaton	$9.95
Blood Lust	J. M. Jeffries	$9.95
Blood Seduction	J.M. Jeffries	$9.95
Bodyguard	Andrea Jackson	$9.95
Boss of Me	Diana Nyad	$8.95
Bound by Love	Beverly Clark	$8.95
Breeze	Robin Hampton Allen	$10.95
Broken	Dar Tomlinson	$24.95
By Design	Barbara Keaton	$8.95
Cajun Heat	Charlene Berry	$8.95
Careless Whispers	Rochelle Alers	$8.95
Cats & Other Tales	Marilyn Wagner	$8.95
Caught in a Trap	Andre Michelle	$8.95
Caught Up In the Rapture	Lisa G. Riley	$9.95
Cautious Heart	Cheris F Hodges	$8.95
Chances	Pamela Leigh Starr	$8.95
Cherish the Flame	Beverly Clark	$8.95
Class Reunion	Irma Jenkins/ John Brown	$12.95
Code Name: Diva	J.M. Jeffries	$9.95
Conquering Dr. Wexler's Heart	Kimberley White	$9.95
Corporate Seduction	A.C. Arthur	$9.95
Crossing Paths, Tempting Memories	Dorothy Elizabeth Love	$9.95
Crush	Crystal Hubbard	$9.95
Cypress Whisperings	Phyllis Hamilton	$8.95
Dark Embrace	Crystal Wilson Harris	$8.95
Dark Storm Rising	Chinelu Moore	$10.95

Other Genesis Press, Inc. Titles (continued)

Daughter of the Wind	Joan Xian	$8.95
Deadly Sacrifice	Jack Kean	$22.95
Designer Passion	Dar Tomlinson Diana Richeaux	$8.95
Do Over	Celya Bowers	$9.95
Dreamtective	Liz Swados	$5.95
Ebony Angel	Deatri King-Bey	$9.95
Ebony Butterfly II	Delilah Dawson	$14.95
Echoes of Yesterday	Beverly Clark	$9.95
Eden's Garden	Elizabeth Rose	$8.95
Eve's Prescription	Edwina Martin Arnold	$8.95
Everlastin' Love	Gay G. Gunn	$8.95
Everlasting Moments	Dorothy Elizabeth Love	$8.95
Everything and More	Sinclair Lebeau	$8.95
Everything but Love	Natalie Dunbar	$8.95
Falling	Natalie Dunbar	$9.95
Fate	Pamela Leigh Starr	$8.95
Finding Isabella	A.J. Garrotto	$8.95
Forbidden Quest	Dar Tomlinson	$10.95
Forever Love	Wanda Y. Thomas	$8.95
From the Ashes	Kathleen Suzanne Jeanne Sumerix	$8.95
Gentle Yearning	Rochelle Alers	$10.95
Glory of Love	Sinclair LeBeau	$10.95
Go Gentle into that Good Night	Malcom Boyd	$12.95
Goldengroove	Mary Beth Craft	$16.95
Groove, Bang, and Jive	Steve Cannon	$8.99
Hand in Glove	Andrea Jackson	$9.95

Other Genesis Press, Inc. Titles (continued)

Hard to Love	Kimberley White	$9.95
Hart & Soul	Angie Daniels	$8.95
Heart of the Phoenix	A.C. Arthur	$9.95
Heartbeat	Stephanie Bedwell-Grime	$8.95
Hearts Remember	M. Loui Quezada	$8.95
Hidden Memories	Robin Allen	$10.95
Higher Ground	Leah Latimer	$19.95
Hitler, the War, and the Pope	Ronald Rychiak	$26.95
How to Write a Romance	Kathryn Falk	$18.95
I Married a Reclining Chair	Lisa M. Fuhs	$8.95
I'll Be Your Shelter	Giselle Carmichael	$8.95
I'll Paint a Sun	A.J. Garrotto	$9.95
Icie	Pamela Leigh Starr	$8.95
Illusions	Pamela Leigh Starr	$8.95
Indigo After Dark Vol. I	Nia Dixon/Angelique	$10.95
Indigo After Dark Vol. II	Dolores Bundy/ Cole Riley	$10.95
Indigo After Dark Vol. III	Montana Blue/ Coco Morena	$10.95
Indigo After Dark Vol. IV	Cassandra Colt/	$14.95
Indigo After Dark Vol. V	Delilah Dawson	$14.95
Indiscretions	Donna Hill	$8.95
Intentional Mistakes	Michele Sudler	$9.95
Interlude	Donna Hill	$8.95
Intimate Intentions	Angie Daniels	$8.95
It's Not Over Yet	J.J. Michael	$9.95
Jolie's Surrender	Edwina Martin-Arnold	$8.95
Kiss or Keep	Debra Phillips	$8.95
Lace	Giselle Carmichael	$9.95

Other Genesis Press, Inc. Titles (continued)

Last Train to Memphis	Elsa Cook	$12.95
Lasting Valor	Ken Olsen	$24.95
Let Us Prey	Hunter Lundy	$25.95
Lies Too Long	Pamela Ridley	$13.95
Life Is Never As It Seems	J.J. Michael	$12.95
Lighter Shade of Brown	Vicki Andrews	$8.95
Love Always	Mildred E. Riley	$10.95
Love Doesn't Come Easy	Charlyne Dickerson	$8.95
Love Unveiled	Gloria Greene	$10.95
Love's Deception	Charlene Berry	$10.95
Love's Destiny	M. Loui Quezada	$8.95
Mae's Promise	Melody Walcott	$8.95
Magnolia Sunset	Giselle Carmichael	$8.95
Many Shades of Gray	Dyanne Davis	$6.99
Matters of Life and Death	Lesego Malepe, Ph.D.	$15.95
Meant to Be	Jeanne Sumerix	$8.95
Midnight Clear (Anthology)	Leslie Esdaile Gwynne Forster Carmen Green Monica Jackson	$10.95
Midnight Magic	Gwynne Forster	$8.95
Midnight Peril	Vicki Andrews	$10.95
Misconceptions	Pamela Leigh Starr	$9.95
Montgomery's Children	Richard Perry	$14.95
My Buffalo Soldier	Barbara B. K. Reeves	$8.95
Naked Soul	Gwynne Forster	$8.95
Next to Last Chance	Louisa Dixon	$24.95
No Apologies	Seressia Glass	$8.95
No Commitment Required	Seressia Glass	$8.95

Other Genesis Press, Inc. Titles (continued)

No Regrets	Mildred E. Riley	$8.95
Not His Type	Chamein Canton	$6.99
Nowhere to Run	Gay G. Gunn	$10.95
O Bed! O Breakfast!	Rob Kuehnle	$14.95
Object of His Desire	A. C. Arthur	$8.95
Office Policy	A. C. Arthur	$9.95
Once in a Blue Moon	Dorianne Cole	$9.95
One Day at a Time	Bella McFarland	$8.95
One in A Million	Barbara Keaton	$6.99
One of These Days	Michele Sudler	$9.95
Outside Chance	Louisa Dixon	$24.95
Passion	T.T. Henderson	$10.95
Passion's Blood	Cherif Fortin	$22.95
Passion's Journey	Wanda Y. Thomas	$8.95
Past Promises	Jahmel West	$8.95
Path of Fire	T.T. Henderson	$8.95
Path of Thorns	Annetta P. Lee	$9.95
Peace Be Still	Colette Haywood	$12.95
Picture Perfect	Reon Carter	$8.95
Playing for Keeps	Stephanie Salinas	$8.95
Pride & Joi	Gay G. Gunn	$15.95
Pride & Joi	Gay G. Gunn	$8.95
Promises to Keep	Alicia Wiggins	$8.95
Quiet Storm	Donna Hill	$10.95
Reckless Surrender	Rochelle Alers	$6.95
Red Polka Dot in a World of Plaid	Varian Johnson	$12.95
Reluctant Captive	Joyce Jackson	$8.95
Rendezvous with Fate	Jeanne Sumerix	$8.95

Other Genesis Press, Inc. Titles (continued)

Revelations	Cheris F. Hodges	$8.95
Rivers of the Soul	Leslie Esdaile	$8.95
Rocky Mountain Romance	Kathleen Suzanne	$8.95
Rooms of the Heart	Donna Hill	$8.95
Rough on Rats and Tough on Cats	Chris Parker	$12.95
Secret Library Vol. 1	Nina Sheridan	$18.95
Secret Library Vol. 2	Cassandra Colt	$8.95
Secret Thunder	Annetta P. Lee	$9.95
Shades of Brown	Denise Becker	$8.95
Shades of Desire	Monica White	$8.95
Shadows in the Moonlight	Jeanne Sumerix	$8.95
Sin	Crystal Rhodes	$8.95
Small Whispers	Annetta P. Lee	$6.99
So Amazing	Sinclair LeBeau	$8.95
Somebody's Someone	Sinclair LeBeau	$8.95
Someone to Love	Alicia Wiggins	$8.95
Song in the Park	Martin Brant	$15.95
Soul Eyes	Wayne L. Wilson	$12.95
Soul to Soul	Donna Hill	$8.95
Southern Comfort	J.M. Jeffries	$8.95
Still the Storm	Sharon Robinson	$8.95
Still Waters Run Deep	Leslie Esdaile	$8.95
Stolen Kisses	Dominiqua Douglas	$9.95
Stories to Excite You	Anna Forrest/Divine	$14.95
Subtle Secrets	Wanda Y. Thomas	$8.95
Suddenly You	Crystal Hubbard	$9.95
Sweet Repercussions	Kimberley White	$9.95
Sweet Sensations	Gwendolyn Bolton	$9.95

Other Genesis Press, Inc. Titles (continued)

Sweet Tomorrows	Kimberly White	$8.95
Taken by You	Dorothy Elizabeth Love	$9.95
Tattooed Tears	T. T. Henderson	$8.95
The Color Line	Lizzette Grayson Carter	$9.95
The Color of Trouble	Dyanne Davis	$8.95
The Disappearance of Allison Jones	Kayla Perrin	$5.95
The Fires Within	Beverly Clark	$9.95
The Foursome	Celya Bowers	$6.99
The Honey Dipper's Legacy	Pannell-Allen	$14.95
The Joker's Love Tune	Sidney Rickman	$15.95
The Little Pretender	Barbara Cartland	$10.95
The Love We Had	Natalie Dunbar	$8.95
The Man Who Could Fly	Bob & Milana Beamon	$18.95
The Missing Link	Charlyne Dickerson	$8.95
The Mission	Pamela Leigh Starr	$6.99
The Perfect Frame	Beverly Clark	$9.95
The Price of Love	Sinclair LeBeau	$8.95
The Smoking Life	Ilene Barth	$29.95
The Words of the Pitcher	Kei Swanson	$8.95
Three Wishes	Seressia Glass	$8.95
Ties That Bind	Kathleen Suzanne	$8.95
Tiger Woods	Libby Hughes	$5.95
Time is of the Essence	Angie Daniels	$9.95
Timeless Devotion	Bella McFarland	$9.95
Tomorrow's Promise	Leslie Esdaile	$8.95
Truly Inseparable	Wanda Y. Thomas	$8.95
Two Sides to Every Story	Dyanne Davis	$9.95
Unbreak My Heart	Dar Tomlinson	$8.95

Other Genesis Press, Inc. Titles (continued)

Uncommon Prayer	Kenneth Swanson	$9.95
Unconditional Love	Alicia Wiggins	$8.95
Unconditional	A.C. Arthur	$9.95
Until Death Do Us Part	Susan Paul	$8.95
Vows of Passion	Bella McFarland	$9.95
Wedding Gown	Dyanne Davis	$8.95
What's Under Benjamin's Bed	Sandra Schaffer	$8.95
When Dreams Float	Dorothy Elizabeth Love	$8.95
When I'm With You	LaConnie Taylor-Jones	$6.99
Whispers in the Night	Dorothy Elizabeth Love	$8.95
Whispers in the Sand	LaFlorya Gauthier	$10.95
Who's That Lady?	Andrea Jackson	$9.95
Wild Ravens	Altonya Washington	$9.95
Yesterday Is Gone	Beverly Clark	$10.95
Yesterday's Dreams, Tomorrow's Promises	Reon Laudat	$8.95
Your Precious Love	Sinclair LeBeau	$8.95

Order Form

Mail to: Genesis Press, Inc.
P.O. Box 101
Columbus, MS 39703

Name ____________________
Address ____________________
City/State ____________________ Zip ____________
Telephone ____________________

Ship to (if different from above)
Name ____________________
Address ____________________
City/State ____________________ Zip ____________
Telephone ____________________

Credit Card Information
Credit Card # ____________________ ☐Visa ☐Mastercard
Expiration Date (mm/yy) ____________ ☐AmEx ☐Discover

Qty.	Author	Title	Price	Total

Use this order form, or call 1-888-INDIGO-1

Total for books ____________
Shipping and handling:
$5 first two books,
$1 each additional book ____________
Total S & H ____________
Total amount enclosed ____________

Mississippi residents add 7% sales tax

Visit www.genesis-press.com for latest releases and excerpts.